NOVA TENNIS:

Onward to Glory

D0547735

Written by: Annette Liem

Illustrated by: Mimmy Shen (cover), Ilan Millström (chapters 1 – 3), Haidan Dong (chapters 4 – 9, 12), Alice Shen (chapters 10 – 11)

Hi everyone! Annette here!

Thank you for buying *Nova Tennis: Onward to Glory*! It was a hectic road getting here, but I hope you will enjoy the work that I have put my heart and soul into writing, along with the glorious illustrations my band of artists have drawn for you.

Major kudos go to my family and friends for their support, my editors for putting up with crappy physics descriptions and grammar mistakes, my illustrators for putting up with my nagging, my tennis coaches and partners for introducing me to this wonderful world, and of course all the professional tennis players I watch on TV while jumping up and down in hysteria. (Because, as any sports fan knows, your shouts of encouragement can be sensed from millions of miles away.)

And, again, my heartfelt thanks goes to you, the readers, for spending your hard-earned money on this novel. Please continue to support me in this venture, so everyone can visit the wonderful worlds of literature and tennis. So, without further ado, please enjoy the first installment of *Nova Tennis*!

Most Sincerely,

Annette Liem

Annette Liem
Fulltime Student, Lifetime Daydreamer

TABLE OF CONTENTS

4/14/13

Dear Kenji,

It's been a blast spending time watching anime and playing tennis with you! I so bad it ended so soon. Let's meet with Wen, Anna, and all the others once we're all successful! We can go to a Japanese hot springs! =^w^=

Anyway, thank you for your support! Keep in touch!

most Sincerely,
Annette Liew

"Your wallet, punk!"

"I-I'm sorry, I don't bring money to school! Ahh – !"

A loud crash resounded through the halls, and the innocent passerby stared before hurrying on.

"Josh White's at it again," a sophomore girl said to her friend sadly.

"He never lets up, the jerk," the brunette agreed, before the pair rushed down the hallway towards class and as far away from the commotion as possible.

Val Hauser watched from the end of the corridor as the lanky boy, who was currently pinned against the wall of lockers, fumbled through his pockets, and eventually turned them inside out, revealing nothing more than a spare HoloStick and a lint-covered piece of candy. "I-I have, this is all I swear! I-I mean, I sw – !"

The burly junior slammed the palms of his hands on the locker behind the first year again. The resulting *clang* of metal rang through Val's ears, and probably the poor boy's as well.

"Quit lying, you friggin' punk!" he roared, grabbing the freshman's collar.

"J-Joth, keep it down, man," his lookout whispered urgently. "Thomeone'th bound to hear you."

Josh was about to snarl angrily in response, but he was interrupted by the unmistakable sound of someone closing a locker. Val took a deep breath, glad that such a simple act had gained their attention, and then stepped forward, dark brown eyes staring straight at the blond-haired person with the disgusting cowlick. Even though he wore a studded leather jacket and faded jeans, the pink undershirt diminished any terrorizing effect Val would have experienced. His lisping friend was dressed like a typical underling, with ripped jeans, a ripped shirt, and other articles of clothing that were needlessly attacked by a chainsaw to become "stylish." The struggling freshman, on the other hand, wore a mop of messy black hair, a green polo, and regular jeans, free of the expensive bells and whistles. Val wondered if the glasses that continued sliding down his nose, and the large amount of sweat that kept facilitating the movement were normal, or merely a side-effect of his current stressor.

Val walked forward slowly, keeping one hand on the bill of the tweed cap that – strangely enough – no teachers had asked to be removed. Josh and his friend glared as Val approached, and eventually reached them.

"What do *you* want?!" the junior barked, spittle flying everywhere. Val inwardly hoped idiocy was not contagious.

"You *do* know bullying is forbidden by section 13.2 of the student manual, right?"

Josh slowly unhanded the freshman, who slid to the floor, paralyzed with fear.

"Cocky punk," Josh growled menacingly, cracking his knuckles. "You wanna die first?!"

Val sidestepped a second before Josh's punch reached its target, then ran up to the freshman gazing confusedly through fogged-up glasses.

"Need some help?" Val asked nonchalantly, extending a hand.

The boy was about to stammer out an answer, but instead squeaked out, "Look behind you!"

Without pausing to think about the warning, Val grabbed the freshman's sweaty hand and literally pulled him down the hallway. Eventually, the boy managed to regain his footing, likely due to realizing Josh and his friend's threatening shouts were mere meters away.

As the freshman tried to make his voice box work correctly, Val led him further down the hall, and turned a corner. Strands of dark purple hair escaped the cap's confines, but Val let them fall, having more important things to concentrate on than bangs.

"Just a bit further," Val promised, trying to soothe the freshman. He seemed to be having a panic attack, but kept running.

Finally, they reached their goal: an open classroom. Upon realizing where they were, the boy seemed to cry with joy.

A computerized voice over the intercoms announced, "Fourth period, it is now fourth period" as the pair stumbled inside the classroom. The freshman doubled over, catching his breath, as Val went up to the teacher, one hand tugging the hat down to tighten it.

"I'm sorry, Ms. Pern, the thumbprint scanners on our lockers were malfunctioning."

"Oh, those are always causing trouble," the middle-aged history teacher complained, shaking her head. "Don't worry about it, Mister Hauser."

Val smiled innocently, looking as if they had not just outrun a bully. "Thank you, ma'am."

"Mister Trenton," Ms. Pern continued sweetly. It took the gasping freshman in the back a few seconds to realize that his surname was indeed Trenton. "Please take a seat."

"Y-yes, Ms. Pern," he stammered, walking awkwardly towards the desk closest to the exit. Upon realizing Josh and his friend were still loitering around outside, growling, he decided against it and made a beeline towards the back corner, as far from the door as possible. Val cocked a head, and decided to pull up the chair next to him. Val thought the boy would object, but he instead held out his hand.

"Th-thank you," he stammered, blushing. Val noticed his glasses were still sliding down his nose, and that his hand was still sticky with sweat, but accepted the handshake all the same, realizing at last that this was his default setting.

"No problem. My name's Valen Hauser, by the way, but you can just call me Val."

They shook hands, smiling widely while ignoring their teacher as she reviewed the main qualities of the Nile. "I-I'm Alan. Trenton. Alan Trenton, I mean," he spluttered. "A-and I have to re-repay you somehow, Val!"

Val chuckled, shrugging. "Like I said, it's no problem, don't worry about it. Us friends have to help each other out, right?"

"F-friends?" Alan repeated uncertainly. Val shot him a quizzical look, and this time blew the strands of purple hair escaping from the front of the hat.

"Well, yeah. Unless you don't want to – "

"NO!" he suddenly exclaimed, causing heads to turn in their direction. Alan blushed magenta, but the teacher instead clapped her hands together.

"Correct, Mister Trenton! The west side of the Nile River was where the Egyptians buried their dead, not the east. Next time, though, please raise your hand."

"S-sorry Ms. Pern," he squeaked out before sliding down in his chair. As their fellow classmates copied down the factoid, Val grinned. The second week at a new city was pretty interesting so far.

~~~

"N-nova tennis?" Alan repeated during Study Hall. The students around them were playing handheld games, or sleeping with their heads on their desks. Even their teacher was nodding off in the corner. Val ignored the sonorous rumbles and continued the topic, grinning broadly.

"I played back in Rejina before moving to Yole City. My coach said I was sure to become a Regular on my old school's team, so I'm hoping the skill level in Neo York is no different from Myraland."

"Nova tennis," Alan said again, as if incapable of saying anything else. "Is that the sport with racquets and balls?"

Val suddenly clenched both fists, turning to the bespectacled freshman. He shrank back instinctively, but instead of beating him up, Val merely waved them around madly.

"It's not just racquets and balls! It's heart and enthusiasm and teamwork and sweat!"

"O-okay, okay!" Alan said quickly, before Val continued on some maniacal tirade. His friend calmed down, and resumed speaking normally.

"But yes, it's a racquet sport. Way back when my dad wasn't old, they played with titanium racquets and rubber balls covered in felt. But now we play with Novara racquets and Novara balls, so it's called nova tennis. Balls are still covered with felt, though, for aerodynamic properties."

"My dad works in a Novara factory," Alan said quickly, before Val went on about something else that would make his head spin. His friend merely nodded, though, fully intent on telling the entire story.

"That's cool! Novara completely revolutionized the way we play tennis, it's like a brand new sport now!" Suddenly, Val's big brown eyes got even wider. "Hey! Why not you join the nova tennis team!"

It was not a question, and Alan could feel it from the way Val carried on. "Signups are afterschool today, and rumor has it they're choosing Regulars this week in some type of round robin tournament. It'll be *awesome*."

"V-Val," Alan interrupted, face growing crimson. "I'm not really cut out for spo – "

Another computerized voice announcing an end to the school day drowned out the rest of his statement. The students around them gave small hoots of joy and raced out, though the teacher continued snoring. Before Alan could object, Val grabbed his hand and yanked him into the hallway. Alan tried to pull his arm back, but Val just tugged it harder until the freshman gave up, favoring to keep his bones intact. He reluctantly followed as they left the building, and walked down the stairs towards the courts, merging with the mass of students that had gathered there. By the time Alan realized Val had let go of his arm, it was too late to make his escape. A redheaded man in a red and white tracksuit had caught their eyes and approached them, grinning even more broadly than Val was. Alan wondered if all nova tennis players were this jovial.

"More freshmen? We're getting a lot this year, that's awesome!"

"I-I-I – " Alan stuttered, but Val made up for it by putting a hand forward, beaming just as elatedly.

"Valen Hauser, Val for short! I'm a transfer student from Rejina, Myraland, and I've been playing nova tennis since I was six!"

The overly cheerful man laughed, accepting the handshake, and then jerked a thumb at his face. Alan could have sworn that one of his white teeth had *dinged*, as if in a toothpaste commercial.

"Nice to meet you, Val! You guys might have recognized me as the P.E. instructor Davide Ercole, but I'm also the nova tennis coach," Davide said as a handful of other freshman surrounded him. "Like I say in class, you can drop the titles and stuff with me. I go by Davide."

"Sir?" one of the freshman interrupted, raising a hand. Davide closed his eyes, as if drowning out the dreaded word, but turned to the boy all the same.

"Yes?" he asked frostily, all sense of his previous warmth gone. The student did not realize his mistake, and continued.

"Where are all the girls?"

His friends snickered. "Dude, didn't you know?" one of them said, placing a tan hand on his friend's shoulder. "The women's team was disbanded a couple years ago because not enough people joined."

The original asker widened his eyes in disbelief, as did many others. Only Val seemed unsurprised. "You serious, Heath? That sucks! I came for the miniskirts…"

Davide cleared his throat authoritatively, but Val noted his ears reddening. "*Anyway*, signups don't officially start for another few minutes, so hang tight. I'll announce everything soon."

With that, the man disappeared into the sea of heads, high-fiving some of the older students. Before Alan could run away, though, the tanned student with windswept bleached hair grinned at Val.

"Hey Val, I'm in your Biology class. The name's Heath Stone, and I've got around five years of tennis experience, so I guess you outrank me." He laughed loudly, holding out a hand. Val grinned, accepting it.

"I'll see your skills on the court tomorrow, I guess! And if you know me, then you know Alan as well." Val motioned towards him, and Alan bobbed his head while rubbing the back of his neck. Heath gave him a familiar look that said, "Oh, this nerd was there too?" but nodded his head in acknowledgement all the same.

After the rest of the freshman introduced themselves, Davide's voice suddenly boomed from the crowd, and when they turned their heads, they saw why. He was standing atop a wobbly student desk he had salvaged from the dumpster, but he did well in keeping his balance even while holding a megaphone.

"Listen up everyone! Glad to see you survived another day of school and want to join the nova tennis team!" Davide shouted, as a large cheer erupted from the crowd. "I see some familiar faces, and some new ones, which is always awesome!

"Signups are simple, just come up here and put your name down! There are two laptops, one for freshman – that's you guys in the back! – and one for everyone else. Everyone who signs up in the second group will be able to compete in the round robin tournament to decide the six Regular positions!"

Despite the loud hoots around them, Val's mouth dropped to the ground. Alan turned to his friend, frightened by the action. "Wh-what's wrong?"

"F-freshmen can't compete?" Val whimpered, sounding somewhat like a hurt puppy. Heath shot a quizzical look at his peer.

"Well, yeah. Didn't you know? Freshmen like us are pretty much stuck as ball boys until next year. The only time we're on the court is when Davide drills us, but for now it's just conditioning and manual labor."

Val's chin jutted out, but instead of speaking up, the first year student merely put a hand on the tweed cap and tugged it lower.

"So without further ado, let signups commence!" Davide finished, completely ignorant of the change in atmosphere in the back. He hopped off the desk, and produced two laptops from out of nowhere, setting them down. "The one on the left's for freshmen, and the right is for everyone else."

A mass of students ran toward the right laptop with no intention of forming an orderly line that even Kindergarteners were capable of doing. Instead, the large blob of students retained its random shape, but with much more pushing and shoving. Heath and his friends hurried towards the left laptop, forming a much shorter and more orderly line. Val reluctantly trudged forward, with Alan hesitantly following.

Suddenly, Val perked up. "Wait, maybe I can ask Davide for an exception!"

"V-Val, why not just wait until next year?" Alan suggested uncertainly. Val's head shook from side to side so violently that he thought it would fall off.

"It'll be too late, then!" was the answer he got, but before he could press for more information, a familiar voice reached his ears. And he did not like it one bit.

"Outta my way, losers!" Josh exclaimed loudly, pushing his way into the front with some help from his tattered henchman. Someone shouted to get Davide, but another informed him that the coach was currently helping the pretty – and more importantly, single – art teacher move supplies from her car into the school. Alan shrank behind another freshman beside him, hoping Josh would not recognize him. Luckily, Josh was busy glaring at everyone else. "I'm taking one of those Regular spots, and you all know it!"

While there was a general wave of shouting from the front, only one word ran out loud and clear.

"Negative!"

The crowd hushed after a while, parting for the speaker. He was about 5 foot 6, with a white T-shirt and shorts that exposed his toned arms and legs. His violet eyes were narrowed, and his black eyebrows were furrowed. He had a crew cut, so the jet-black hair he was known for was short and spiky on his head.

Alan shuddered involuntarily, realizing the jock looked similar to one of his middle school bullies. But instead of running away, he leaned forward and whispered, "Who's he?"

"Didn't you know? That's Percival Parrish, a sophomore," Heath explained, as the boy in question strode towards Josh. "People say he's a shoe in for one of the Regular positions. Even though he's only played tennis for a year, he's so strong that they call him Powerhouse Percival. And Porcupine, but they say he'll punch you if you call him that."

Alan withheld a sigh of dread. Everyone here *was* a bully.

Percival had at last reached Josh, and although he was a year younger, the sophomore matched him in height. "Ignore the rules and we'll get the captain to kick you out of here."

Josh scoffed at his underclassman, and proceeded to cross his arms and snicker while his henchman did the same. "Heh, look who's trying to play the hero. Why should I listen to you, Mr. Wannabe Powerhouse?"

Percival creased his forehead again and clenched his fist, shaking it angrily. "You may be tough when there's lunch money to steal, but this is *my* turf now. If you do even one more thing to tick me off, you'll be out of this school by your disgustingly oiled-back hair!"

The crowd cheered at Percival's enthusiasm, but Josh laughed yet again, his sour breath reaching even Alan. "At least I didn't fashion my hair after some dirty animal!"

Percival reacted almost immediately, narrowing his eyebrows. Even his hair, the target of the insult, began bristling in anger. Heath smacked a hand to his forehead.

"Oh, don't go there!" Percival shouted even louder than before. "Don't you even dare – !"

"*Porcupine head!*"

"You went there!" Percival roared, a vein on his forehead bulging. He made to grab Josh by the scruff of his neck. However, someone calmly placed a hand on Percival's shoulder, and he froze like an ice sculpture.

"Stop it, Parrish," the newcomer said. "That is enough."

Even though he barely spoke above a whisper, those six words resounded through the courtyard in a voice that completely mesmerized Alan, as well as those around him. As if in a trance, Heath answered Alan's question before it left his lips.

"That's Christian Cuyler, the current captain," he said dreamily which, when combined with his tanned skin and bleached hair, made him look like a surfer boy from Kaliphornia. "He's a senior and has won every single official match of his high school career. He's got good grades, and everyone respects him, even teachers. He's just *awesome*."

Alan could not disagree. It seemed like each syllable was spoken with the clarity of the most experienced orator, and his mere presence was so overwhelming that it took Alan a while to realize he had been holding his breath for about ten seconds.

"Captain Cuyler," Percival said in surprise. He looked ashamed to be caught, but pulled his arm back and muttered a brief apology nonetheless. After Cuyler nodded, Percival shot one last glare at Josh before walking away from the scene, rubbing the back of his neck.

Cuyler's long, seemingly golden blond hair shone in the afternoon sun and fluttered to the middle of his back as the captain turned to Josh. Alan resumed holding his breath upon realizing a right eye so shockingly blue stared out from through Cuyler's lengthy bangs. Heath did the same because of what was on the captain's back, something only two other people in the crowd wore. It was what many dreamed of someday wearing: the team jersey.

The light red jersey had a crimson phoenix flying next to six bright yellow tennis balls stitched onto the back, underneath "C. CUYLER" written in bold print. The cuffs near the neck and wrists were white, as well as three stripes on each sleeve, above, below, and on the elbow. Made of the finest quality cotton, and custom made to order at the largest clothing factory in the state, having one was proof that a member had clawed his way up the ranks, and deserved to wear it upon his shoulders. In many ways, it was a cloth trophy more valuable than silk, synonymous with the title "Regular." Every tennis player present yearned to wear one, and even Alan found himself longing for it.

The bully still wore a haughty look on his face, though his partner in crime had backed up several paces.

"White," Cuyler began, his voice as cool as the September breeze. It sent another curious chill down the spines of everyone present, apart from the person right in front of him. "I can assure you that if you disrupt the peace at these courts again, you will be banned from ever participating in any clubs in school. Do you understand?"

Cuyler stared at Josh, calm and serious. The fact that a bang covered the left side of his pale face offered an element of mysteriousness to his façade, something many girls dreamt of at night. Although teachers gave many of his classmates grief for their choice in "hip" hairstyles, none dared ask if he could see the board. His straight A's were all the proof they needed.

Onlookers watched Josh with bated breath to see what his reaction would be. Unfortunately, he responded with his typical demeanor.

"Yes *sir*," he answered without a hint of truth to the words. And with that, he strutted away from the crowd, his follower apprehensively trailing behind. Once he was gone from sight (but not from smell) Cuyler apologized to everyone for the circumstances, but a few rushed forward to thank the captain for his interference, before reforming a blob with no order whatsoever.

Alan exchanged relieved looks with Heath, and it took him a few moments to realize he had made friendly eye contact with a *jock*.

Before he could ponder this further, he was in front of the laptop and typing his name down. The second he pressed the last *n* in his name, he blinked.

"Awesome, so you *are* joining the team!" Val exclaimed happily from behind him, clasping a hand on his shoulder. Alan buckled under the weight, nodding weakly.

"Uh-huh," he squeaked out as Val led him away. "And I don't know why."

Val laughed, a hand on the tweed cap, ignoring the comment. "I'm glad. Nothing's more fun than playing nova tennis with friends!"

"With friends," Alan repeated, still blinking foolishly. He slowly realized Heath waving at them.

"You guys had better get home," he heard him call out. "Didn't you know? Bio homework is always *killer* in the first weeks!"

As Val shouted back a reply and headed off in another direction, Alan suddenly broke into a wide smile. "Yeah, nova tennis with friends!" he exclaimed, raising both hands over his head to wave at Val and Heath. He was delighted to see both Val and the Neo York surfer were waving back.

"I have friends," he finally said. The wave of realization sent a chill of ecstasy down his spine.

~~~

"Hey Valley, how was school?" Richard Hauser asked as Val kicked both sneakers off. He withheld a sigh as they landed in a disorganized heap in the corner.

Val laughed, a hand on the tweed cap, ignoring the comment. "I'm glad. Nothing's more fun than playing nova tennis with friends!"

Val's father had short purple hair and glasses with a thin golden-painted frame. He was only one inch taller than Val, but was slowly losing. His build, though muscular in his prime, had been overcome by the avoirdupois of age, as evidenced by his flabby sides. However, he was still rather fit for a man of nearly fifty, and could outrun Val on a good day, much to his child's embarrassment. His main feature was a fading birthmark on his right cheek, in the shape of a leaf, which he occasionally rubbed for good luck.

"It was great," Val replied cheerfully, removing the tweed cap, as well as the ornate butterfly clip that held her dark purple hair in place. The moment it was taken off, more than eighteen inches of hair tumbled down. Val tossed her head back, and ran her fingers through the locks, still grinning at her father.

"This year is gonna be awesome."

belleofthetennisball has entered the chatroom.
carrottop: HI VAL, HOW ARE YOU?
speedangel has entered the chatroom.
speedangel: hey, its val! whats up?
carrottop: oops, Caps Lock
belleofthetennisball: good, thanks you guys :)
belleofthetennisball: the coach looks like a real goofball so far
speedangel: lol
speedangel: how were your signups?
belleofthetennisball: some genius made a rule that said freshmen couldn't compete
speedangel: say whaa?
speedangel: thats dumb
carrottop: sorry about that, Val. :(did you ask the coach for an exception?
belleofthetennisball: don't worry
belleofthetennisball: I got it covered ;)
belleofthetennisball has exited the chatroom.

"Alan, we don't have to take a completely different route to every single class," Val said crossly, rolling her eyes. The bespectacled freshman shook his head and peered around the corner before finally turning to walk down the hallway.

"No, Josh is going to *kill* us the next time he sees us. We were lucky he didn't notice us yesterday, but if we run into each other again we'll be slaughtered!"

"He's on the nova tennis team," Val reminded him flatly as they walked into the Biology classroom. "We'll see him every day." Alan tensed up, as if he had forgotten that simple fact, but shook his head when he reached his seat in the far corner.

"W-well, we'll just hang around Mr. Ercole, then."

"Davide's the coach, not a babysitter," Val muttered, taking out her regulation HoloStick. It was a thin, thumb-sized rectangle, with a round, red "activation button" smack-dab in the middle. The quality was garbage, if the graphics and voice recognition were of any indicator. Worse still, Yole High insisted on being "high tech" and continued assigning students the "most up-to-date equipment" without realizing they were distributing models two years obsolete. Every student received one, and they contained the textbooks for each class, a map of campus, and other things most people never used more than once. Naturally, the only reason students bothered bringing them along was to log onto the school database accessible at every desk of the school. If not for that anti-hacking software, most would use their own HoloSticks, which had much more storage space, more amusing games, and were *not* the ugliest shade of gray known to man.

She tightened her hat absentmindedly while plugging the HoloStick into her desk. A keyboard appeared at the surface, while a touch screen hologram popped up in front of her.

"Heath was right, this homework was horrible last night," she whispered, navigating through the apps as their teacher slouched in. "I mean, twenty pages of readings *and* five essay questions? I barely had enough time to do anything else!"

"Silence everyone!" Mr. Luntey barked before Alan could reply. The scowling instructor turned on the HoloBoard in the front of the classroom, and crossed his arms. "Forward your assignments now!"

The students withheld groans as they e-mailed their files to their teacher's inbox. Mr. Luntey turned his back on his students and scanned the names of the pupils who had done as he had told.

"Hmph, looks like everyone's here. Then let's get started. Today we'll talk about orga – "

"Will Valen Hauser please come to Davide Ercole's office?" a voice over the floating intercoms drawled. "Valen Hauser to Davide Ercole's office."

Val shrugged as she got up. She had been expecting this all day, and to be truthful, fifth period seemed a little late.

"May I be excused, Mr. Luntey?" she asked politely, with a hand still on her chair in case he decided against it. But the man grunted, and motioned towards the door.

"Make it quick, Mister Hauser."

Val nodded, unplugged her HoloStick, and quickly left the room while hushed whispers followed her out. Mr. Luntey once again demanded quiet as she hurried down the hall.

She pressed the red button on the HoloStick to turn it on, and waited for five irritating seconds before the start screen finally popped up: a rotating hologram of a bright yellow smiley. "Say a command!" it said, mouth moving with the words, in what was undoubtedly too happy a voice. Its white teeth and large eyes were unsettling, but Val tried to ignore it. In Rejina Middle School, *their* screen was a slightly less creepy talking apple.

"Yole High School Map," she commanded clearly, hoping the words would be recognized. On more than one occasion, even lunchroom chatter could not drown out a distressed freshman shouting, "For the love of technology, SHOW ME THE FREAKING BATHROOM!"

Luckily, the HoloStick Gods were lenient, and the overly cheery face turned into a map of the high school's corridors and rooms. A red dot in the science wing depicted Val's position.

"Davide Ercole's Office."

A golden dot appeared in a chamber in the third passageway to the left, next to the gymnasium locker rooms.

"Figured as much," she muttered, tossing the lanyard around her neck as she walked. *Well, let's get this over with.*

~~~

"Hi Davide, it's Val," she said, opening the door. The tennis coach quickly hid the candid photo of the art teacher, Rose, behind his back nervously. Upon seeing it was not the principal, he calmed down and stuck the HoloFrame in a drawer in his desk, before gently sliding it shut.

The "office" was more of a storeroom full of sports equipment and other related items, scattered here and there in no particular order. Lacrosse sticks were twisted in with the volleyball nets, and golf balls mingled with hockey pucks in the corner. Only nova tennis equipment was set apart from the others, but still in the same disorder. It seemed like the only tidy part of the room was the desk, the size of which was comparable to two student desks glued together. At least the stench was manageable; Val barely had the inclination to gag.

"Val, come on in!" he said as warmly as the day before, beckoning to a seat in front of his desk. Val quietly closed the door and did as Davide suggested, wondering if she should smile or not.

A holographic nameplate hovered over the front of his desk. When Val's eyes were inexplicably drawn to it, the coach smiled proudly. The nameplate was definitely a worthy investment. Indeed, it was the most impressive item in the entire room.

"Pretty sweet, eh?" he asked, staring at the golden letters. In large capital, bold, italicized, and cursive letters, read his name: DAVIDE ERCOLE. Then, in smaller, yet still bold, italicized, and cursive font was his position: PE Instructor and Nova tennis Coach. Although most teachers opted for more modest styles on their virtual plaques, Davide seemed to enjoy going all out. He waited for Val to take in the immense beauty that took him nearly an hour to design, and even longer to admire.

"Yeah, it's, uh, it's nice," Val replied curtly, smiling as politely as every other student he had asked. Davide stared at her, waiting for more words. When she did not even venture a "very," he sighed. It seemed like no one understood its beauty.

"Well, anyway, it's good to see you again. I suppose you're wondering why I called you here," he began, clasping his hands together authoritatively.

"Is it because I signed up for the second tennis group?" Val asked, as if things like this happened all the time. Davide nodded slowly, taken aback that Val did not even attempt to plead innocent. Another student might have crafted an elaborate story before walking into his office, like Benjamin Jefferson had last year. Davide hung his head dejectedly. He was *so* looking forward to catching a student red-handed. That was what teachers were for, after all.

"Well, yes." Sighing, he took a HoloPad out of the second of his two desk drawers. Like their students, all teachers received a complimentary device during their employment, but unlike their students' HoloSticks, the HoloPads were actually useful. Davide's touch screen model was 6 by 8 inches, which was too big to carry in his pocket for day-to-day needs, but it proved most advantageous for whacking students who got on his nerves. He pulled up the signup sheets from the day before, and showed Val the hologram of the sheet in question. *Val Hauser* was typed right below THE *JOSH WHITE*. "I guess I don't need to ask you *why*, but how'd you do it?"

Val shrugged and answered truthfully, this time grinning with a smidgen of enthusiasm. "I signed up when that Josh person was fighting with Parrish. I doubt anyone noticed me, especially when that blond guy came."

"Josh White, Percival Parrish, and Captain Christian Cuyler," Davide sighed, leaning back in his swivel chair, the second best thing in the room. He made a mental note to punish Josh later on, or at least attempt to exert some kind of authoritative power over him. The delinquent was not exactly known for orderly conduct.

At least he had no reason to worry about the other two. He expected Captain "Lap-crazy" Cuyler had already forced Percival to run an impossible distance in the sky. It made him shudder just picturing the sophomore running with Hover Outsoles attached to his shoes while under the watchful gaze of Cuyler. The captain was a talented tennis player, and an intelligent, well-behaved senior, but he still managed to invoke this indescribable awe into him and many of his peers. Why? He had no clue. Nobody did. It was just another thing teachers accepted in the school setting, like why HoloBoards malfunctioned the moment someone wanted to use them, or why fire drills occurred only during the most stressful of times.

"Um, can I go now?" Val piped up, sending Davide back into reality. He sat upright in his chair again, shaking his head.

"I'm afraid not, Val, I'm not quite done yet. Sorry about that," he added apologetically, upon seeing his student's crestfallen face. "I don't know how things worked in your old school, but I thought it was quite clear that the second group was only for sophomores, juniors, and seniors. You're only a freshman. I mean, the captain was a freshman regular, but he's…the captain. You'll have a chance at the end of the year."

Suddenly, Val tugged her tweed cap tighter, and levelly matched Davide's gaze. "I assure you, Davide, that I have the same skill level as those in the second group. I've been playing since I was six, like I said. If the captain was a freshman ace, I'm pretty sure I deserve a chance."

Davide could not help but chuckle. "Heh, that's pretty big talk for such a skinny guy! No offense, but Cuyler left a more striking impression. You don't even have one muscle on you, and you're shorter than most of the others."

Val ignored the height comment. "No, seriously! I honestly think that if I play against any of my upperclassmen, I will match up perfectly with each of them, and maybe even beat them." Val paused a nanosecond before adding, "And I drink milk three times a day, thanks."

Davide gave a low whistle, and smiled. "Well, if you're so sure of yourself, how about a deal? I'll set up a challenge match, and if you win, you can compete in the round robin tournament."

Val grin grew even larger, and she could not stop a laugh from escaping her lips.

"Thanks, Davide!"

Davide ran a hand through his shaggy red hair, smirking. "Don't thank me, I just hate seeing talent go to waste. Anyone you want to play against?"

"Captain Cuyler."

The coach chuckled as he took notes on his HoloPad.

"All right, the Capta – ARE YOU CRAZY?" Davide exclaimed, instantly standing up and pounding both palms onto the table. Even Val shrank back at the sudden movement. "No one can beat the captain! Probably not even me! He's way out of our league! He'll probably – no, DEFINITELY play professionally next year, you know!" Davide sat back down, and picked up his stylus as if nothing ever happened. "Pick someone else."

Val gave a sigh of annoyance, but grudgingly nodded. "Fine."

"Excellent, glad we're finally on the same page. But Val, trust me," Davide said with all the seriousness of the teacher he strove to be. His eyes flickered to see his student listening attentively. "If the Captain sees something in you, he'll challenge you himself."

He allowed that statement to sink in, and continued filling in the challenge form.

"Then he's my goal."

Davide blinked, before lifting his head to see Val's enthusiastic face staring back.

"I'm, uh, I'm sorry?"

Val's thin lips were curved into a determined smirk, dark brown eyes brimming with anticipation. "If he's as good as you say, then by the end of the year, I swear I'll beat the captain!"

Davide felt his jaw go slack, and quickly pushed his chin up with his fist once he got over the initial shock. Suddenly, he too grinned.

"Wow. Now you've got even me rooting for you. You know what? I honestly hope you do win your challenge match, Val. We could use gutsy kids like you."

Val passionately beamed back before announcing the name of her desired opponent.

~~~

After everything was said and done, and both had filled out various forms, Val left Davide to his privacy. He leaned back in his wooden chair, gazing at the aureate letters that shone in front of his desk. ELOCRE EDIVAD stared back. Once again, a smile made its way to his lips.

"Valen Hauser, huh?" he asked aloud, swiveling his chair around to look at the empty tennis courts on the other side of the window. Every year, something interesting happened on those four battlefields, but Davide knew the tales they would tell after this year alone would far surpass anything from the past.

"Heh, there's more to you than meets the eye."

~~~

"What?" Josh asked, looking up from tying his sneakers.

"I told you everything I know, Joth," his peer said defensively. "Davide thaid that frethman who thigned up in the thecond group challenged you to a nova tennith matth. It'th the thame guy from yetherday, the guy with the cap!"

Josh jokingly shook his head and rose, putting on a faux worried voice. "Wow Derek! I hope I don't get stood up by this punk! It would be the end of me!"

"Don't be tho thared, Joth," he comforted. "There'th no way you'll looth – "

"Of course I won't, you lisping moron!" Josh snapped back. "Make yourself useful and get my Ravolat."

When Derek raised an eyebrow, Josh slapped his forehead and shrieked, "My racquet, you idiot, my racquet!"

Derek jumped a foot into the air. "R-right away Joth!"

~~~

"YOU DID WHAT?" Alan exclaimed hysterically, as he, Val, and Heath began the trek from their lockers to the courts. She had thrown on her favorite long-sleeved white shirt and black shorts in the bathroom before meeting up with her friends.

"I told you, it wasn't *me*," Val replied for what felt like the tenth time, carefully weaving in and out of the crowd. "It was Davide. He set the whole thing up. *I* wanted to play the Captain."

He ignored the last part as Heath gave a low whistle from Val's other side. "Still, *you* signed up in the second group!" Alan cried, exasperated and still getting over the fact that his best friend was suicidal. His glasses were uneven on his paling face, and his expression was more panicked than usual. "The *second group*! You couldn't be patient and wait until next year?"

"Like I said yesterday, it would be too late then," Val muttered irritably. Heath shook his head in disbelief.

"Yeah, but dude! You'd better back up your words, or else you'll be living with a target on your back! Didn't you know? The guy went to juvie until they kicked him out!"

Val sighed but said nothing, and just tugged her hat lower over her eyes. Alan gave a groan of frustration while Heath continued recounting rumors, and eventually the freshman trio found themselves at the courts.

"Well, well, well, what do we have here?" Josh smirked, surrounded by some of the members of the team. The round robin tournament had been postponed for a day to get the challenge match out of the way, and upon hearing who was playing, a handful of people had decided to stick around.

Davide was standing nearby, his HoloPad in hand, keeping a close eye on the cocky junior. Alan instinctively hid behind Heath, who had stepped backwards as well to avoid being marked by Josh. Val stood as composed as Cuyler would have, and pulled the tweed cap lower to hide the bully's hideous body from view.

"Valen Hauser, your challenger," she replied coolly.

"Uh, I think that'th the frethman guy!" Derek exclaimed as gleefully as a little boy in a video game store.

"I can see that, you idiot!" his boss snapped, shoving his tattered henchman out of the way to march towards Val uninterrupted. Val kept silent and steadfast as Josh bent down nearly a head to sneer at her. Val returned the gaze unflinchingly, trying not to inhale his musk of unwashed body parts.

Josh straightened up, and said, "All right, punk, let's see what you've got!"

He took something out of his pocket, and Val's eyes flickered downwards to see it was a cylindrical tube, with *Ravolat Sharp* emblazoned in blue letters down its six-inch length. The otherwise white racquet handle fit snugly in Josh's large grip. Alan gulped, and Heath exhaled quietly. "Well? Where's your racquet?"

Val lowered the tweed cap again, performing her carefully planned speech. "I haven't unleashed it at the moment. But don't worry. Once I get on the courts, you'll see it, and have plenty of time to take in its glory."

Josh snarled menacingly, while whispers of "cocky runt!" and a couple giggles from the few females present arose from the crowd. If Josh was not satisfied with beating the newbie at tennis, it was likely a second meeting in a dark alley would finish the job.

A well-timed cough from Davide quieted the crowds, but Josh glared at both coach and opponent before turning around and stalking towards the courts. "Whatever! You can play with a stick, for all I care! Hurry up and get on the courts!"

Val nodded and turned to follow, but Alan was a little less willing.

"Val, shouldn't you rethink this?" he pleaded anxiously, voice returning to that of a pre-pubescent state. His hands shook as he pushed his glasses further up the bridge of his nose, but the immense volume of sweat from his overactive glands just caused them to slide down again. "He looks really strong."

"And that's a Ravolat Sharp, man," Heath said urgently, shaking his head. "It's, like, one of the newest models on the market!"

"Stop worrying, guys, I'll be fine," Val replied calmly, placing a hand on the tweed cap, and the other on Alan's shoulder. She grinned at both of them reassuringly. "C'mon, why don't you cheer for me? You'll probably be the only ones."

Alan gulped nervously, as Val stepped onto the courts.

"Good luck!" Heath shouted as he and Alan stood behind the chain link fence that surrounded the courts to stop stray balls from leaving. Davide stood beside them, ready to see if Val was truly skilled enough to beat Josh. The cocky junior was not as good as he bragged to be, as evidenced by the lack of a jersey on his back, but he still had a reasonable amount of skill.

If you can't even beat this guy, you stand absolutely no chance against the Captain, Davide thought, absentmindedly twirling the HoloPad stylus.

So Val, please win.

Josh was already situated upon the courts like a king on his land. When Val observed him silently from the baseline, Josh sneered and pressed the Ravolat logo button at the bottom of the handle. A sliver-blue light shone at the other end, which vaguely reminded Alan of the flashlights his father would bring along when they went camping. Of course, parts of a nova tennis racquet never emerged from flashlight beams.

Two thin, blue "arms" slid out from the handle, and slowly unfolded to create the shaft and the entire circumference of the frame. Once they had clicked into place and finally met at the top, Josh held the racquet high above his head for the grand finale. White lasers shot out from the frame, and crisscrossed to form strings, bearing Ravolat's blazing sun logo. The player lowered his arm and leered at Val through the face of the racquet.

"This is my racquet," Josh announced arrogantly. "A state of the art Ravolat Sharp. This baby just got off the production line last week."

Val clapped lazily, combining annoyed boredom and dry sarcasm like a professional. "Congratulations, I hope you two will be very happy together."

"The dude really is suicidal," Heath muttered, shaking his head in a combination of awe and pity. While Alan turned as white as a sheet, Davide tried not to bark out a laugh.

Josh scowled, and he thrust the racquet forward, clearly wishing so intensely to punch his opponent in the face.

"Can it, punk! Nobody makes a fool of me, especially not newcomer losers! Show me your racquet if you're all high and mighty!"

"Okay," Val said, taking it as her cue. "Since you asked me so nicely, I will!"

Val straightened up, her feet shoulder-width apart, and then clearly roared, "Unleash! Amethyst!"

At first, it seemed like nothing happened, and a few derisive snorts could be heard. Josh was about to join in, when he – and everyone else – realized a silver chain around Val's neck was *moving*. Gone unnoticed before, the necklace dangling from Val's neck had indeed become animate. The charm, an inch-long purple racquet sporting silver wings, slowly rose in the air, still tethered by the chain. Eventually, it broke off from its anchor, and lay suspended long enough for people to realize it was glowing as brilliantly as a violet star, before gradually succumbing to the laws of physics. Val caught it at chest height in an open palm, grinning.

Now for the best part.

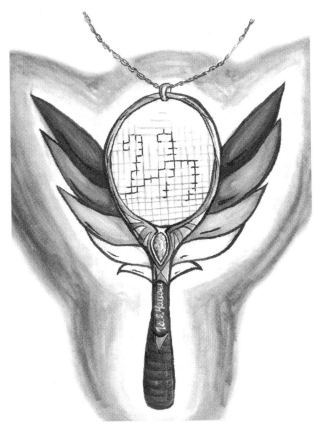

The charm, an inch-long purple racquet sporting silver wings, slowly rose in the air, still tethered by the chain. Eventually, it broke off from its anchor, and lay suspended long enough for people to realize it was glowing as brilliantly as a violet star.

Slowly, it began to enlarge, until it had grown to the size of a standard racquet. Finally, the racquet's blinding radiance faded, revealing its true colors. Once the crowd had stopped rubbing their eyes in disbelief, they gazed in awe at the piece of artwork before them.

The racquet head was approximately a foot long, with a gleaming violet frame that matched the original charm. The equally lustrous shaft met the octagonal handle, which was wrapped in what seemed like a pure white grip that fit Val's right hand like a glove. Val, too, grinned through the racquet face as the same white lasers formed a barrier of strings. However, instead of a logo depicting the brand, *V.H.* was boldly written on the racquet face in beautiful, black cursive. Heath whistled, a faraway expression taking over his face again.

"No make or brand," Val declared proudly, pointing it directly at Josh's contorted mug. "Just a plain, old, one-of-a-kind, custom racquet made with the latest in space-saving technology."

"I've heard of these," Heath said dreamily. "They're super light and made with all the specs the player wants. Only the top professionals who can afford *not* to advertise racquet companies use them, and each one is in the top ten. Dude must be *loaded.*"

"Yeah, Val is so cool," Alan agreed, speaking aloud without meaning to.

"It *is* quite impressive, Val," the coach smiled, writing down notes intently. "I can't wait to see what you've got in store for us."

"I'm ready, when you are," Val said, eager to show off her skills in front of the coach.

"Enough talk, brat, just start the match so I can pummel you already!" Josh snapped, getting into position. Val continued playing along and shrugged.

"Whatever you say. Hey, coach, can I have a tennis ball please?"

Davide wasted no time in pulling a bright yellow ball out of his pocket.

"You got it," he said, tossing it over the chain link fence. Val nimbly caught it and, after receiving a good-luck thumbs-up from Davide, turned to Josh, gleaming with pride and determination.

"Well? What'll it be? Red or blue?"

Puzzled, Alan turned to Davide, since Heath still seemed to be in a trance. "Um, sir? What's he talking about?"

The lower corner of Davide's mouth twitched. Why did these freshmen insist on calling him *old* names?

"It's just *Davide*," he said tiredly, looking down at the boy. Alan immediately nodded, face reddening. Before he could stammer out an apology, the coach continued. "Alan Trenton, right? Well, you know how in old-school tennis people would spin the racquet to start the match?"

Alan nodded, remembering something Val had told him when she was on a tennis rant. "Yes, the players would call the logo on the bottom of the racquet, right?"

"Yeah. That was before we started using Novara on racquets. Since continually landing on the ground in such away could damage the Novara frame, players needed another way to start the match. Of course flipping a coin is okay, but people decided to redesign the tennis balls with Novara too, so they were changed in a way that would let players start a match fairly."

Davide took a deep breath. This was one of the most long-winded speeches he had ever given, trailing behind the awkward "the birds and the bees" talk he had given his little sister. He noticed Josh had outstretched his arm and curled his hand into a fist with the thumb sticking upwards, so Davide motioned towards him. "Okay, just watch the match here. Josh just gave a thumbs-up, which means red."

Still thoroughly confused, Alan turned back to see Val nod.

"Okay, red it is," Val said before throwing the ball onto the ground. Alan watched the yellow nova tennis ball intently, determined to see what this color talk was all about. After impact, it turned blue, then bounced back upwards. Alan's eyes widened, and he turned back to Davide as Val swiftly caught it and showed it to Josh.

"Oh! So the ball developers enhance the Novara so it turns a different color on impact?"

Davide nodded. "You got it! Every nova tennis ball can become either red or blue, but it's a 50-50 chance which one shows up when you hit it. On a side note, you know how nova tennis balls are fuzzy, right?"

Alan nodded, and surprisingly figured the answer out on his own. "I guess they add something that makes it fuzzy?"

Praise the gods, the boy gets it. Davide grinned, bringing his attention back to the courts. "Not bad, kid. Learning the basics is the first step to playing nova tennis. I'll make a player out of you in no time."

Alan had tuned out at "not bad"; it was the first compliment a P.E. teacher had ever given him. With a dreamy expression that matched Heath's, he turned back to the match.

"Sorry, it's blue. My serve," Val said, pulling her hat down.

Josh growled irritably, but, finding nothing else to complain about, readied himself at the right end of the baseline. Val did the same, prepared to do all the introductions. However, Davide cleared his throat and proceeded with the trivialities.

"One set match! Hauser to serve!"

Val took a moment to compose a game face, following the routine of all the professional nova tennis players she admired. She twirled the racquet in both hands, bounced the ball up and down, and secured her hat tightly one more time. The last thing any player wanted was for a hat to fall off in the middle of the point. And to Val, guaranteeing that it would not be blown away during the game was absolutely vital. Then, after a deep breath, the freshman threw the ball into the air.

"All right," Val muttered, bending both knees. She threw her left arm upwards to follow the ball, and dropped her right arm behind her back for momentum: the standard serve taught to all players, and practiced to perfection. Everyone watched curiously as the yellow ball reached its zenith. When it did, Val struck.

"Ugh!" came the universal grunt, after she jumped up and slammed the ball with the sweet spot of the racquet face.

Compared to serves from players of the same age, it was quite slow, but Davide was already impressed by Val's fluid form, as well as the faint violet glow from the bottom part of her racquet face.

A sixth of the way already? he thought, making a note. *Not bad.*

Josh, on the other hand, was unfazed.

"What a lame serve!" he sneered, running towards where the ball would soon bounce. He returned it with ease, hitting it back with a normal forehand. "TAKE THIS!"

The ball sped down the line, but the freshman was swift, and raced to the left side of the court. Val held her racquet in both hands, and then bent both knees in time to do a two-handed backhand crosscourt.

"Crap!" Josh growled, turning his body to react in time. *That was quick!*

The junior ran as fast as he could to make it to the left side of the court. He got there in time, and then positioned his right arm for a one-handed backhand, hitting it right back at where Val was standing. He realized too late what he had done. Val grinned in anticipation, and hit it directly down the line.

"Not today," Val whispered under her breath, after Josh failed to return the ball before the second bounce. Alan's mouth dropped to the ground in surprise, and he exchanged incredulous looks with Heath. Val, their *friend* Val, had scored a point on Josh! *The* Josh!

Alan felt his face and neck turn extremely hot, but he did not care. Watching Val playing excited him, and scared him to death, but he did not care. His glasses were fogging up and greatly askew, but he still did not care. At that moment, all he cared about was cheering on his friend – no, his *best* friend! – until his lungs burst.

"Go, Val!" he cheered in unison with his tanned classmate.

Josh cursed irately while walking sullenly to the left side of the court. Val followed suit, unable to stop her face from breaking out in an excited smile. After Josh grudgingly threw the ball back, Val chanced a glance to where Davide was standing. He paused writing on his HoloPad to give his new secret weapon a wink of encouragement.

"15-Love."

~ ~ ~

"Game and match to Valen Hauser," Davide said, shaking his head not in disbelief but in delight. "Six games to love."

Val walked to the net and extended a hand. She was barely sweating, but Josh was utterly drenched. It made him smell even worse than before.

Josh flung his racquet onto the ground before stomping off, ignoring both Val and Davide. When a flabbergasted Derek came up to him, Josh shoved him away too. Val rolled her eyes.

"Sore loser," she muttered, stepping off the courts as Derek scrambled to retrieve the discarded Ravolat. Alan and Heath began running towards Val, but Davide got to her first.

"Great job Val, it'd be wrong for me *not* to let you play this year," he laughed heartily, clapping her on the back. She kept her composure, but smiled back just as brightly. "Sorry guys, can I talk with he – him for a sec?"

The freshmen stepped back, nodding, unaware of the stutter.

"No prob, Davide! We'll be back tomorrow!" Heath replied, still staring at the racquet in Val's right hand, before he turned around and ran off. "Catch you later, guys!"

"See you," she said, waving. Alan nodded and turned to go as well.

"Y-you were really awesome out there, Val," he squeaked, blushing. Val chuckled, rubbing the back of her neck.

"Thanks, Alan."

With that, Davide led her away, and Alan walked off in the opposite direction, glad that his route home was completely different from Josh's.

Davide shook his head again, still laughing. "I just can't believe it. No, I *can* believe it. You totally beat him up!"

"He has fists, I have Amethyst," Val replied, looking at the racquet in her hands.

When they had walked far enough so that no students were around, he put both hands on Val's shoulders, and turned so they were looking at each other face to face. Instead of his usual jolly demeanor, his expression was completely serious.

"Who else knows you're a girl?"

"So far, only you, and anyone else who looks at my transcripts," she answered, shrugging. Davide closed his eyes and nodded, already planning his steps for the year.

"Okay, this makes things easier. As long as none of the other students know, I think it'll be fine. With your permission, I'll tell your teachers."

Val considered this, and finally nodded. "Sounds good."

The two broke into matching grins, and Davide slapped her on the back before walking towards his green minivan.

"Awesome. Get some sleep, then, I'll see you tomorrow."

Val nodded and made her way to the street. Davide watched her go before getting into the driver's seat. He exhaled loudly, and turned to the person sitting next to him.

"So, what do you think?"

Cuyler stopped watching Val's retreating figure, and turned to his coach.

"I think you're right."

Davide grinned victoriously as he started the car and backed up. "I knew you'd agree. He's a promising candidate, Valen."

Cuyler looked like he was going to say something else, but instead held his tongue. The two sat in silence as Davide continued driving down the street, still beaming. Those empty courts would *definitely* have interesting stories to tell.

belleofthetennisball has entered the chatroom.
carrottop: val, how'd it go?

belleofthetennisball: I'm in
speedangel: you're a Regular now?!
belleofthetennisball: not yet
belleofthetennisball: one step at a time
speedangel:???
speedangel: your weird, Val
belleofthetennisball: ;)
belleofthetennisball: sorry, gotta go, old man's calling
carrottop: OK, see you on the courts soon then?
belleofthetennisball: haha, that'd be great
carrottop: everyone else back home says hi!
belleofthetennisball: cool, hi from me too
belleofthetennisball: ok, bye
speedangel: lol!
belleofthetennisball has exited the chatroom.

PRELIMINARIES

Intra-school Ranking Tournament

	Q. Harris	B. Jeffer-son	K. Beaure-gard	L. Korin	O. Carroll	C. Cuyler
Q. Harris	X					
B. Jefferson		X				
K. Beaure-gard			X			
L. Korin				X		
O. Carroll					X	
C. Cuyler						X

	D. Dwyryd	J. Zawisza	R. Dwyryd	M. Lapointe	R. Malnar	H. Burn-ham
D. Dwyryd	X					
J. Zawisza		X				
R. Dwyryd			X			
M. Lapointe				X		
R. Malnar					X	
H. Burn-ham						X

	H. Hamilton	V. Hauser	P. Par-rish	S. Roz	E. Duff	P. Wit-ter
H. Hamilton	X					
V. Hauser		X				
P. Parrish			X			
S. Roz				X		
E. Duff					X	
P. Witter						X

"Hamilton, Henry. Junior." Davide said monotonously, reading off the name on his HoloPad. Including Val, there were eighteen students on the list, and each person would compete in the intraschool ranking tournament for the six free Regular spots, five if the captain was ignored. Intraschool ranking tournaments took place in September, February, then once more before Nationals. *If* the school made it that far; the last time Yole High had held such a prestigious honor was when Davide was captain six years ago.

While half of the Regulars from last year remained, three seniors had graduated, leaving a handful of coveted places of honor. The former captain, Troy Bruins, had named the then-vice captain Cuyler as his successor, and as long as Cuyler played as flawlessly as everyone knew he would, the title would stay.

The brunette stepped forward and typed his name into the laptop from the other day. It registered his name, ready to spit it out next to someone else's when the time came. After the junior was done, he mingled with his friends once again, and Davide glanced down at the next name on the list. Upon realizing who it was, he said it more enthusiastically than he had the others.

"Harris, Quincy. Sophomore."

A skinny boy with silver-framed rectangular glasses and black hair in a ponytail that reached his shoulder blades stepped from the crowd of uncalled people, walking briskly to the laptop. He wore a long-sleeved white shirt like Val, and long black pants. Neither article of clothing looked wrinkled in the slightest. Davide paused from reading off the names to look at the sophomore type in his name.

"Rumor has it you want to be captain in a few years," he whispered nonchalantly. Quincy was likewise indifferent, and adjusted his glasses by his temple to let the sunlight reflect off the lenses.

"Hn," he sniffed smugly. "Most assuredly. I'll never lose."

The coach smirked and shook his head before reading the next name with equal keenness.

"Hauser, Valen. Freshman."

Many people whispered amongst themselves. Ever since "he" had defeated Josh so easily, rumors had spread like wildfire, and Val had a sneaking suspicion that Heath had everything to do with it. Most of the buzz regarded how Val had defeated Josh and a slew of his cronies in less than twenty minutes, had trained with the top coaches in underground Russia, and could shoot lasers out of his synthetic eyes. Val paid neither the gossip nor the spreaders any heed as she walked up to the laptop and bent down to type her name in.

"Be sure to put me in a block with the captain, Davide," she muttered after she was done, though it was hard to tell if she was serious or joking.

Nevertheless, Davide's lips curled upwards as he suppressed a laugh. "It's random, but I'll do my best."

Val grinned, lowering her tweed cap slightly before retreating to where Heath and Alan stood. Davide resumed the list with his previous air of boredom. "Jefferson, Benjamin. Sophomore."

The list went on and on, until the senior Jeremy Zawisza had signed up at last. Josh White's absence was clearly noted, and personally celebrated by them all.

Dispersed in the crowd were the three skilled enough to wear team jerseys, and everyone looked at them in both awe and envy, especially Val.

I'll join you all, soon, she thought, biting her lip. *And one day, I'll beat you too.*

Heath sensed her thoughts, and grinned, slapping her on the back. "Dude, you're totally going to be one of them by the end of the week! I can feel it!"

"Y-yeah, you'll definitely win all your matches!" Alan said quickly, not wanting to be outdone. Val smiled at both of them, nodding.

"Haha, thanks, but I can't take it easy just yet," she replied, shaking her head. "These guys are Regulars for a reason. Heath, you seem to know everything. What can you tell me?"

Heath puffed out his chest proudly. "Informant Heath Stone, at your service!" As Alan tried not to feel useless, Heath pointed out two redheaded twins in the crowd. They wore their jerseys in the same style around their waists, and it made Val wonder if cloning machines really did exist.

"Those guys over there are the twins Donald and Ronald Dwyryd, juniors. They made the lineup last September, and they've been in first doubles ever since because of their awesome serve-and-volley play. They rarely play singles, but don't let your guard down! They're also renowned pranksters, and have information on pretty much everyone in the school." Heath looked at them, another dreamy expression overtaking his face. "I wanna be like them…"

"I think you're well on your way," Val muttered under her breath.

"Which one's which?" Alan asked, trying to distinguish between them himself. Heath ignored the question, but Alan did cheer up upon realizing the tips of his tanned ears were redder.

"Moving on, you know the captain, Christian Cuyler," he continued, gesturing to the tallest teenager in the crowd. His blond head was clearly visible, but as usual, his left eye was not. At six feet, only Davide could see him eye to eye. "He's cool and collected, and when he was a freshman, he beat all six Regulars *and* the coach before Davide. At least, that's how the rumor goes. He's been a Regular ever since, and was vice-captain last year. There's no way he'd lose his position, it'd be like the Apocalypse or something."

"Val would be able to beat him," Alan said confidently. Val turned to him and grinned widely, laughing, while Heath shook his head.

"Sorry dude, never gonna happen. Cuyler's trained in underground Russia, and his left eye was replaced with one that can shoot lasers."

"I thought *I* trained in underground Russia," Val said, narrowing her eyes smugly. Heath blinked and cleared his throat as his friends exchanged amused glances.

"A-anyway, there are other people you need to watch out for too!" He motioned towards Percival and Quincy at opposite sides of the crowd. Percival was joking around with some of his friends, but Quincy stood alone, cleaning his glasses with an embroidered handkerchief. "Parrish and Harris were the super freshmen last year, and they both challenged senior Regulars in May, Collim and Sierna. It was the upset of the month when Quincy and Percival won, so Collim and Sierna gave them their jerseys as proof."

"Why aren't they wearing them?" Val asked curiously, watching Percival run his hands through his hair. Heath put his hands in his pockets, apparently out of dangerous players to point out.

"Didn't you know? Apparently, they said it didn't matter unless it was their name on the jersey, so they gave them back. But everyone started treating them like Regulars anyway, and it didn't really matter, there weren't any more tournaments to compete in."

Just thinking about the five godlike figures gave Alan goose bumps. "They're so...so *cool*," he decided after an intense ten seconds of struggling for an appropriate adjective. "What do you think, Val?"

Val cocked her head, then stared at both of the sophomores. "From his nickname, I'd guess Percival's an aggressive baseliner, but Quincy's probably a counter puncher."

"Oh," Alan replied uncertainly, although Heath nodded beside her. Clearly the only one without any idea of what she was talking about, he added, "what?"

Val's eyes shimmered as she clarified. "Their playing styles. Aggressive baseliner means you stay in the back and hit powerful ground strokes all the time." When she received another blank stare, she rubbed the back of her neck. "Um, really strong players who hit hard."

"Okay," Alan said slowly. "And, uh, counter puncher?"

"They go for accuracy and consistency over power. The best of them can go on forever, for a single point. Sometimes they're walls, people who can return anything." For some reason, she began snickering, and added, "People like me."

Alan seemed to ignore the momentary bout of laughter and widened his eyes. "Jeez Val, you know so much!"

"Didn't you know?" Heath asked, tossing back his bleached hair. "It's fundamental knowledge once you start playing yourself. You always want to know what type of players you're better against. I'm an aggressive baseliner myself...anyway, I bet Val can just tell who's who with a glance."

Alan blushed, but Val shrugged.

"Not really, I only stereotyped Percival and Quincy because he looks like a jock and he looks like a nerd."

"So could I be a counter boxer too?" Alan asked a little too excitedly, judging by the general turning of heads in their direction. Val chuckled uneasily as Heath shot him a quizzical look.

"Ah, I guess?"

Alan's face lit up to such an extent that Val decided against correcting the name. Instead, she left her friends and joined the crowd of players.

"If everyone's ready, I'll start the randomizer," Davide announced while typing a lengthy password into the laptop. Every few seconds, he double-checked his HoloPad to ensure he did not miss a single digit. Unfortunately, the twins hovered over him, engaging in their favorite activity: being annoying.

"Seven! Twelve! Forty-eight!"

"F as in forever, S as in single, D as in Davide…"

Without looking up, the coach swung his HoloPad to the side, just missing one brother's buttocks. He and his twin pranced away and bowed to the laughing crowd as Davide grudgingly cleared the field and started over. The juniors continued their antics from afar, but eventually Davide got it right and clicked "submit."

There was some rapid, high-pitched beeping, which stirred whines and covered ears from the crowd, and finally a long deep one. Davide pressed another button and a giant hologram of the tournament blocks popped up, hovering at eye-level. There were three blocks, each one representing a group of six players. They were organized in a chart such that every member would play against their opponents at least once, for a total of fifteen matches per block. The program was usually rigged so that two current Regulars were in each of the blocks, but Davide had further tampered with the software to ensure Val ended up with only one jersey-sporting opponent. (He generally strayed away from playing favorites, but this was a special circumstance.)

Quincy was in the first block with the captain (the sophomore's skin turned even paler upon seeing this, but Cuyler was expectedly impassive), and the twins were together in the second. Val picked one of her opponents out from the crowd, and found him busy running his hands through his hair once again. It appeared to be bristling in excitement.

"How über positive," Percival stated, turning to Val. "I get to test out the new guy before anyone else. Hope I don't shatter your dreams too quickly, freshman!" Then, to end his monologue, he gave a cocky, narrow-eyed smirk. Val matched his grin with her own smug look.

"Try me."

Percival's smirk grew wider, but a certain bespectacled sophomore interrupted.

"Hn, be careful not to lose your jersey before you earn it."

A growl escaped Percival's lips as he whirled around, Val forgotten. "Shut up, Stylus!"

His teammate returned the glare. "Back off, Porcupine!"

"Skinny nerd!"

"Prickly jock!"

Within seconds, the two were standing face to face, fists clenched, an obvious and overwhelming animosity emitting from their eyes. The friction between them could have sanded a diamond. Davide did nothing to stop it because, after all, their rivalry was as old as the stars. Also, he was never able *to* discourage them from arguing even when he did try. So, he left it in the capable hands of the captain. Indeed, Cuyler wasted no time in stepping forward.

"Stop it, both of you," Cuyler ordered, holding his racquet handle between the pair. He did not even need to activate the racquet; the two averted their gazes quickly, muttering quick apologies. Everyone feared punishment from Cuyler, and with good reason. Percival's legs *still* ached from the rounds the day before, and Quincy had absolutely no intention of suffering the same fate. However, they no doubt planned to continue the fight later on, when their superior was out of range.

Val's eyes widened slightly when she realized he was holding the handle with his left hand. It was no wonder that he was captain; most lefties made better tennis players than right-handers, and after quickly scanning the other players, he seemed to be the only one. Due to their rarity, it was difficult for players to adjust to the "southpaw" playing style, and would be caught off guard when strategies had to be changed. Backhands would become forehands, weaknesses would become strengths, and balls would bounce slightly differently on returns. Only those with a firm grasp of concepts and technique would be able to pull ahead. Val thought herself one of those people, and licked her lips in anticipation. *The captain is my goal this year,* she reminded herself, tightening her hat. *I'll do it. No matter what.*

Relieved that the situation had resolved itself without requiring him to lift a finger, Davide clapped his hands to get everyone's attention. (It took quite a bit of time, and his hands were raw by the time he got his desired level of quiet. He decided to dig out his whistle in time for the next practice.)

"Listen up! We'll hold tryouts today, and after school tomorrow and Friday. You know the drill: to become a Regular, you must either win the most or second-most one-set matches in your block. If Cuyler loses," he paused for a round of laughter to fill the air, "the new captain will be picked after the Regulars have been decided.

"Remember everyone! We were able to go to the State competition last year, but lost, so we weren't eligible for the Grab Bag Tourney."

"Um, sir?" one of the freshmen near Alan piped up. "What's that?"

Davide wanted to say, "The next person who calls me that is running laps," but the twins cut him off. The grinning pair suddenly popped up beside the new student, and enlightened their underclassman in the alternating speech pattern for which they were famous.

"That's the one where the top six schools from each state are mixed up with the others schools and sent to random locations in the country," one of them began.

"We could end up playing anywhere, against anyone," interjected the other.

"*In all thirty states!*" they finished in faultless unison.

Val suddenly perked up, staring at the twins. "I could play against any team? In all thirty states?"

"Hey, freshman!" Hamilton called, shaking his finger mockingly at her. "You'd better become a Regular before you plan on going that far!"

Val lowered her head, but leered cockily at her upperclassman from below the bill of her cap.

"Worry first about yourself, Hamilton."

A chorus of *ooohs* reverberated through the crowd, and the junior even nodded his head in acknowledgement. Davide once again had to sacrifice his palms to gain the spotlight.

"Guys! Don't forget, our goal is first place in all five tournaments: Districts, County, States, Grab Bag, and finally Nationals!" he roared, concluding his speech at last. "We're gonna put Yole on the map, and make YHS a place to be proud of! So, without further ado, let's get started!"

Everyone let out a cheer, and set out towards the courts. Since there were only four, there would be many antsy players waiting for their turn to play. Davide assigned the first two students of each block into their respective court, as well as the next two players of Block A to Court D to speed up the process. With fifteen matches per block, each day of tryouts would be packed with five matches per block for a total of fifteen matches a day. Many wished that the school board would give up some money to get a few more tennis courts, but that day was far from here. They would have to make do with what few courts they had.

Luckily, some matches went by quickly.

"Game and set to Parrish, 6-0."

"Game and set to Dwyryd, 6-0."

"Game and set to Cuyler, 6-0."

"The Regulars are amazing!" Alan exclaimed, eyes shimmering in awe, as he watched through the chain link fence. Heath had volunteered to be a ball boy on court B, and was currently tracking down the leftover balls from Donald Dwyryd's court. "They all won their matches 6-0! And in less than twenty minutes!"

"Of course, dude!" someone said from behind him. Alan looked back to see the twin who must have been Ronald. He had been watching his brother's game intently, as usual. "We're all Regulars for a reason, you know! We've gotta bagel our opponents, or else!"

His team jersey was tied around his waist, as both twins always did while doing nothing. His messy, strawberry red hair was short, but several stubborn tufts in the front always stuck up and leaned to the right. His brother was indistinguishable, except his hair continually slanted to the left. (Despite this glaring difference, however, only their mother could differentiate between the two of them. The fact that they walked out of the house in near-identical clothing everyday did little to help.)

Alan gulped, Ronald's steely look sending a chill down his spine. "Or else?" he repeated breathlessly.

The red-head drew a line across his neck, and grinned devilishly. "Coach'll kill us. They still haven't found the remains of our *last* singles two."

"And do you want to join poor Johnny in the weeds?" Davide asked frostily, coming up from behind, nostrils flaring. Alan's heart leapt from his throat, but Ronald was unfazed, and smiled broadly.

"Hey coach!"

"Stop making up rumors, you punk!" Davide commanded, getting his student in a headlock. Alan watched uncertainly as Davide ruffled Ronald's hair in a disciplinary, yet oddly friendly way, and wondered if Heath would one day face the same fate. Ronald's cries of distress mixed with his laughter, and eventually he freed himself just as Donald walked off the courts.

"Sorry coach, but I've got a match to win!"

Ronald skipped up to his brother as he walked past the fence, and held out his right fist. Donald slammed it with his own, smiling widely.

"17 minutes, 29 seconds, beat *that*! And nice escape, by the way."

"Oh, I will! And thanks, better not get caught yourself!"

"Hey coach! Buried any dead bodies lately? Or have you turned to cannibalism?"

Alan watched as Davide made a lunge for Donald, missed, and chased the guffawing junior around the area. Eventually, the freshman turned back to the courts just in time to see Cuyler shake hands with his abashed opponent. The captain was especially awesome, as he had defeated his challenger without giving up a single point. *And hopefully you can do the same, Val.*

Cuyler stepped onto the grass coolly, looking as if he had just enjoyed a cup of tea on the veranda, instead of playing a match. However, the sophomore opponent who followed in his wake seemed like he had run fifty laps around the country. The moment he exited the courts, he toppled sideways onto the grass. It took two of his teammates to help him off the ground.

Percival also appeared unfazed by his challenger, a junior now busy massaging his blistering palms. But as he passed Val entering the courts, he paused and declared, "I'll be waiting for you."

Val kept her cool and nodded. "Likewise."

Percival grinned as she continued forward, eyes still focused in front. Throughout the entire encounter, neither had looked at the other. After the doors shut, the sophomore shook his head and began his trek to the water fountain.

Things are going to be interesting this year, he thought, running a hand through his hair. *Über interesting.*

~ ~ ~

"It's amazing that freshman can hold up against these guys!"

"Seriously! I mean, his shots are so deep, it's amazing!"

"But, you know, he's pretty weak. He only uses his opponent's energy against them."

"You're right about that. Plus his serve is kinda, well, lame."

"…You wanna take my place then?"

"What? No way, I don't want my career to end just yet!"

Alan listened to the conversation, and could not help but grin. Sure, Val was not *strong*. But consistency and stamina more than made up for it.

Val won 6-0 as well, to most people's amazement. She would play one more match before the end of the day: the one against Percival.

"Hey, Val!" Alan exclaimed, running as fast as he could. She looked his way and smiled as he held out her blue water bottle, trying to stifle his panting. "I refilled it for you, you were running low."

"Thanks Alan," she said, taking large gulps of the thirst-quenching liquid. Her coach had always told her it was vital to drink plenty of fluids, no matter how easy or short a match seemed. Sudden dehydration could lead to dizziness, fainting, or worse: a loss.

"So," Val began, after finishing off more than half a liter. "What've you been up to?"

"Oh, I've been looking for the balls that landed in the woods with the rest of the first years," he said proudly, jerking a thumb in the direction of the nearby forest. It was a few yards away from the courts, but many inexperienced players hit more than one ball over the fence, and few were driven enough to want to go and find it. Besides, the area was covered in burs. Unfortunately, all of the freshmen would be doing this for the rest of their first year as part of their "conditioning" (and in regulation shorts until winter). The non-Regulars would be able to practice, but on a different court than the Regulars, provided one was free. For the others, the stone wall that stood on one side of the area was always ready for a good pounding.

Val and Alan walked up to Davide, who was sitting near the scoreboard at another salvaged desk, to deliver her score.

"Valen Hauser won against Henry Hamilton, 6-0," Val stated, as Davide wrote it down, wearing a face of pure glee.

"Another straight set. And people said a spot had Hamilton's name on it. Well, I guess you're aiming for it, huh?"

But Val was not listening, because she was already five feet away, walking to the courts to scout out her opponents. Alan stared at her, and then looked at Davide, who was shaking with mirth. This year was *definitely* going to be out of the ordinary.

~~~

"Last match of the day: Parrish versus Hauser!" Davide announced. "Please make your way to the courts now!"

Val looked up from her chat with her friends to see Percival walking towards the third court. He wore only a white t-shirt and shorts, so his toned muscles and hairy legs were visible for all to see. His racquet was already engaged, and Heath widened his eyes in wonder.

"That's a Heel Firebrand," he explained, as Val analyzed it from afar herself. It had a slightly thicker handle than her racquet, and the black grip was worn from overuse and squeezing it too tightly during play. The rest of the racquet was in better shape, with a vibrant red frame and small orange flames that surrounded the checkmark-shaped arrow in the center of the strings. "It's made for 'explosive power' and Percival is the only one on the team who can use it, and believe me, he'll use it. He's the best aggressive baseliner in the school, so watch yourself."

"G-good luck," Alan stammered. Val grinned in anticipation, one hand on her hat, as she began her trek to the courts as well.

"Thanks."

Once both she and Percival were on opposite baselines, she faced him and smiled good-naturedly.

"Let's have a good match, Parrish," Val said, tightening her cap. Percival grinned back, pointing his racquet at her.

"Of course, I always go all out. Well, red or blue?"

After some thought, Val gave a thumbs-down, indicating blue. Percival wasted no more time, and flung the ball onto the ground. When it came up, it was red.

"How positive," Percival said, laughing. Then, after seeing Val standing at the baseline, he grinned. "Ready to go?"

Val nodded. "Unleash! Amethyst!"

Once again, the charm detached and enlarged in a shimmering display. More exclamations grew from the crowd, and Percival, too, had to keep his jaw from dropping. The freshman tried not to blush, but in all honesty, watching her racquet reveal itself still hatched butterflies in her stomach.

After Val caught it, she instinctively edged three feet behind the baseline, bending her knees and trying to keep loose. With power players, it was better for her to take a cautious approach. She nodded to indicate she was ready. Percival inclined his head as well, then prepared himself.

Finally, the sophomore (who was a good four inches taller than his opponent, hat included) threw the ball into the air. He then heaved his racquet upwards, and slammed the ball. While the shot was slightly off from the sweet spot, its power more than made up for it. The ball sped across the net at an extremely high velocity, completely unlike Val's; it turned blue at impact, but maintained its shape.

"Seems like Porcupine's going for victory from the start," one of the upperclassmen said to his friend. "That's his special serve: Explosion!"

"Yeah! The twins say it goes over a hundred miles per hour!" came the enthusiastic reply. His friend turned to him slowly, forehead wrinkled.

"Steve, you believe the twins?"

"Yeah! Why?"

"How are you still alive?"

Alan had taken a break from fetching balls to overhear the first part of the conversation, and cringed. Something that powerful would break Val's skinny arm like the twig it was! Yet as he watched the ball speed near, a resounding *crack* did not echo through the courts.

Something that hard has to be hit with a backhand! Val thought, as she calculated her next move. She quickly backed up to buy herself a few milliseconds of time, which also allowed her to adjust her feet. Doing so put her in an ideal position to return it with a two-handed backhand. She grunted when the nova tennis ball slammed into her racquet, and gritted her teeth in strain. Her strategy paid off, and she was able to return it straight down the line, exactly where Percival was not. Quincy, who was watching the match from Percival's side of the court, gave a low whistle.

"Hn, nice," he stated, impressed. "He knew returning it with only one hand would put immense strain on it, but with two hands it's not that bad." Quincy smirked and cupped both hands around his mouth. "Watch yourself, Porcupine! If you don't concentrate, you'll lose to me!"

"SHUT. UP!" he snarled, as he maneuvered himself. He hit another powerful shot near the baseline, but it was simple for Val to return it with a forehand, since – like many others – Percival's normal hits were weaker than his serves. Although, as Val quickly noted, the difference was not by much.

Her aim was true, and the return flew crosscourt. Percival grimaced as he put everything he had into running there in time to hit it. He made it, but unfortunately for him, he put too much power and not enough accuracy into the return, so the ball landed out.

"Out," Val said, while holding up an index finger to designate the return was long.

"Aww, über negative," he sighed in disappointment, as their ball boy, a freshman named Gilbert Walime chased down the ball and hit it back. Percival caught it, and then took a deep breath, ready for the next point. He grinned at Val before serving, catching her off guard. "But man, you're good, you know?"

"Hey thanks!" she replied, quite pleased. Points felt even better when compliments were tagged on.

"Anytime."

"Hey, Porcupine! Stop flirting with him and get on with it!" one of his peers, Jefferson, jeered from the sidelines. Percival spun towards the speaker and shouted some indignant obscenities back before taking his place at the baseline. (Val, meanwhile, tried to keep blood from rushing to her cheeks.)

His next serve had much more power: another Explosion. Val was faster to get it as a backhand, since she was on the backhand side this time. With the "perfect aim" the rumors said she possessed, she returned it down the line. This time, however, Percival was ready.

"That trick won't work twice in a row!" he shouted with glee, powering one over the net crosscourt. Val, who instinctively ran crosscourt of where she hit the ball, was prepared and tried again, hitting it down the line. Percival was a little slower in getting to that one, but made it nonetheless. Alan watched with an open mouth as the rally went back and forth.

Val always hits it where Percival isn't! He thought in bewilderment. *And Percival always hits it so hard! He has the power, but I wonder…is accuracy better?*

For that point, precision won, after strength hit it into the net. It bounced off and rolled to where Percival was standing, hands on his knees, panting. He bent lower, picked it up, and then stared at it, replaying the point in his head. Percival smiled, feeling his will rise almost immediately.

"Come on, Perce, it isn't over yet. I'll just have to risk it! Love-30!" He straightened up, a determined expression on his face. Val grinned in response. Defeating an opponent who did not give his all was just as bad as losing to someone 6-0.

Well, she thought, bending her knees a bit lower, *almost as bad*.

Percival put all his might into the next serve, grunting louder than he ever remembered. The ball landed right at Val's feet, giving her no time to move into a backhand position. Gripping her racquet as tightly as possible, she hit the shot on the rise. A slight tingle ran through her arm, but the ball was sent flying over the net. Unfortunately, it landed within Percival's attack radius, and her arm was still numb. Percival took advantage of Val's momentary shock, and grinned as he slammed the ball crosscourt. Even though she reached the area where the ball landed, she had not recovered. The resulting backhand was too weak, its aim off. Although she expected it to interrupt Zawisza's match on the neighboring court, the tennis ball landed merely inches away from the net on the Percival's side. The baseliner cried aloud as he ran as fast as he could, to salvage at least one point. Cheers from the crowd goaded him to do it, and he held his racquet so that its face was nearly parallel to the ground. The ball bounced harmlessly off the strings and, with a little push from Percival, landed on the other side. Such a perfect drop shot drew applause from the onlookers, even a reluctant Quincy.

Val was too far away to reach it, and her arm was still too weak to return it fully as well. She massaged her forearm muscles, smiling widely.

"Nice shot, Parrish."

Percival beamed, a surge of adrenaline rushing through his body. "Please. You can just call me Perce. 15-30."

By now, many students were crowded around the match, as well as Davide. The other two matches were forgotten by all but a few. While most of the guys were rooting for Percival, nearly all of the freshmen cheered for Val. Quincy joined them too, but he had a different reason, and he made it painfully clear.

"Take note, Porcupine, you're being defeated by *another* counter puncher," Quincy goaded when Percival ran to the fence to retrieve the ball. A couple veins bulged on Percival's forehead, but he managed to keep his cool. He would deal with Stylus later.

Donald and Ronald stood upon a hill overlooking the match. Neither of them really had a taste for singles. They were strictly doubles people, and would only partner with each other. However, since one of their favorite pastimes was poking fun at people when they lost points (or did anything else that warranted a joke), they decided to watch this match just for fun. Besides, what did they know? This Valen may become one of them.

"That guy's good, isn't he, Ron?" Donald asked, standing akimbo.

"Yeah, sure is," replied his twin. "I wonder if he's got what it takes to beat Porcupine?"

Both brothers looked at each other, snickered, and whirled around to face the captain behind them. "What do you think, Captain Cuyler?" they cheekily asked in seamless synchronization. Cuyler stood with his arms crossed, and looked down at the twins, before turning back to the match.

"At this moment, it is hard to say," he began, watching the intense rally go on. When Percival concentrated too much on power instead of aim, he hit the ball a couple inches out. Val held up three fingers, the sign for a wide shot. "They both played matches already, so they seem to be pacing themselves, as they should.

Knowing limits is a crucial skill we all need to possess if our goal is truly victory at the National tournament. To be frank, this match could go on for quite a whi – "

Cuyler stopped when he heard laughs and whispers from behind him. And they were from *girls*.

"Hee hee, Ashley, Christian is talking to himself!"

"I know, right? Isn't he soooooo cute?"

Cuyler looked around to see the twins were no longer in hearing range and turned bright red as the girls continued to giggle flirtatiously. Then, while avoiding eye contact with them by facing a direction opposite of where they were walking, he cursed this almost constant occurrence. No matter what, he was always caught in these awkward situations, and he knew they were all courtesy of the twins. After all, the first time he was caught with egg on his face was the first day they joined; that was no mere coincidence. The locker room incident still haunted his nightmares to this day.

Cuyler exhaled through his nose. After one year, he had faced enough hardship. As the girls passed him by, he vowed this "running gag" of theirs would cease by the end of the semester. If either Ronald or Donald managed to trick him again, all three of them would run twenty sky laps.

(The twins snickered from behind a nearby dumpster. Cuyler was much too easy a target.)

Meanwhile, the match fiercely raged on, with neither side giving an inch to the other. At least, that was how it seemed to Alan. Quincy had shouted himself hoarse in the first ten minutes of jeering at Percival, and had since fallen silent, but still clapped approvingly when Val won the point. Eventually, Val broke Percival's serve, which shocked nearly everyone except for Davide and, of course, Val. The players passed each other to grab their water bottles during the between-game break, both trying to hide how tired they were. The brief twenty seconds elapsed silently, with the only exchanged word being "here" and "thanks" as Percival handed Val the three yellow balls. She nodded and pocketed two of them, then passed her opponent without another word. Onlookers whispered amongst themselves again. Percival usually *always* cracked some joke during the breaks. The sophomore in question overheard this, but merely looked at his racquet head. The entire face was glowing a faint red. A grin crept onto his face. This match was not over yet.

"One game to love!" Val called from the other side, bouncing the ball a couple times. She had noted the tinted strings as well, and was excited to see what tricks Percival had up his sleeve. She tossed the ball up and served it over before instinctively recovering behind the baseline. *Come at me!*

"Take *this*!" Percival roared, as he pressed a button in the groove where the open throat met the handle. His strings glowed even brighter, and when he slammed the face into the incoming ball, the resulting forehand was different from before.

The ball shot over the net down the line, where Val had dashed to prepare a backhand. She met the shot on the rise, and immediately gained even more respect for her opponent.

"Gahh!" she gasped, as her racquet was blown backwards several feet. It clattered behind her, and the ball struck the fence, frightening the freshman onlookers who had not known the golden rule of nova tennis at Yole High: never stand in the way of Percival's shots. Val stared at her hands, and realized that they were *trembling*.

"Sorry about that, but I can't let you win so easily!" Percival called over the net. Val looked up to see the grinning sophomore pointing his racquet directly at her. Its strings had returned to their default white color. "That's my Firebrand's special power, and I can use it after seven hits to the sweet spot! It doubles the strength of my shots. To date, no one has been able to return it."

"I can see why," she shouted back, a likewise wide smile on her lips. "No wonder they call you Powerhouse."

Loud hoots of applause filled the courtyard, though a gaping Alan barely noticed it. He was still trying to wrap his mind around the fact that it was possible for Percival to get *stronger*.

"Surprised?" Davide asked, clasping Alan's shoulder. The freshman nodded dumbly, still too flabbergasted to overreact to the coach's sudden appearance.

"Wh-wh-wha?" he squeaked out, as Val calmly retrieved her racquet and ball. Her hands were still shaking. "Racquet glow why power wha?"

Davide did his best not to burst out laughing. "Yeah, that's pretty much everyone's first impression."

"Didn't you know, Alan?" Heath asked, materializing just as magically beside him. "Every racquet has its own unique special ability."

"Take this!" Percival roared, as he pressed a button in the groove where the open throat met the handle. His strings glowed even brighter, and when he slammed the face into the incoming ball, the resulting forehand was different from before.

"Each racquet has its own cool power like that?!" Alan gushed once he was able to form complete sentences. Davide nodded, grinning jovially.

"C'mon Trenton, get with the program! They wouldn't redesign racquets with Novara and *not* give them special powers, right? See, look at Val's racquet face, at the strings."

Alan numbly turned back to the match, where a seemingly unperturbed Val stood bouncing the ball. Her racquet strings were colored violet, but only five-sixths of them. The top part of the face was still white.

"You can think of the racquet face as a sort of meter," Davide explained, as Heath continued rooting for Val. "However, it only fills up when players hit the sweet spot, or the center part of the face. That area is generally the best place to hit a ball, because it gives the best shot for the least energy. If they don't hit that area, the meter doesn't fill up, and the strings don't change color. Once the meter is full – that is, all the strings are colored – you can unleash the special ability related to that racquet. Some are related to power, like Perce's, but others can enhance speed, accuracy, or other *fun* things."

"But how could you return something like that?!" Alan exclaimed. Davide laughed, thumping Alan on the back.

"That's the whole point, Trenton! Usually you can't! But that's what makes nova tennis so interesting, when players try to defeat their opponent's special power with their own."

Bewildered, the freshman turned back to watch the match once again. Nova tennis was definitely not this *confusing* when he was playing with his father. Granted, he was more concerned with getting the ball over the net than unlocking any type of special ability.

Val, what're you gonna do now? he thought, biting his lip and cheering alongside Heath. *If he does that again…*

But Val continued playing normally. It was as if that one point had never happened. As soon as her hands had calmed down, every hit was just as consistent as before. Her strings were all violet, but she showed no inclination of unleashing her ability, to everyone's dismay. Percival gritted his teeth in frustration as he slammed through a forehand.

Why isn't this guy affected by my power?! He asked himself angrily. *Even Davide was shocked when he saw it!*

"Grahh!" he growled, after accidentally sending another backhand out of bounds, to award Val a second game. He leaned over, panting heavily, and stared at his right wrist in contemplation. *No, he thought, blinking away the sweat. I've gotta risk it to get ahead! Can't lose here!*

"Love to two! Let's go!" he shouted as he served. It sped across the net, but at a noticeably slower speed than before. Val took no chances, however, as she hit a backhand crosscourt. Percival, expecting a down the line shot, was taken off guard, but managed to hit it down the line anyway. Cuyler's perceptive eye observed his underclassman wince after hitting what seemed like an easy forehand. Then, without wasting a second, he walked down the hill to Davide, who was busy taking notes.

"Coach, I think you should stop the match," he declared matter-of-factly. Everyone looked up from the two passionate players with puzzled looks plastered on their faces. Davide, too, was perplexed as to what brought about the sudden suggestion.

"What for? It's just getting good!" Davide stated, looking at him eye-to-eye. "Look, Perce is a good guy, I'm sure he won't mind losing to Valen. You know, probably."

Cuyler shook his head, and gestured to Percival, who was still attacking the ball with his famed power. "That's not what worries me. It's *that*."

At that instant, Percival momentarily lost his concentration, and hit an easy ball into the net, gasping for breath. Davide's brows furrowed, and he immediately got serious. "Here, Christian," he muttered, hurriedly shoving the HoloPad into Cuyler's arms. "Hold this." And with that, he opened the door to the courts and stepped inside.

"This match is over!" he said, holding both arms up in the air. Percival looked up from serving to see Davide come over to his side of the court. "Percival, there's no way you can win. Just retire."

"Wh-what?" he exclaimed angrily, letting his arm drop. "How can you say that? What kind of coach are you?"

Davide sighed and seized Percival's right forearm. The sophomore grimaced at first, and then let out a full-blown whine when Davide pinched an area of his wrist. He immediately dropped his racquet, which clattered onto ground and pointed directly at Val.

Davide shook his head, released Percival's arm, and then began walking back to the exit of the courts, speaking matter-of-factly.

"You sprained your wrist, Perce, probably because of hitting the ball too hard in your first match. You'll be okay as long as you default right now, and get to the nurse. Of course, I can't force you to, but if you'd like to end your nova tennis career right now, who am I to tell you not to?"

Percival groaned, feeling his revealed injury tenderly. Then, with a slight reluctance to his voice, he held up his arm and said, "Fine. Sorry Valen, but I default."

Val nodded, and made her way to the net.

"It was a good match so far, though," she said, smiling, and holding out her hand. "I hope we can finish it sometime, once you've recovered. I want to face you at your full strength, so I don't feel bad about defeating your special ability."

Percival had just begun to outstretch his hand when the last comment made him freeze. He looked at the bold expression on his underclassman's face, full of pure determination and confidence, and broke out in laughter.

"Davide wasn't lying, you *are* as cocky as me!" he guffawed, grasping her hand as tightly as his would allow. "You know what? I'll look forward to seeing you try, dude. I wanna see your special ability too, before I crush it."

Val broke into a smile as the two firmly shook hands, and left the court together to cheers from the crowd. Alan managed to run up to Val before anyone else and clasped his hands on her damp shoulders.

"Wow, that was amazing Val!" he exclaimed, his eyes literally shining with wonder. "I can't believe how cool you were out there! You even won after Percival used his special power thingy!"

Val chuckled, shaking her head. "Nah, I wasn't anything special. But hey, thanks for your cheering Alan, it really helped a lot!"

Alan blushed, and continued blabbering his stream of compliments. Meanwhile, Percival was making his way to the school to see the nurse when Quincy joined him.

"Hn, what kind of moron plays with an injured wrist?" Quincy scoffed provokingly, shaking his head. "Even a six year old knows better." Percival narrowed his eyes, but had his retort ready.

"What kind of idiot doesn't care about his rival's injuries?" he countered. Quincy paused, confused.

"What do you mean?"

Percival grinned as he opened the school doors. "Come on Stylus, admit it. You'd *miss* me. I mean, if I wasn't around, who would kick your butt at nova tennis?"

Finally, with one last goading smile, he entered the school. Quincy stared silently at the departing figure through the transparent doors. Suddenly, his lips curled into a small smirk.

"Hn, get better Porcupine," he mumbled, turning around and walking back to the courts. "I can't improve without a decent rival."

belleofthetennisball has entered the chatroom.
powerbarbie: hey Val, long time no see!
belleofthetennisball: same to you, how's it going?
powerbarbie: its ok, I heard you had a match today?
belleofthetennisball: yeah, haha, it's funny, the guy I played was sort of like you
powerbarbie: oh?
belleofthetennisball: I mean powerful, haha
powerbarbie: you had me worried for a second, lol
belleofthetennisball: hahaha, you're not that hairy
belleofthetennisball: so how's the rest of the team?
powerbarbie: good
powerbarbie: Adam's crazy as ever, he's hyped over being captain
belleofthetennisball: oh, good for him! ☺ any new recruits?
powerbarbie: lol, a few. Alex'll whip 'em into shape
lonewulf has entered the chatroom.
belleofthetennisball: speak of the devil
lonewulf: i ain't no devil! 'sup val
belleofthetennisball: hey, good to see you
belleofthetennisball: well, not really
belleofthetennisball: I'm shutting up now
lonewulf: rofl
lonewulf: so how's the regular hunt? make it yet?
belleofthetennisball: not yet, today was only the first day of matches
belleofthetennisball: in two days I think they'll announce the lineup
powerbarbie: you can do it!
lonewulf: yup
belleofthetennisball: thanks guys, sorry, but I gotta go
lonewulf: ok, laters
poewrbarbie: good night!
belleofthetennisball has exited the chatroom.

"Well, aren't you up early?" Richard Hauser asked as he entered the kitchen. As usual, he had worn gray sweatpants and an old white T-shirt to sleep; they were the same ones he had been using for years, as evidenced by the multitude of coffee stains down the front.

Val had been awake since six, when she drowsily pulled off her pajamas and threw on jeans, a gray polo, and a red blazer before stumbling down the stairs. Since then, she had smeared peanut butter on a slice of bread and pulled up the daily comics on her HoloStick. Val glanced upwards from looking at an orange-striped cat gobble down three pans of lasagna to greet her father.

"Morning. How's your back?"

"Eh, getting on," came the response from within the refrigerator. He reached in to get a container of sliced cheese for his breakfast, groaning to make his point. "It's not fun to get old, you know."

Val nodded, though she was not really listening. She zoned everything out after she asked the required question that separated her from other teenagers her age. Her father went on, talking about some work-related subject as he selected what flavor coffee to brew, so he did not notice his daughter quietly slip out, the remainder of her bread crammed in her mouth. She could still hear him yammering while and even after brushing her teeth, which both amused and worried her.

Val crept up the stairs like a mouse, wondering how long it would take him to realize her absence this time. The current record was twenty minutes, but only because his co-workers had been particularly annoying. When she arrived at her bedroom at the end of the hall, she walked in and quietly closed the door, her father's voice still audible.

Val's room was rather plain, with only one true decoration, which hung above her bed: a poster starring her favorite nova tennis player, Kawamura Kei as he struck a valiant pose and held a golden-framed, King brand racquet high above his head. The Japanese-American was currently eighth in the world, but Val had been a proud follower since his teenage debut five years ago, and she was fully determined to see him all the way to the top.

Her desk was only slightly more garnished, with her laptop and a small stuffed teddy bear she had had since she was seven. (In the past, its full title had been Lord Timothy Plushie Bearman

III, but now Val just called him Tom.) Her single bed was messily made, but Val had no intention of fixing it.

After gazing admirably at Kawamura (and his meticulously groomed sideburns), she sat at her desk, and plugged her school HoloStick into her laptop to upload the many assignments she had toiled at the night before. Then, as she watched the green bar increase as slowly as molasses in liquid nitrogen (as school HoloSticks were apt to do), she decided to open her blinds to let in the sunlight.

"It's too dark in here," she muttered, walking over to the window and pressing the up/down switch. After a quick whirring, the blinds folded upon themselves and rose upward, pouring sunlight inside and instantly transforming the interior through the magic of InstaScene technology.

The hardwood floor transformed to green grass, and white lines appeared in familiar outlines. The walls were plain and boring no longer; lifelike faces of screaming fans now surrounded Val on four sides, silently cheering. The still image of Kawamura suddenly jumped to life, performing forehands and backhands with flawless form. She closed her eyes, fully immersing herself in the experience, imagining the thrill of millions of spectators chanting her name.

Val had envisioned the sensation of being on Center Court many times in her life, and each time it got better, more believable. The pre-match jitters, the deafening applause, (and when she had a bad day) the blistering sun and uncompromising wind. She even imagined the aroma: freshly mown and watered grass with just a hint of sweat. Val slowly brought herself out of her daydream to gaze at the artificial scene, adrenaline pumping as hard as ever. This was *not* just a fruitless wish to her; it was a premonition. And one day, she would meet Kawamura on the court not as an adoring fan, but as an opponent.

But I'll still ask for your autograph, she thought, marveling at his well-toned arms and legs. *And find a way to steal your towel.*

She jumped slightly when her laptop "dinged," but unplugged the HoloStick and threw the lanyard around her neck. After a few moments of pause, she opened one of her drawers to grab her personal HoloStick, just in case boredom struck during Study Hall. She had gotten addicted to Quadtris over the summer.

"Okay, now the only thing I need left is *that*," Val said, walking towards her bedside table, stationed by the net like an obedient ball boy. As plain as her desk and walls, only an alarm clock, HoloBook, and a silver chain lay upon it.

She had had the analog clock for the past seven years, and absolutely adored it. Three racquets acted as the hour, minute, and second hands, and a nova tennis court was displayed in the background. Instead of a loud beep announcing the start of the day, a built-in nova tennis ball model would detach from the top and continually hit any living being in the room until someone could no longer take the abuse and put the ball in its proper place. She found it a brilliant piece of technology, and always wondered why classmates despised bunking with her during school field trips.

The HoloBook was a present from her aunt, and while she did enjoy reading the occasional novel with "breaking edge technology," Val missed the paper books she had to leave behind in Rejina. Something about manually turning pages delighted her, although she did take pleasure in the lack of paper cuts.

At last, her eyes rested on the silver chain. It looked rather empty with just one charm on it, but due to price restraints, she could not afford another one without selling a kidney or two. Nevertheless, Val grinned as she fastened it around her neck. Her Rejina tennis friends had actually pooled the money to purchase it as a going-away present. Upon receiving it, and after tearing up, she named it "Amethyst" because of its brilliant color. Val had considered more threatening names to use when unleashing it, but decided it would be too embarrassing to shout "Excalibur!" at the beginning of each match.

She gazed nostalgically at it. Every time she saw that tiny handle and racquet, reminiscences of her Rejina teammates came flooding back.

Many children had taken lessons from her coach Ms. Bonnie, but only she and five others had come year after year. Group lessons had been so fun back then! From having a "hole in her racquet" to clumsy serving, all six of them had grown under Ms. Bonnie's watchful eyes to become Regulars. Because she was sure to become a Regular. There was no doubt about it. Ms. Bonnie had trained her too well. (If, by some unaccountable twist of fate, she lost her next matches, she had already decided hitchhiking back to Rejina could not possibly be *that* difficult.) And when the time came for her to play against her old teammates, she would show her greatest rival no mercy.

I swear I'll defeat you this time, she thought, staring at the figure across the net. While Kawamura gazed back, the opponent that burned in her mind's eye was someone else. *But I have to win against everyone here first.*

Val sat on her bed and leaned against the net with her head resting near Kawamura's ankles, recalling her match with Percival. She knew she had caught a lucky break the other day. Percival would have been a much tougher opponent if he had not been injured. But after having a day to heal, his wrist was sure to be at full strength. Though one day, she hoped the two would play a match to completion, and she would do her best to win.

No, she thought firmly, standing up and balling her fists. *I will win.*

Val finalized a few things, patted out the wrinkles in her shirt, tightened the tweed cap on her head (another good-luck present), and then before she left the room, closed the blinds. The interior turned into its original, boring state, and even Kawamura was static once again. With a nod, she left the room.

"Bye Dad," Val hollered, as she slipped her sneakers on. "I'm going to school now!"

There was a pause as an electric razor was turned off. "What?"

"I'm going to school now, bye!"

Richard poked his head into the hallway, shaving cream from the right side of his face dropping onto the carpet. "What?"

Val shook with visible annoyance, and spun around to face her father.

"BYE I'M GOING TO SCHOOL NOW!"

"Ow, not so loud, Valley," Richard cringed, bringing a hand to his ear. Val rolled her eyes and scoffed.

"Oh, forget it, old man," she muttered, heading to the front door. "Go invest in – GO INVEST IN A HEARING AID!"

"Hey now, who's the one paying for your food? Clothing? Home?!" he retorted, annoyed and hurt at how cold-hearted his once loving daughter had become. "I'll have you know that in the past, I was…"

Val ignored the lecture she had heard many – *too* many – times before. After putting her sneakers on ("Ladies asking for my autograph, those were *worth* something back then, whether they were on a check or not!"), she reached for the doorknob of the main entrance, threw the door open, and raced outside to face the second day of tryouts.

~~~

"I'M SO LAAATE!" Val whined, pulling up the clock on her HoloStick. It was 7:58. She had two minutes. *Argh, I wonder if Ms. Till will believe I helped an old woman cross the street.*

She glanced down again. 7:59.

Better make that two.

Val's feet put up with the early morning abuse, and she sped down the sidewalk, arms and legs pumping, trying to block an image of the vile tardy slip from her mind. She was going faster than she ever could on a nova tennis court. To her, having a mar on her permanent record was more dangerous than losing 5-0 in a match. After all, three of them meant expulsion from clubs and sports for the month, and there was no way she was suffering through such an everlasting fate.

She raced past houses, around tree branches, and below armies of wild squirrels stocking up on food for the winter. It was only September, but sometimes the autumn could be as cruel as the frost.

Okay, the school's right there! Val thought excitedly, eyes set on the building at the far end of the street. It was a dull gray, two story building, with a parking lot in front that only had room for the teachers. Those who drove cars to drop of their children would have to be extremely fast and early to avoid the 7:45 traffic jam.

A couple other students were rushing into the school, but two distinct differences set them apart from Val. For one, they were closer to the building than she was. And for another, they were not as nice.

"OH, COME ON!" she screeched as the door slammed shut seconds before her fingers could grasp the handle. The boy who had entered last turned around and grinned apologetically before proceeding to run down the hall. Val continued panting, gulping down air as if it was cake. *Yup*, she thought bitterly, pressing her forehead against the door. *Just like Rejina.*

~~~

"I'm sorry I'm late!" Val apologized, thrusting the door open and leaning against the wall, clutching a stitch in her chest. She had caught a lucky break when Davide, just coming from the art room, saw her tugging at the doorknob, as if that would somehow unlock the door. He had waved at her for a few seconds, just to mess with her, but let her in before she threw any obscene words at him.

The English teacher merely continued sipping her coffee at the front of the room, and shook her head calmly.

"Not at all, Mister Hauser," she smiled, winking. "In fact, the bell has not yet rung."

"Oh, awesome," she sighed in relief (both for punctuality and her teacher's acting skills), before walking to her seat in the back of the room. As usual, Alan was waiting for her, in his typical khakis and tee. While he sat there to avoid being a spitball target, Val did so to read up on nova tennis strategies without teachers catching on.

In addition to him, a pair of other girls, Liana and Emile, sat with them. Val knew little about them, except that they were more inseparable than Siamese twins.

Liana was taciturn and reserved; the bang that covered the left side of her face made her seem even more withdrawn. Her flaxen hair and cerulean eye were familiar to both Alan and Val, but neither of them could really put their fingers on where they had seen it before.

Emile had short red hair, tamed with a long yellow and blue bandana that trailed to her waist. It was completely against school dress code (apparently, a "safety hazard") but Emile feared nothing, not even write-ups. Eventually the teachers decided to stop arguing with her, and let her wear whatever she desired. She was the antithesis of Liana: extroverted and brash. Her brown eyes glinted with a rebellious gleam. Now, however, they were glazed over in pre-class boredom. She, too, looked like someone Val and Alan knew, and once again, that person eluded them.

Both were members of the Journalism Club, and always worked together on stories as a two-girl team. While Emile frequently interviewed sportsmen, Liana followed in her wake with the school camera, taking pictures of small animals, blooming flowers, and on rare occasions, the people assigned to them.

Alan waved, Liana smiled meekly, and Emile gave a bored, "yo" as Val took her seat. Seconds later, the bell rang.

"I thought you weren't gonna make it," Alan whispered out of the corner of his mouth.

Val was about to respond when the teacher stood up from her stool.

"All right class, please access page 1942 in *The Anthology of Shakespeare*..."

~~~

"Ah, thank you, Mister Harris, that is correct," the calculus teacher said after Quincy finished solving a warm-up problem on the SmartBoard. The sophomore stepped back from the board to admire his work, while straightening his red tie at the same time. (He always dressed for success with a white shirt and dress pants, which impressed the teachers. Truthfully, though, he had little choice in the matter; his mother still bought all his clothing for him.) As expected, his penmanship was impeccable. The balding Ph.D. candidate quickly cleared his throat, and brought a new equation onto the board. "Ahem, you may be seated now."

Quincy nodded, and returned to his desk in the front row. His classmates gave him looks of awe and jealousy, and several murmurs reached his ears.

"Dude, that took me three hours to solve!"

"How long did it take him, thirty seconds?"

"I think his eyes were closed too."

Although his classmates lauded his intellect, Quincy felt little pride. It was a hollow victory, being in an advanced junior class as a sophomore. Knowing that his brother and sister had achieved the same thing several years prior soured the taste. The only thing that truly set them apart was sports: he was the only one ever to play a varsity sport, let alone hold a Regular position, as he was sure to do. Of course, what did this matter to his father? Not much. Quincy fiddled with the cuffs on his dress shirt absentmindedly. At least his mother understood his hobby.

"Ah, now how about Mister ah, Donald Dwyryd, you answer the next one?"

Several heads turned to face the far corner of the room, a place the class clowns usually occupied. Two figures in black hoodies sat there, but made no movement. "Ah, Mister Dwyryd?"

Suddenly, one of them stood up and slowly made the way to the front of the class, shoulders hunched. Before he reached the board, though, he tripped over his untied shoes, and fell with a *thud* in the front of the classroom. Those in front stood up, including Quincy. The Donald *he* knew was much more nimble than that! And on top of that, since when did he have brown hair?

"Ah, Mister Stews?"

"I'm sorry Mr. Tersdon!" the student cried, still prostrate on the floor. "They made me do it!"

"Wh – ?"

Before the question could leave his mouth, a shout of glee erupted from the hallway. A handful of students raced to the door to see what the commotion was about, despite the teacher's protests. Quincy, not quite as thrilled to fight his way through a crowded doorway as his classmates were, stayed put. Without even opening his eyes, he knew who was responsible. Or rather, who *were*.

"Fork over the cash, Don!" Ronald exclaimed with glee. He wore a navy blue T-shirt with the Roman numeral "I" on the front and back, as well as jeans with a hole just big enough to expose his left kneecap. "I told you with enough Hover Insoles a desk could float!"

His brother ran behind him, trying not to laugh. His shirt was dark green, with the numeral "II." Naturally, his jeans had a tear for the right knee.

"You still can't steer it, tho – WALL!"

CRASH.

As Mr. Tersdon nervously paced the room, wondering whether to report them or not, Quincy heaved an audible sigh. At times, he wondered why he associated himself with such dolts.

~~~

"…So as you can tell, the Silk Road was indeed a very important trade route, spanning from Europe to Asia and even Africa when counting the oceanic routes, MISTER PARRISH!"

"Yeff ma'am!" Percival jerked his head up, a pretzel still sticking out of his mouth. Crumbs littered his T-shirt, and even made their way to his cargo shorts. His teacher stomped forward, heels clicking sharply, while classmates around him snickered.

"Mister Parrish, I have told you countless times that there will be no eating in my class!" She snatched the bag of trail mix from Percival's helpless hands, and slapped the top of Percival's desk with her pointer. He looked away guiltily.

"'M forry, Mfef O'Hare," he muttered.

"You should be, you know!" she exclaimed, walking back to the board. "All you do is eat and eat and eat in my class, and what do I get? A measly salad, without any dressing! Just a couple of lousy croutons…"

Unsure laughter rippled through the classroom, but was immediately silenced with a hostile glare. Mrs. O'Hare leaned against the board and crossed her arms.

"Now then, Mister Parrish, when you're done chewing, why not *you* read the next section?"

Percival swallowed quickly and began reading, while his confiscated snacks made their way to someone else's mouth.

~~~

Cuyler admired the butterflies fluttering outside the window of the physics lab, as well as the bluebird's nest comfortably situated against the oak's bough. He fondly remembered last spring when he watched an egg hatch there before his very eyes.

"Mister Cuyler, stop your woolgathering and tell me the difference between quantum and classical mechanics!"

Nearly all of his classmates glared daggers at their teacher, Dr. Gacedes. How dare he address Cuyler that way! In fact, he was the only teacher in the entire school – district even – who showed an open dislike for the one who most extolled as a model student. The majority of the student body thought he was just jealous of Cuyler's golden hair.

The senior, unfazed, looked directly him in the eyes to answer clearly and concisely.

"They are both subfields of mechanical physics. Classical mechanics is related to the motion of specific bodies under a system of forces, while quantum mechanics describes matter and energy with particle and wave-like behaviors."

As if on cue, the girls in the class applauded enthusiastically while his lab partner thumped him on the back, passing him a grin.

Dr. Gacedes growled, but turned back to the board, wire-drawn comb-over again revealed for all to see. "Wipe that smirk off your face, Mister Cuyler! You haven't graduated yet! And do something about that atrocious haircut!"

Cuyler decided against saying that he never "smirked," and continued staring out the window, his back still as straight as a board. The butterflies had gone, but something else caught his eye: Val.

Apparently, it was time for freshmen Physical Education, and she was running laps with a boy with glasses. Perhaps "with" was the wrong term, considering he was always left behind as she continued to make rounds. However, following each lap she would pause to chat with him briefly before starting again. Cuyler smiled again, surprising himself.

That one is definitely promising.

"Mister Cuyler! The Schrödinger's cat thought experiment!"

"Doc, that's not until chapter 28!"

"Quiet, Miss Geetse!"

~~~

"Radioactive mush again?" Val sighed, poking at the mound of matter the lunch lady had plopped on her plate. It looked like rainbow colored mashed potatoes, but when prodded with a fork, a putrid, yellow, bubbling liquid oozed out. It had the consistency of honey, but smelled like a fish market. Val blinked twice, and then pushed her tray away. She would rather take her chances with the food left behind in gym lockers.

Alan, from her right, laughed. "Yeah, that's why I've learned to bring my lunch. Wait."

He proceeded to split the peanut butter and jelly sandwich in two, and handed half of it to Val. "Here, you need to eat something if you want to win your matches today!"

Val smiled, and took the offering. "Thanks Alan, I owe you." Alan shook his head, and continued to eat. Suddenly, he felt a hand on his shoulder, as did Val.

"Hey freshmen!" two familiar voices stated in unison. They looked around to see Ronald and Donald sliding over and sitting across from them. Ronald was holding an ice pack wrapped in a towel to his left eye, but he looked more jovial than ever. Alan quickly waved in greeting.

"He-hello, Ronald, Donald," he stammered nervously, nodding at them in turn. They both laughed instantly.

"Haha, he's Don!" the twin on the right chuckled, jerking a thumb at his brother.

"And he's an idiot," the second one snickered. Alan stared as Ronald whacked his brother with the ice pack before returning it to his eye. The right side of his face was quite red and bruised, and made him look as if he had picked a fight with the wrong end of a cargo train. While both freshmen were sure there was an interesting story behind it, neither were brave enough to ask.

"And *you're* a lousy navigator," Ronald grumbled, taking out a thermos and setting it on the table before him. "You could've warned me a couple seconds earlier."

"I'm sorry," Donald apologized, sounding genuinely sincere. He then turned to his brother, who was still digging through his bag for something, and asked just as seriously, "Do you want me to kiss the boo-boo better?"

Without even looking up, Ronald brought a spoon down on his twin's head, and returned to his lunch.

A horrible gagging noise erupted from Val's direction; she was beating on her chest with a clenched fist.

"Okay, I'm okay," she said quickly, holding up a hand. Donald paused from rubbing his head long enough to exchange triumphant glances with his brother.

"An' you're Alan Trenton, right?" Ronald asked, unscrewing the cap on his thermos. Alan nodded quickly, suppressing the urge to sing, "An upperclassman knows my name!"

"Five foot three, president of the Laider Glee club, your first username was skullcrusher86?"

Val shot Alan an inquiring look after Donald stopped reading from the HoloStick he carried around to scare newbies.

"I-I was younger," he mumbled, blushing. Alan looked down dejectedly, too afraid and humiliated to ask how in the world Donald had known that.

The twins shared a sly smile. They had dirt on every single person who had ever walked through the school doors, students *and* staff. Transcripts, family history, and even medical information were backed onto one Master HoloStick, kept in a safe place within Donald's underwear drawer. Though some records were incomplete, there was always *just* enough for their own purposes. The twins constantly wondered how the school technicians had overlooked so many breaches in the system's firewall, and had every intention of telling them to beef up the security. *After* graduation.

Before the twins could scoop out a spoonful of clam chowder, another figure walked up to the table.

"I didn't know we were claiming a team table! How positive!" Percival exclaimed, sliding beside Val, with a huge grin. He was carrying a school lunch tray, but before he began his meal, he held his fist out to Ronald.

"Heard about the hovering desk," he smirked, as both twins slapped their hands down.

"And not even a detention, Tersdon's such a pushover."

"Über positive!"

Finally, his eyes flickered down to the plate before him. Val expected his reaction would mimic hers, but he just shrugged and started digging into the odiferous mystery meal with unbridled relish. She simply stared; her mind had gone blank with astonishment. When Percival eyed Val's lunch, she wasted no time in flicking the unwanted tray towards him.

Suddenly, Percival looked up and groaned. "Ah, negative! ÜÜÜÜÜÜÜBER negative!"

"Shut up, Porcupine!" Quincy snarled, sitting on the other side of Ronald, and slamming his tray onto the table forcefully. "I could be taking an extra-curricular right now, but nooooo, the school board says I need to eat within lunchroom boundaries! Pah, what? All this is just tasteless calories, no nutrition whatsoever!" Quincy began to poke angrily at his lunch, as if doing so would somehow curb his rage. "I *told* Elizabeth to save the last slices of bread for me. She even ate the banana…"

"Tch, not like *you* can do better, Mr. Calculus!" Percival snorted, his mouth full of food. A few flecks flew out, landing dangerously close to Quincy's hands. Quincy flared up and threw his fork on the table with a *clang.*

"What was that?" he whispered irritably, leaning into the table so his gaze met Percival's head-on. Percival leaned in too, goading his rival on.

"You heard me!" Percival stated, smiling like a shark. He would have looked more menacing had it not been for the crumbs on his cheeks and the food in his teeth. "You'd fail at making a sandwich!"

Lightning emitted from their eyes as the freshmen looked on. Val absentmindedly shifted closer to Alan, afraid that being too near to Percival would burn her to ashes. Ronald and Donald completely ignored the spat and continued to eat their soup.

"They're always like that," Ronald commented, stuffing a potato into his mouth. "Dunno why."

"They never stop unless *he* shows up," Donald said, digging around for his favorite part: the elusive oyster crackers.

"'He'?" Val asked quizzically. "'He' who?"

Before either twin could stifle a full-blown guffaw, the final member of the would-be team showed up, carrying a white tote bag with "Christian Cuyler" embroidered on it in red string. He was wearing plain brown pants, a cream collared polo, and a frown.

"Parrish, Harris, cease arguing," Cuyler commanded, standing beside them both. His voice rang clearer than the school's fire alarm, resounding across the lunchroom and resulting in two seconds of eerie silence. Donald would have bet every penny in his and his brother's name that the girl named Annabeth Jenkins was swooning near the windowsill. And probably the middle-aged cashier, too.

The sophomores immediately stopped their glaring war, and looked down at their food in shame. "Yes sir," they said in unison. Cuyler nodded, and then walked over to the other side of the table. As he did, though, Percival mouthed, *He said MY name first.*

Quincy fixed his glasses, but said nothing.

"Good afternoon Dwyryd, Dwyryd, Hauser, Trenton," Cuyler said, nodding to each of them in turn. The twins jokingly saluted back as Val gave a curt nod. Alan, on the other hand, hastily scrambled to his feet, thinking of a proper way to show his admiration.

"Ca-captain Cuyler!" he exclaimed at the top of his lungs. *Not only the twins, but the CAPTAIN!* the freshman thought, red in the face. *Okay Alan, just like we practiced! One, two!*

"Itissuchanhonortomeetyou!" he jabbered. Before his brain could register how much he had deviated from his speech, his mouth tried to make up for it. A nanosecond later, Alan realized it should have stayed shut.

Cuyler stared as Alan continued to stammer various phrases that very well could have been in another language, considering the amount that everyone actually understood. Both twins were on the verge of exploding with laughter, and Percival had even stopped shoveling forkfuls of gruel into his mouth to gape at the over reactive freshman. Quincy felt a little pity for the boy; he had the same mindset about the captain the previous year, but he acted more socially acceptable in public. Val stared quizzically at her friend, wondering if she should intervene. She supposed good friends would prevent each other from looking like wet hens, but in the end, she presumed she would do more harm than good and stayed silent. The captain merely watched until Alan seemed to choke on his tongue thirty seconds later.

"Ah, I am honored you think that way," Cuyler managed to say. Alan stopped mid-sentence and suddenly straightened up, red in the face from both his workout and the compliment. His glasses were fogged up and completely askew; it was a miracle they were still on his sweating face.

"Hey Captain!" Ronald jeered, cupping his free hand over his mouth while his brother snickered uncontrollably. "Looks like you've got a fanboy!"

Both Cuyler and Alan turned redder than humanely possible, and faced the mirthful twins. While Alan tried to deny the accusation, only squeaks emerged from his mouth. The captain, on the other hand, managed to keep his voice level as he spoke. "Both of you, please cease these antics." Donald and Ronald both put on solemn faces, and looked their upperclassman in the eye.

"Sorry, captain!" the older one shouted, attracting looks from the surrounding tables. "Won't happen again!"

"Until tomorrow," his brother finished with just as serious a façade. Cuyler exhaled softly. It was better than nothing.

Alan suddenly regained his composure, and grabbed his lunch bag from the table. "H-here Captain, please sit here!" he said hopefully. Cuyler regained his composure, and nodded.

"Ah, thank you, Trenton," he replied, sitting down next to Val, across from a still smirking Ronald. He put his bag on the table, and took out the contents. Everyone stared.

"I-is that a five-course meal?" Val asked breathlessly, as Cuyler used the bag as a plate for his roll.

"Yeah, I think so," Percival answered, watching the captain take out a container divided into tomato soup and Caesar salad.

"I wonder if Mother would cook me a lunch like that if I asked her," Quincy wondered aloud, subconsciously drooling from another container with a drumstick of chicken and rice.

Ronald and Donald said nothing. They simply looked from their finished thermoses of chowder to their upperclassman's dessert: a cup of tiramisu.

Alan's glasses completely slid off his face.

Cuyler was about to daintily dip his roll into the tomato soup when he felt a vibration surge through the table. Val clutched her stomach, blushing crimson, and the twins' laughing did not ease the situation.

"Err, sorry," she muttered, clutching the bill of her cap in an attempt to hide her face. Percival meekly slid her half-finished lunch tray towards her.

"You want it back?"

"N-no, it's f – "

"Okay," he said, snatching it back at the speed of light. The next second, he had resumed his gormandizing.

"Hauser," Cuyler said sharply. Val cringed, and looked up. Cuyler's visible eye was icy as ever, and his mouth was a thin line. He was staring at her with all the intensity of her middle school Music teacher when she caught her lip-synching.

"Y-yes Captain?" She did her best not to sound like a dog's broken chew toy, or even worse, Alan. Cuyler's hard gaze was utterly agonizing. *Forget about beating him in a match,* Val thought. *I can't even beat him in a staring contest!*

Suddenly, he held out the roll, and slid the soup and salad in front of her. She blinked, now blushing for a different reason. She sat, eyes transfixed on his. In fact, everyone sitting at the table froze. Never before had the captain offered *them* food! Only laps and the occasional nod of approval. (Percival made a mental note to "forget" his lunch card someday.)

About ten seconds passed before Cuyler held the roll out further. "Well?"

The movement snapped Val back to reality, and she lowered her hand to accept the offering. "Er, thanks."

The bread exchanged hands, and Val brought the soup closer to her. The scent of herbs and spices wafted upwards, but she was unable to bring herself to enjoy it. She cast a glance at Cuyler, who had moved onto the main course. With great reluctance in her voice, she solemnly said, "Captain, I can't accept — "

"Hauser, are you disobeying an order?"

Percival and the twins snickered as Cuyler tilted his head in her direction, once again transfixing that captivating eye on hers. (She slowly felt herself turning to stone.) "You have yet to make the Regular lineup. If you cannot follow the simplest of directions, I have the capabilities to bar you from joining the team."

To finish his monologue, he turned his lips upwards the smallest amount, and his gaze softened. Again, Val's heart leapt out of her throat. "You can pay me back tomorrow, if you so desire."

Val slowly broke into a grin, respect for the captain growing hundredfold. She nodded and accepted the food.

"Yes sir! Thank you for the meal, sir!"

"Hey Val, looks like you have a fanbo — !"

The rest of Ronald's statement was cut off by a well-aimed kick to the shins from across the table.

Alan, after sliding his glasses up his nose, grinned, and left to find a different, hopefully deserted, lunch table. After all, a geek like him could never fit in with the others. They were too *cool*. He just hoped Val would enjoy himself. For some reason, that was all he wanted.

He eventually spotted a secluded corner table next to the door; the best place for a quick escape if ever a food fight occurred. Alan re-opened his lunch bag, and took his pudding out. Breathing a sigh, he peeled back the cover, and ate his dessert in accustomed silence.

A few minutes before the period ended, someone came up behind him.

"Mind if I join you?"

Alan whirled around and saw Val beaming, carrying her now-empty tray in both hands.

"You're not sitting with the Regulars?" he asked, confused. Val shook her head, seating herself beside her friend.

"Nah. It got too noisy," she replied, as one of Percival's louder shouts reached their ears. "Besides," she continued, smiling slightly. "You're much more fun to talk to."

If Alan had died at that moment, he could not have been happier. He simply grinned idiotically, as Val twiddled her thumbs. Suddenly, she sighed. Before Alan had a chance to ask, she smiled ruefully at him.

"After today's matches, remind me to pay the captain back tomorrow. I don't want him to rethink his opinion of me."

Alan nodded, overwhelmingly pleased with being given a mission. "Got it. I'll remind you to pack a lunch too."

~~~

"Another bagel, you're on fire today!" Davide said after Val reported her score. "You're in first place for Block C, after your match with Perce. As long as you don't burn out in your last two matches, you're a shoe in."

Val grinned, pleased, and read the hologram score chart above Davide. "Looks like I'm not the only one, all the Regulars are winning just as easily."

The coach nodded, looking up as well. "Yeah, I'm sort of surprised the twins are winning this easily. They usually don't do as well in singles, so it's awesome that they're getting love sets."

"Well *sorry* for sucking at singles!" a twin shouted, stomping up to the table. Judging by the sweaty towel on his head, it was Ronald to report his finished match. "Maybe I was better in it, I'd be able to win eight games to negative one, but I guess you're stuck with a lame 6-0 against Clemmens!"

"Congrats, Dwyryd," Val said, as Davide inserted the scores. They popped up behind him, filling Block B halfway. "I was watching your match, you're really good."

Ronald pointed both index fingers at Val, scowling at Davide. "See? Freshman likes me!" The redhead beamed at Val. "And drop the Dwyryd, me and my bro go by a first name basis here. 'Cept for the captain and Stylus, but they're weird."

Val chuckled after making sure Cuyler was nowhere in sight. "I'll keep that in mind, Ronald."

Ronald guffawed with her, but then threw his arms into the air. "EH?! How'd you know I was Ron?!"

The freshman shrugged, putting her hands in her pockets. "I dunno, I just had a gut feeling."

The twin stared at her for a few moments, and suddenly burst out laughing. "Good lie! It's because Don's playing Zawisza now, isn't it?"

"Yeah," she admitted, rubbing the back of her neck. "B-but I promise I'll figure it out eventually!"

Ronald beamed, and brought his hand directly onto Val's head, up, then down again. She gripped her hat tightly, shutting her eyes with every impact. She felt like an arcade Whack-a-Mole game. "Hahaha, I like you, kid! Davide, can we keep him?"

"If you promise to walk and pick up after him every day," the coach answered while updating the chart with Hamilton's scores.

"Yaaay!" Ronald shouted, throwing his arms around Val in a bone-crushing hug. It knocked the wind out of her, and she blushed at all the hoots of laughter around them. "I'm gonna love him and pet him and name him Fedora!"

"It's not a fedora," Val corrected, gasping for air. "It's a chimney sweeper's hat."

"I thought it was a newspaper boy's hat," Davide commented idly, though nobody was listening.

"Sweeps, even better!" Ronald laughed, finally freeing Val. She backed away quickly, sucking sweet oxygen into her lungs. "Makes sense, you're winning straight sets anyway."

Val considered the nickname, still breathing as heavily as during a match. "Sweeps, huh? I guess I can live with that."

Ronald grinned, crossing his arms. "Even if you couldn't, we'd still call you that!"

"Hey Val, Court D's open now," Davide interrupted, pointing towards it with his stylus. "Grab Witter and start a match, if you're – "

"Yes," she said immediately, fleeing from the scene. Ronald watched her, snickering.

"A nickname, huh?" Davide asked, leaning back in his chair. "You nicknamed Perce and Quince last year too, but not anyone else. They stood out to you that much?"

The twin shrugged, placing his hands on his head. "No, but they did to the captain. And his gut feeling is usually right."

~~~

"Game and set to Hauser, 6-0!" Davide roared on the third and last day of tryouts, after Val hit a winning overhead smash. Her opponent, the sophomore Samual Roz, collapsed in a sweating heap on the ground, his dark skin shimmering with sweat.

"Ah snap! That guy shows no mercy," he panted, as Val walked up to the net, reaching her hand over the barrier to shake. When Roz did not get up, she shrugged, and left the courts.

Alan slammed his fist into the air while doing a little victory dance with Heath. "All right! Five straight wins! That means – !"

"Gather 'round everyone!" Davide shouted through a megaphone. The team members raced to form a circle, or at least tried to. The best they did was a dented ellipse. "The Regulars are now set for the next five months!"

There was a simultaneous cheer, even from those who had lost. Roz was still too tired to make any unnecessary sounds, so he leaned on Hamilton for support. Jefferson, who had haplessly lost to the Captain, was still spread-eagle on the court. No one had bothered helping him up.

Davide motioned for everyone to quiet down so he could start the introductions.

"First up, the man who will lead as Captain! Christian Cuyler!" Davide began, as Cuyler coolly entered the middle of the circle. His hands were in his pockets, and he was looking around nonchalantly. The team cheered wildly, and a few fangirls watching from afar squealed and collapsed onto the ground, apparently felled by Cupid's arrows. While the latter did so due to his charm, the former applauded simply because it was the captain, and he was better than the rest of the team put together. He had gone undefeated in the State competition last year, but due to the rest of the team's losses, was not able to proceed. Everyone hoped that this year would have a different outcome.

"Secondly, the Diamond Duo who went undefeated until States!" the coach continued with equal excitement. "Ronald and Donald Dwyryd!" The twins walked into the middle of the group, bowing elaborately, raising their hands, and blowing kisses as if they were famous celebrities. In truth, they were still quite sour about the loss last year, even after infecting their opponents' mainframes. This year, they were out for revenge.

Alan leaned over to Heath, who seemed to be worshiping them with some awkward hand gestures. "Diamond Duo?"

"Didn't you know? It's because their doubles play is as valuable to the tennis team as diamonds are to anyone," he answered vaguely. "I wonder if Val would get me their autographs if I asked…"

"Third, it's the Porcupine Powerhouse of Yole High, Percival Parrish!"

Percival stumbled into the empty area seething, "I'm not a Porcupine!" Eventually, he straightened up and performed a flourishing bow before the crowd. One particular fangirl in the distance made a horrible banshee scream. Val covered her ears with her hands; this was one thing that definitely did NOT happen at Rejina.

"Next is the man known for accuracy and precision! Introducing Quincy Harris!"

Quincy smirked, and made his way to the center of the huddle. Once there, he adjusted his frames, paused for a giggle or two from the crowd, then began his hourly glaring match with Percival.

For this final introduction, Davide took a deep breath to signify extreme importance. All eyes were glued on him and the people in the middle, anticipating his next words. Even though everyone knew who the obvious final Regular was, such tension never hurt anyone.

"And now, the moment you've all been waiting for," Davide goaded, taking as long as possible to enunciate every syllable. "The *first freshman* to join the Yole High Nova Tennis Team in a whopping *three years*! VAL EN HAU SER!"

Most everyone on the team raised a gigantic cheer, and the freshmen were loudest of all. Val gladly joined her Regular peers, tugging her hat lower. She stepped between Percival and Quincy, accepting a victory slap on the back from the former.

Davide waited until it was quiet enough to continue with one of his favorite parts. He brought the megaphone to his lips, took a deep breath, and shouted, "Who are we?!"

"Yole High Phoenixes!" his students screamed back, voices ringing loud and clear. Cuyler and the twins brought their dominant hands to the center, and motioned for Percival, Quincy, and Val to do the same. Val excitedly followed suit, feeling the bonds of teamwork hold them together.

"What'll we do?!" Davide continued, putting his right hand on the very top of the pile.

Most everyone on the team raised a gigantic cheer, and the freshmen were loudest of all. Val gladly joined her Regular peers, tugging her hat lower. She stepped between Percival and Quincy, accepting a victory slap on the back from the former.

"Yole will win! Phoenixes will win! YOLE PHOENIXES WILL WIN!"

Davide repeated the mantra twice more, each time with increasing volume. Even Cuyler participated in the chant, his deep voice easily discernible from the rest of the chorus.

At last, a final deafening cheer arose from the crowd, and the arms of the Regulars flew up, towards the sun. Once the chatter had died down, he carried on.

"Practice begins again on Monday. Everyone, just relax this weekend, and be ready to work twice as hard when we come back. That is all."

And with that, Davide shut off the megaphone, but motioned for the new Regulars to stay. After accepting congratulations from both the twins and Cuyler, the three turned to their coach.

"You guys need to order your jerseys now," he explained, bringing up a file on his HoloPad. "I'm e-mailing you the order forms now, so once you fill it out just forward it back to me."

The three of them brought out their own HoloSticks to access the file, and Val shuddered with excitement.

"My jersey, with my name on it," she said, savoring the taste of the words. "Man, have I been waiting for this!"

"Some of us longer than others," Quincy muttered coldly. Val looked at him quizzically, but Davide quickly patted both students' backs.

"C'mon guys, play nice," he joked, though Quincy merely fixed his frames and walked away without another word. Percival cupped his hands around his mouth to jeer after him, but Davide shot him a warning glance. "Don't mind Quincy, Val, I just think he's upset he didn't become an official Regular as a freshman."

"He's just über negative," Percival agreed before walking away. "See you tomorrow, coach, and welcome to the team Val!"

"Thanks, see you later," Val called back, leaving Davide as well. The coach shrugged, thinking about the team dynamics.

Sierna didn't really like the twins, he thought, casually humming a love song as he walked to his minivan. *But that didn't affect much, so hopefully this year will be okay too.*

Alan and Heath had approached Val after she had left the coach, but now a swarm of the other six freshmen surrounded her.

"You were so awesome, Val!" Alan tried to say, but he kept being drowned out by his classmates' wishes for her to teach them tennis. She held her hands in front of her, shaking them back and forth.

"Whoa, whoa, one at a time, guys!" she cried, moments away from activating Amethyst just to defend herself. "What's with the sudden popularity?"

"You're the hero of the freshman, dude!" Heath enlightened her, with the grin of someone who was responsible. "Of course everyone wants to emulate you!"

"Well I can't teach you guys tennis if I'm training as a Regular," Val replied, to the dismay of many around her.

"At least tell us your secret," Gilbert pressed, and his friends repeated the question, curious. Val shrugged, shaking her head.

"No secret, I just like playing nova tennis," she said simply. "It's fun."

With that, she turned around to walk away, hands in her pockets, leaving the freshmen to ponder her words. Alan stared after her, admiring Val's aura. He was so absorbed in approbation that he did not notice Davide screaming after the twins, who had pilfered his keys, broken into his van, and were leaving tread marks across the baseball field.

~~~

"Yo, Don," Ronald muttered as he scrolled through the Yole High School student database. Donald tossed his GameStation Portable aside and leapt off their neon green couch, coming up behind his brother in a flash.

"What's up?" he asked, leaning over his Ronald's shoulder.

His twin pointed at his computer screen, his finger hovering over a certain name. Donald peered at the screen, and then rubbed his eyes in disbelief. "Whoa, did I read that right? Why the heck is Val set as *female*?!"

"That's what I was going to ask you," Ronald replied, turning around to face his older half. They looked at each other, mirroring confused expressions.

"This can only mean one thing," Donald began slowly, furrowing his brow. Ronald nodded, narrowing his eyes.

"Right. There's been a breach in security."

Donald pulled up the chair next to Ronald and turned on his own computer. "Ron, we gotta figure out who else is hacking into Yole!" he commanded, stretching his arms in front of him to crack his knuckles. "This is our territory! Kill all invaders!"

"Aye aye, sir!"

somechriskid: val's late
speedangel: yeah, she's usually on before u
powerbarbie: hope she's ok
carrottop has entered the chatroom
carrottop: HELLO EVERYONE!
powerbarbie: hi Bonnie
carrottop: oops, Caps again
speedangel: lol
powerbarbie: Bonnie, do you know where Val is?
carrottop: she's not here?
somechriskid: nope
speedangel: no
carrottop: good
speedangel: ???
somechriskid: thats not very nice
carrottop: no, Val said she wouldn't have time to log on today if she made the team
powerbarbie: oh yeah, results come out today
speedangel: so that's good news then!
speedangel: oh yeah, what'd you get for Q5 on the quiz today?

capnsword has entered the chatroom.
de_macho: hey valen, glad you could make it!
capnsword: thanks, um...
capnsword: de_macho? really?
aimtrue100: That was what I said too.
aimtrue100: Hello, Valen. I apologize for my actions earlier today. I'm looking forward to playing with you this year.
capnsword: thanks Harris, don't even worry about it. Congrats on becoming a Regular, too.
aimtrue100: Congratulations to you as well, for thrashing Porcupine so.
powerknight: stop tryin 2 impress every1 with "perfect grammar" Stylus!
de_macho: wait, what's wrong with my chatname?
aimtrue100: Better this than insufferable "txt-tlk", Porcupine!
capnsword: I dunno, it's just like...the prefix "de" is like "un", right?
powerknight has challenged aimtrue100 to a duel on Knightworld
de_macho: No wonder those dating chatrooms file out so quickly...
capnsword: where are the others?
de_macho: christian is rarely on, and the twins show up when they feel like it
c.c.cuyler has entered the chatroom.
de_macho: so you're on today
c.c.cuyler: Congratulations on becoming a Regular, Valen. Keep up the good work.
capnsword: oh, thank you Captain.
c.c.cuyler has exited the chatroom.
de_macho: cold as always...
capnsword: ...
capnsword: that's it?

aimtrue100 has defeated powerknight
aimtrue100: Satisfied yet? I would be more than happy to trounce you again.
powerknight has challenged aimtrue100 to a duel on Knightworld
de_macho: consider yourself lucky
de_macho: I guess…
capnsword: um, thanks?
aimtrue100 has defeated powerknight
aimtrue100: Give up, will you? My father dislikes it when I play on Knightworld too much.
powerknight: well 2 bad, Stylus!
powerknight has challenged aimtrue100 to a duel on Knightworld
capnsword: right. okay, I'm logging off now
de_macho: no problem, thanks for swinging by. good night, Valen
capnsword: good night, coach
capnsword has exited the chatroom.
de_macho has exited the chatroom.
powerknight has defeated aimtrue100
powerknight: PWNED!
aimtrue100 has exited the chatroom.
powerknight: sore loser, lol!
powerknight: oh, i'm the only 1 left?
powerknight: the captain was on?
powerknight: whos "capnsword"?
powerknight has exited the chatroom.

ROUND ONE

District Tournament

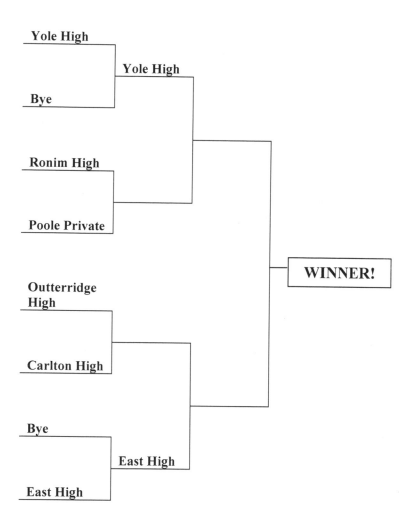

Yole High

Bye

    Yole High

Ronim High

Poole Private

    WINNER!

Outterridge High

Carlton High

Bye

East High

    East High

"This is my uniform?" Val asked, breathlessly. She had just opened up the box Davide gave her, and she was already impressed.

"It's great, isn't it?" Davide laughed heartily, as Val carefully took the clothes out of their packaging. "The company's filled our orders since before I was here; the best part is they're yours to keep."

"Seriously? Awesome!" she exclaimed, jumping with joy, unable to contain her excitement. "I've been dreaming of this day for so long, you have no idea how amazing this is!"

Truly, Val had always wanted a jersey of her own. She would often raid her friends' closets for their jerseys, but they were too loose, too tight, or smelled like the wrong type of sweat. But, this one fit like a glove, smelled like victory, and was hers and hers alone. The polo shirt also looked like a perfect match, and both the red-and-white track pants and shorts had two pockets big enough to fit two nova tennis balls each. The back of the jersey, though, was the best part, the part she stayed up at night thinking about. There, above the team logo of a phoenix and six balls, read "V. HAUSER."

In one fluid motion, she wrapped the jersey over her shoulders, turned around, and jerked a thumb towards the words. "Well?" she asked, beaming. "How cool do I look?"

Davide laughed again, clapping his hands. "It definitely suits you, that's for sure. Hurry up and get changed, though, or the other guys will barge in on you. I called for them fifteen minutes after you."

Val hurriedly gathered the clothing in her arms and disappeared into the locker rooms, still grinning toothily. Davide watched the door slam shut, and briefly returned to his office to prepare for practice.

Ordering the jersey for her was simple; it was her father who would be billed later anyway. The *real* work had come in the late morning, when Davide tried to get her on the team "legally." This entailed coercing one more person to help him hide Valen Hauser's true identity from the higher-ups of the sports world. All the teachers were privy to her secret already, so the only one left was the big man himself. After giving himself an hour-long pep talk (and practicing "mean" faces in the mirror), he left to face his boss.

In one fluid motion, she wrapped the jersey over her shoulders, turned around, and jerked a thumb towards the words. "Well?" she asked, beaming. "How cool do I look?"

The principal was completely against the entire idea. Having a girl on a boy's team was one thing, but to have her as a *Regular* was another thing completely. To have him, Nelson Nareba, keep the secret was absolute blasphemy. He would rather lose his title as District Principal of the Year to Old Mimsy from Ronim! (And that was really saying something. He had held that position for ten consecutive years and was not going to let one girl ruin his streak.)

Davide had fought for nearly an hour, saying Val could bring "infinite glory" to Yole High, but Nareba refused to budge from his position. "No" was his one and only answer to nearly everything.

When Davide offered to take him and his wife out to dinner at the fanciest restaurant in town: "No."

When he offered to hand wash his two cars every month: "No."

When he offered to shovel his driveway in the winter: silence.

"Sir?" Davide had asked hesitantly after a pregnant pause. His superior had been staring at him, clearly contemplating the toothsome offer.

"That's actually quite tempting, Davide," he had mused, leaning forward and stroking his beard. The coach rubbed the back of his neck diffidently. It was too late to admit he was kidding now.

"Every morning, before seven?" Nareba had asked with a voice of a man who signed paychecks.

"Um. Suuuure. Why, uh, not," he had managed to reply, straining his smile as widely as possible. He felt each of his cheek muscles groaning.

"Weekends too?"

Davide's eye twitched, and he tried not to grind his teeth down to the gum. It had taken him ten seconds to force the full word out of his mouth. "Yeeesss."

"Done deal then," Nareba had said, slapping his palm onto the table. His voice admitted defeat, but his eyes sang hymns of triumph. "She can stay. But on the one condition that any problems she causes, law suits included, are your problem and yours alone."

Davide immediately nodded, and began taking notes about Nareba's favorite brand of antifreeze on his HoloPad. A hollow victory, perhaps. He was saying hello to waking up at 3:30 AM or earlier for a good four months or more. But still, a win was a win, and if he had to forfeit one thing for Val, for his *team*, it might as well be his back health.

~~~

"Hey, now you're officially one of us!" Percival said as he walked up to Val hitting against the wall. "Über positive!"

Val swiftly caught the ball and shoved it in her pocket, again jerking a thumb at her back. "I know! It's so awesome!"

The twins suddenly appeared at her back, and while both were smiling, Ronald was cracking his knuckles for some reason.

"Not so fast, Sweeps," the older twin said, shaking his head. "You're not one of us 'till the ritual's done."

Percival met their eyes and began leering at the befuddled freshman as well. "That's right. It's your *initiation*."

Val backed away from the group, unsavory visions dancing in her mind. "I-I don't follow yo – oof," she muttered, finding herself against the stone wall. Her three teammates grinned devilishly, flanking her on all sides: Ronald on her right, Percival on her left, and Donald directly in front of her. Others had arrived, and were repeating the same mantra: "Read! Read! Read!" Even Heath had taken up the chant, but Alan was as horrified as Val. She threw her hands in front of her face, shuddering.

"Valen Hauser AKA Sweeps, ninth grader, 14 years old, originally from Rejina, Myraland before moving to Yole City, Neo York."

Val blinked and looked up. Donald was reading aloud from a HoloStick, as the surrounding students closed in to listen.

"5 foot 2, 110 pounds – "

"Dude, that's so *short*!" Ronald chortled, while Val tried not to blush about her weight. "No wonder we've got, like, two heads on you!"

"Allergic to penicillin, fully vaccinated, not currently on medication, blood type is B+, contact lenses for 20/40 vision – oof, that's worse than Stylus! Straight A's in everything except for History, which is a shameful C."

"Hey, just like me!" Percival interrupted, smiling broadly in her direction. "Well, the C part anyway."

"Emergency contact is her father, Richard Hauser, who works as a..." Donald trailed off suddenly, and gave Val an inquiring look. "Racquet tester? Seriously?"

Val nodded slowly as both Ronald and Percival leaned over his shoulder to take a better look. "Y-yeah, we moved here 'cause he was hired as a beta-tester at the new racquet factory an hour south. He said this was the best school in the area…"

Impressive murmurs rippled through the crowd. Percival gave a low whistle, and pointed at her necklace. "That's über positive, Val! Man, no wonder you get all the awesome new prototypes!"

Val shook her head quickly, still recovering from the shock. "Oh, n-no, Amethyst is from Rej – "

"Dwyryd."

"Oh, hi captain!" Donald said brightly, the HoloStick still displaying Val's personal file before him. While his brother smiled innocently beside him, Percival quickly spun around and walked away, whistling innocently. "You're a little late for the hazing, we couldn't find much info so I think I said everything embar – "

In one graceful movement, Cuyler grabbed the HoloStick from Ronald's clutches, took Val's racquet with his left hand, tossed the stick in the air above him, and served it into the bur-filled fields with a firm "Ungh!" The tiny piece of Novara flew forward, though how far, nobody could tell. It had disappeared from view before it – presumably – exploded, as many things Cuyler served were rumored to do.

"NOOOOOOO…" the twins moaned in exaggeratedly suspenseful unison. Ronald dropped to his knees as Donald trudged toward the grassy area, both crying into their hands. "Now we only have *five* copies left!"

The captain turned to the crowd behind him and placidly announced, "Fifteen warm up laps, everyone."

Everyone scrambled to the box of Hover Outsoles Davide was just bringing outside, squabbling over the "fastest pair," but the captain was far from done.

"Dwyryd, Dwyryd, and *Parrish*," he boomed as the air suddenly turned several degrees colder. Percival tensed up and turned around, chuckling nervously. Cuyler made eye contact with each student in turn before continuing. "You will each run thirty."

The three gawked at him as their teammates flew off to complete their rounds. When neither the twins nor Percival made any movement, Cuyler pointed Val's racquet at the sky.

"Now."

"YES SIR!" they cried. As they hurried to a bewildered Davide, Cuyler turned around and handed Val her racquet.

"Th-thank you, sir," she said, accepting it.

"It's a nice racquet," he said simply, walking over to the coach. "The sweet spot is a good size. Take good care of it."

Val swallowed and nodded, hugging Amethyst to her chest, before following Cuyler to grab the last pair of Outsoles.

~~~

"All right team, gather 'round!" Davide exclaimed after fifteen minutes of warming up. All the players ceased their hitting and headed to where Davide was standing with a HoloPad. Cuyler was right beside him, with his arms crossed, and his mouth firmly molded into the shape of a frown.

"Okay you guys, listen up," he began, looking at all 23 members of the team. "The District matches are going to be held at the end of the month. That only gives us two weeks to prepare. Even though most of the schools were pretty week in past years, things may have changed. East High is probably one to watch out for, but we've beat them every year for a decade, so don't be worried. They got second place last year, but went on to County to lose. Still, be on your toes.

"However, there's another school out there now: Outterridge High. It's not because they're powerful that they're a threat. We've never faced them before, since they just made a nova tennis team out of the blue. We have no info on them, so we've got to be prepared for anything.

"There are six teams entering the District matches. We and East High have 'byes', so we get to skip the first round and only play two matches instead of three. Both East and Outterridge are in the second block, so we won't meet either until the finals."

Everyone gave a cheer of upcoming victory, until Davide motioned with his hands that something more serious was about to be announced. The team immediately simmered down, curious about the news to follow.

"Now, on a more somber note," the coach began, with a face of utmost solemnity. "The School Board decided that providing the sports teams with free Fract-brand Granola Power Bars – "

"Ah, I *live* for those things!" Percival exclaimed out of nowhere, rubbing his hands together in glee. Val stared quizzically at him as Percival promoted Fract so greatly that she suspected the company had bribed him. "Man, if you ate one of those, you could take on the wor – !"

" – was not as important as supplying the Golf team with new clubs for their upcoming season," Davide finished, waiting for the bombshell sure to follow. It never came, however Percival did huddle in the far corner of the courts in the fetal position, hands over his head. His normally well-maintained spiky hair seemed like a field of wilted dandelions. His teammates simply stared at him, and then referred their attention back to Davide.

"Uh, well, everyone please try to get through this horrible loss to the team."

He turned to the stern captain, who had nodded at everything his superior had said, except for the appalling loss of free food. (While he had to agree that it was a letdown, Davide saying it was such an atrocious problem was rather irking.) "Anything you want to add, Christian?"

Cuyler turned slightly red, to everyone's amusement. For one reason or another, he was always embarrassed when someone called him by his given name, so he did his best to discourage it. No one had any idea why; they felt Christian was a very respectable name. Still, everyone followed his insistent suggestions except for the twins and Davide, when he felt Cuyler was being too stiff.

"No, I believe you covered it all," he answered, after clearing his throat to regain any lost authority. "Continue practice!"

"Yes sir!" the normal team members exclaimed, engaging their racquets and running off. While the Regulars usually used two courts, the other two were available for anyone quick enough to seize them, but seniority did come into play. However, the other three seniors had quit to pursue track and field, so the four juniors were next in line, followed by five sophomores. The eight other freshmen would not have a chance to get onto the courts until the last ranking matches, except for when Davide drilled all the non-regulars together.

"Let's practice doubles first, you guys," Davide said to his Regulars, bringing up his HoloPad screen. "Pair up, and two of you will do singles."

"Hey, wanna be partners bro?" Ronald asked, as though the idea had never struck him before. Donald pretended to muse over the thought with great intensity, crossing his arms and cocking his head to one side.

"Hmm, I wanted to play with the Captain, but I guess family comes first!" he joked.

"Hauser, would you like to team up with me?" Quincy asked, trying to make up for his actions on the previous day. Besides, he had three more years of high school including this year. He needed allies, not enemies, if he was to beat Percival to the coveted position of captain in their final year.

Unfortunately for him, Val shook her head, and trudged to the adjacent court with a hand on her hat bill. "Nah, I'm not that much of a doubles person. Thanks for the offer though."

Percival perked up, and pointed a finger at Val. "Hey, then you wanna play singles against me again?"

"Sure!" came the delighted response. Quincy withheld a sigh at losing to Percival, but was unable to stifle it when he realized the Captain was the only person left with whom to pair up, the person who always played first singles. He would have to work extra hard to please Cuyler, and guarantee there were absolutely no faults in his play. *Then again*, Quincy thought, adjusting his glasses with a smirk, *there are no flaws in my play in the first place.*

"So you don't like doubles either, huh?" Percival asked, his wrist perfectly healed now. Val shook her head as they continued to rally lightly.

"It's not that I don't. To be honest, I've never played doubles before," she admitted, hitting another backhand. "Either way, though, it doesn't really seem like my style." She shrugged. "What's all the hype for anyway?"

"It's nothing special, but the twins would kill me for saying that," Percival answered, chuckling. "It's full of you and your partner not getting along, mis-hit balls, and lots and lots of communication problems."

Val looked somewhat relieved. "Gotcha."

Hamilton and the rest of the juniors immediately took up Court C as the five sophomores on Court D squabbled over who would be stuck on the sidelines first. All students wished that Regulars would see their wonderful skill and power, and perhaps Davide would even kick someone off to make room for them. Sadly, such a thing was only a fantasy. Their best bet was to become a reserve player in the case of an injury or if the score was a two wins and two losses. In the latter event, which occurred quite frequently between evenly matched schools, teams had a choice between having a match between coaches or non-Regular players. While in the higher ranking tournaments Davide usually took up the gauntlet, if he thought they stood a chance with someone else, he would let that deprived player take his place.

The remaining freshmen began hitting against the stone wall and working on the conditioning regime Davide had e-mailed them: pushups and sit-ups. Alan struggled through them, and he felt even more tired when exercising next to Heath, who was going at quadruple the pace. Still, whenever he admired Val holding her own against Percival, he returned to his practice with renewed vigor.

"Okay, switch it up!" Davide exclaimed, after Donald and Ronald had won best three out of five games against Cuyler and Quincy by winning three in a row. "Don, Ron, play singles. C'mon Valen, Perce, hustle!"

Quincy bowed his head to Cuyler in apology, as if that would make up for the ghastly loss they had suffered. Cuyler, who was drinking some water, gave no acknowledgement. Percival chuckled mockingly, coming up from behind.

"Ha, looks like you couldn't stand a chance against the twins!" he goaded, bringing his own water bottle to their court from the previous one. Quincy gritted his teeth in annoyance.

"Back off, Porcupine," he snarled back, as Val and Cuyler ignored the quarrel and shook hands. "Let's watch your skills on the courts."

"Oooh, I'm so scared."

The rivals glared at each other, then turned on their heels and retreated to the baseline without exchanging formalities.

Percival and Val positioned themselves on one side, and Quincy and Cuyler did the same on the other. Davide looked up from his HoloPad to watch the four warriors intently.

Percival stood valiantly at the baseline, his racquet balanced neatly on his shoulders and a cocky smile on his lips. Cuyler was as noble as a king on his throne, even whilst standing. He towered over pretty much everyone and anyone, at a whopping 6 feet. Thanks to Heath, all the freshmen knew Cuyler used a Bilson Radix, with a silver frame that shimmered like Val's Amethyst, and was equipped with the same black grip as Percival's. (More specifically, Percival used the same grip as the captain. In fact, the only reason Percival chose Bilson grips was that Cuyler preferred them.) However, his grip was in much better shape, and showed no clear signs of wear. His strings displayed Bilson's logo, a bold "B."

Quincy, on the other hand, played with a Conex Aeradz, which Heath said gave him the accuracy for which he was known. It had a light blue frame and a silver grip that looked like it would slip out of his hands at a moment's notice. The water waves of the Conex logo adorned the sweet spot of his racquet face. He was about an inch shorter than Percival, but he carried his air of superiority all the same.

Val appeared the most out of place due to the large height difference, but she either did not realize it or she simply did not care, and Davide had a strong suspicion it was the latter. Her uniform complimented her nicely, and her hat added an extra personal flair. Davide could not put his finger on exactly what it was, but so far, it seemed like a good thing. When she gripped her pure white handle, and let sunlight filter through the strings, she looked like she could take on anyone.

"Okay, start!" Davide exclaimed, throwing a ball to Quincy, who would be serving first if they won the toss.

"Red or blue?" the sophomore shouted to the duo on the other side.

"Blue!" Percival called out, holding out a thumbs-down, before Val could even ask which one he wanted. Quincy heaved the ball onto the ground, and when it came up, it was red.

"Our serve, I'm afraid," he declared, as Cuyler positioned himself at the net, between the left doubles sideline and the dividing line separating the left and right sides of the court. Quincy went to the right side of the baseline, bisecting the double's sideline and the hash mark. Doubles players did this to increase serving percentage (as well as to avoid hitting the back of their partner's head), but for singles most players stationed themselves a little closer to the center mark.

Percival and Val spoke briefly, and then carried out their strategy: Val would keep the ball in play while Percival overwhelmed them with power. They would both pray that Quincy made all the mistakes.

Percival went to the right of the baseline to receive the serve first, while Val stood at the line separating front and back areas on the left side. Thus, Val was facing Quincy, who was serving to Percival diagonally, who was in front of Cuyler at the net.

(Davide smirked cynically as he drew the diagram, recalling how many a past girlfriend would just give him a blank stare when he tried to enlighten them about tennis positions. Nova tennis, while very entertaining, was extremely confusing and hard to explain to those who were not raised with the sport.)

Quincy adjusted his glasses by their frames one more time before bouncing the ball to prepare the point. He followed a very specific routine that most blamed on OCD. While he claimed no such disorder plagued him, the fact that even his shoelaces had to be perfectly symmetrical convinced people otherwise. Once the ball had hit the ground ten times, he exhaled.

"Take this!" Quincy yelled, thrusting the ball into the air. He struck directly in the sweet spot, and the ball sped right towards Percival's side, landing precisely on the intersection point of the two lines that separated the left box from the right, and the front from the back. It was good, just like the many times before.

"That's Quincy's Supersonic Serve!" one of the juniors said, awestruck. "Always somewhere on the line, never once has it ever landed out!"

"It's amazing!" agreed another. However, Percival had other things to say about it, as he ran up to the ball.

"Huh, 'amazing', you say?" he exclaimed, hitting a backhand with so much force that it turned red. His shot whizzed over the net back at Quincy; Cuyler was too far to get it. "It's got no power! A little kid could hit harder than that!"

Quincy growled in annoyance, and ran up to the ball. "A simpleton like you could never understand!" he shouted back, hitting it on the rise, straight to Val.

"Here I go!" she cried, excited to be doing something. She quickly dashed towards its would-be landing point. By the time Percival realized what Val was doing, it was too late.

"Val, don't hit it to the captain!" he yelled. It was all for naught, though; Val had already followed through, the ball zooming directly at Cuyler.

If anyone blinked, they would have missed Cuyler hit a drive volley directly down the centerline, between a flabbergasted Percival and Val. Donald and Ronald, who had stopped practicing to watch the match, burst out in maniacal laughter. Val had just committed the most sinful of all Doubles mistakes: hitting to the net person. Even Percival, who scoffed at strategy, knew that such a move was never a smart idea, unless they *planned* to lose a point.

Davide was chuckling it off, despite the clear annoyance spreading across his face, and wrote a note in the upper left corner of his board.

"Val to *never* play doubles," he muttered, as Percival decided to tell his teammate exactly what she did wrong.

"You never, never, never, never, NEVER hit it to the net person in doubles!" he exclaimed, mostly in surprise that a player as seemingly knowledgeable as Val had made such a novice mistake. He was shaking Val back and forth by her shoulders as violently as a rag doll. Once she finally broke free and regained her senses, she opened her mouth to protest.

"How was I supposed to know?" she asked defensively. "I told you, I've never even played doubles before! And," she hesitantly pointed to the wider sidelines of the alley, blushing scarlet. "Is that the doubles sideline?"

"YES!" Percival seethed, his hair seemingly bristling in emphasis. While Cuyler still stood in a ready stance, unfazed, Quincy withheld a laugh. The twins were on the ground howling.

Percival took a deep breath, and then shook his head.

"Okay, you know what, never mind, just return Stylus' serve," he said, aggravated. "And just…just don't return it to the captain." Val nodded, keeping her head down, and proceeded to walk slowly to the left side of the baseline.

Quincy waited until everyone was in position before thrusting the ball up into the air. "15-Love!"

Quincy's accuracy was just as perfect as before, just skimming the center mark and bouncing up to Val. Val managed to hit it back at Quincy, who immediately aimed a return back at her. Percival cast a critical eye on her movements, but she proved a fast learner and sent a high lob directly back at Quincy. The bespectacled sophomore licked his lips. *A lob, eh? Well, two can play at that game.*

He backed up a bit and parroted Val, sending the tennis ball high into the air in a beautiful arc. However, this was exactly what Percival was looking forward to.

"Bad move, Stylus!" he exclaimed, as he ran backwards to get into position. "I am the MASTER of overhead smashes!"

Val readied herself in case Percival missed, but nevertheless exclaimed, "Do it, Perce! Return the favor!"

Percival was just too happy to oblige, as he jumped up with the perfect timing he spent hours of his freshman year honing. Using all the muscles in his right arm, he slammed the ball towards the middle of the court with such intensity that it turned red far before passing over the net. Unfortunately for them, he forgot one important fact.

Cuyler was a southpaw.

In the blink of an eye, the captain had stepped towards the back left, and performed a delicate drop shot on Percival's side, with all the grace of a swan. The sophomore was still in the air by the time it passed him, and even though Val raced as quickly as she could to the net, her racquet hit only empty air. Davide quickly added Percival's name and a couple of exclamation points to his previous notes.

Percival landed on the ground, disappointed. Val, too, welled with irritation; she could have won that point in singles, no problem! Granted, it was partially – if not mostly – her fault for being too focused on solo strategies to care about anything else. She pondered whether she would have had to play this dreaded game of pairs if she stayed in Rejina, and glumly accepted that the answer was "yes."

Percival and Val drowned out Quincy's sycophantic words to the captain, and got into position while avoiding each other's eyes. Cuyler, on the other hand, wanted to take this opportunity to lecture both opponents, and made his presence explicitly clear.

"You both got careless, bred from overconfidence," he said, voice carrying over to all the courts, though he did not even try. "That is an impossible pleasure if any of us desire to make it to Nationals. You must remember to keep your defenses high; all of us do."

The pair nodded, and stood at the ready, determined to take back all the points they had lost with sweat and, if necessary, blood.

It was all for naught. Quincy and Cuyler won three games in a row to Percival and Val's zero. While Quincy glided off the court with a sly smirk (Cuyler still had the ever-present frown), Percival and Val swayed away with disheartened faces. Davide put hands on both their shoulders, but pulled them back when he felt how saturated with sweat their clothes were.

"Come on, now," he said cheerfully, but even he could hear the fakeness in his voice. "Everyone has strengths and weaknesses! We'll just have to, you know, always, um, put you in…in singles." Davide tried to smile but it came out strained. All three of them knew that if Percival and Val always had to be in second singles, they would have to forget Nationals. Even the County tournament would be a hopeless fallacy.

He expected them to nod solemnly and head to the showers to let the hot water drown the sorrow, like he used to do. Maybe Percival would punch a wall or two, but he wondered if Val would have some excuse plausible enough to explain how in the world a player of her caliber managed to make it to high school without learning the basic rules of doubles. Davide waited for them to do *something* other than look dreadfully miserable.

After a few moments, the losers gave each other sidelong glances.

"I hate losing to Stylus," Percival muttered monotonously.

"I hate losing, period," Val replied, in the same fashion.

"We'll drag down the team if both of us are in singles all the time," the sophomore continued.

"And we can't pair Harris with the captain every match," the girl added. They stared at each other through tired eyes for several seconds, studying each other. The fatigue eventually gave way to determination, and the pair broke into simultaneous grins. Suddenly, they whipped their heads around and, with pleading faces, exclaimed, "Coach! Put us in second doubles!"

Everyone, including the non-Regulars, paused what they were doing to stare at them in disbelief.

"Why do they *want* to play doubles?" Alan asked Heath, who had likewise stopped exercising to watch the commotion. "They were so bad!"

Heath shrugged, blowing the windswept hair out of his eyes. "Dunno. Maybe because Districts is the weakest tournament, so it'd be okay if they lost. Or it's pride. I mean, let's face it. Nobody likes to lose."

Davide looked from Percival, to Val, to Cuyler (who was still frowning, but gave a curt nod), and back to the pair. Finally, he groaned and agreed, either because he thought it was a good idea, or because two high school students with such persistent eyes put him in an uncomfortable position. He got enough of *that* from his sister.

"Fine, fine, you can play doubles!" he snapped, thrusting his peeved hands into the air. "You were going to anyway once I trained you enough, but if you want shorter coaching time, fine by me. Just don't screw up! We'll probably win the other three matches, but don't go making us look bad in the first round!"

With that, he stormed off, darkly muttering something about puppies. He continued his grumblings while overseeing the other students practice.

Percival smiled contentedly, and then clenched a fist, offering it to Val.

"So, wanna get some extra practice in?" he asked, winking. Val nodded, and held her hand out too.

"You got it," she said, bumping her fist against Percival's. "Partner."

aimtrue100 has entered the chatroom.
thing1tweedledum: then BAM, Ron cracks the password!
de_macho: why do I tolerate this behavior...?
tweedledeething2: cause u know we'll do the same 2 u!

de_macho: sadly that's true
de_macho: hey there Quince
aimtrue100: Hello Coach. Is Porcupine here yet?
de_macho has changed his username to cantgetadateloser
tweedledeething2: score!
thing1tweedledum: should've reported it!
cantgetadateloser: you guys are running laps tomorrow
tweedledeething2: worth
thing1tweedledum: it
aimtrue100 has exited the chatroom.
thing1tweedledum: i think we scared him away
tweedledeething2: a geek like him'll have a tough password, gimme a minute
thing1tweedledum: so LOSER, wheres perce?
cantgetadateloser: you're super lucky I'm so forgiving.
cantgetadateloser: he's still practicing with Val
thing1tweedledum: still?
tweedledeething2: oh, think I got it
tweedledeething2: no, nvm, got his sister's
cantgetadateloser: well considering today's practice they need it
thing1tweedledum: true
tweedledeething2: crap, why the heck would i need his dads credit card number?!
thing1tweedledum: tag out, lemme try
thing1tweedledumSFXERROR
thing1tweedledumSFXERROR
thing1tweedledumSFXERROR
thing1tweedledumSFXERROR
thing1tweedledumSFXERROR
thing1tweedledumSFXERROR
thing1tweedledumSFXERROR
thing1tweedledumSFXERROR
thing1tweedledumSFXERROR
thing1tweedledumSFXERROR
thing1tweedledumSFXERROR
can'tgetadateloser: ooookaaay…
can'tgetadateloser has exited the chatroom.
aimtrue100 has entered the chatroom.
aimtrue100: Just for the record, you should never mess with a geek and his computer.
aimtrue100 has exited the chatroom.
tweedledeething2: well played Stylus. we admit defeat.
tweedledeething2: for now
tweedledeething2 has exited the chatroom.

EXTRA PRACTICE

The front door opened and slammed shut within the span of two seconds. Richard barely had time to look up from his Chinese takeout to see his daughter standing before him, finger pointed at his face. She was huffing, her hat was lopsided, and from the moment she set foot in the kitchen, the smell of her sweat had diffused through the room. Her pained face stared at him breathlessly. Richard guessed what was wrong and immediately put on his "stern father" façade.

"Look, if you wanted egg rolls, you should have told m – "

"Teach me doubles!"

Richard realized he was mistaken and took the opportunity to snatch the last fried wonton while Val's eyes were still focused on him.

"Is that why you're home late? Anyway, I told you doubles was good to know, remember?"

"Yes, fine, you were right, I was wrong," she answered quickly, although the next morning she would never admit to saying it. "I should've listened to you before, but since I didn't, teach me doubles *now*." She took a deep breath and relaxed somewhat. "Please."

Richard chewed slowly, enjoying that persistent look in his daughter's eyes. It looked so familiar, from a time long past...

"Set everything up in the basement, then," he decided. "I'll be there in ten minutes."

Val immediately brightened up and gave her father a peck on the cheek.

"Thank you so much dad!" she exclaimed, running out of the room as quickly as she had entered. Her footsteps echoed down the stairs. "I love you!"

Richard sighed, but it was full of an old man's contentment. This was one of the few times that he and his daughter ever saw eye-to-eye on anything. Gleefully looking forward to the night's future events, he reached out for the platter of vegetable dumplings. In a blur of motion, a hand seized the plate, and yet another grabbed a fortune cookie. After stuffing an entire dumpling in her mouth, Val scanned the table for anything else to take, ignoring her father's flabbergasted expression. Finally, she swallowed.

"What, no chopsticks?"

~~~

"You look like death," the twins said in unison, when Val showed up at practice the next afternoon. She had bandages covering her arms and legs, and bags under her eyes. Her hands, too, were raw, and her arms hung by her sides limply, like seaweed.

"I, ah, got some extra training in yesterday," she answered quietly, tugging her hat lower as she recalled the previous night.

Her father was a tough coach, and his special training session had lasted until dawn, as usual. She had slept through most of her classes, begging Alan to be both a note taker and an alarm clock. He was more than happy to oblige, even more impressed at how fervent a player she was. Meanwhile, Heath took the initiative to create several more rumors to tack onto her legacy.

"Seems like someone else did too," Donald said in surprise, pointing behind her. "Look."

She painfully turned her neck to see someone else hobble up the path.

Percival.

Her jaw dropped to the ground. Not only were his legs wrapped like a mummy's, but his face was home to several adhesive bandages too. When he saw Val's condition, though, he stopped dead in his tracks. The two stared at each other for a while, eyes as wide as tennis balls. Different feelings raced through their minds, but there was one common thought:

I can't believe someone else is as stubborn as me!

It took Davide to break the silence.

"Yo!" he said cheerfully, as he came up behind Percival. He proceeded to slap him on the back, as was their usual greeting. This time, however, the sophomore stumbled forward and fell, legs sprawled out behind him.

"Ow."

~~~

"I can't tell if you're both idiots, stubborn idiots, or clones of the same stubborn idiot," Davide sighed, replacing the bandages Percival had inexpertly applied. The two players sat side-by-side silently on the bench, exchanging rueful grins. Cuyler had let them skip laps – this time – after seeing just how pathetic the two looked. "You really shouldn't train this recklessly without adult supervision."

"My dad was watching me," Val argued back, somewhat annoyed. "And we're high school students!"

"You look like death," the twins said in unison, when Val showed up at practice the next afternoon. She had bandages covering her arms and legs, and bags under her eyes.

"Yeah, and I was on school grounds," Percival added, though he knew how week an argument it was. Davide gave them both exasperated looks, and stood up, motioning for them to do the same.

"Fine, whatever. You can play, right?"

"Don't underestimate me!" Percival roared, activating his racquet to make a point. Val clenched a fist, brown eyes flooded with ambition.

"No pain, no gain!"

Davide smiled, admiring their attitudes, but bittersweet memories had begun to rise to the surface as he watched them hobble to the courts. Recklessness and enthusiasm had led him far, and he was glad his students shared his ideals. It would make the team stronger in the end, but only if they knew when enough was enough. Without any notion of their limits, it was the coach's job to stop them from going over the edge. He just hoped he would be capable of the task.

~~~

"Davide, I feel sort of guilty beating them up like this," Ronald hollered to his coach. "It's like running over a piece of road kill with a steamroller."

Val suppressed the urge to vomit. "Please don't say that," she begged while massaging her arms. Percival hoisted himself off the ground, wiping the dirt from his shirt. *Even if it is true.*

Their coach was training the other students on the far court, while Cuyler and Quincy played doubles with two juniors, and over the din, it was impossible for Davide to hear anything. Donald sighed, and crossed his arms, walking up to the net.

"Well, we're really not getting anywhere with you guys torn up like that."

"Sorry," they said simultaneously. Ronald put one hand in his pocket, the other twirling his racquet around his wrist.

As Heath had told Val almost a million times already, it was a beautiful Lundop 2000, with a bright yellow frame and a neon orange grip covering the handle. His brother had a similar racquet, except Donald's frame was orange with a dazzling yellow grip. People often asked why they did not opt for more conservative colors with which to garb their handles, but the answer was always "because these colors annoy our opponents!" said with a devilish grin. Indeed, it gave Val a headache just watching Ronald spin it around and around.

Suddenly, the younger twin caught it, sighing. "I'm bored. Bro, think of something."

Donald nodded and clapped his hands, seemingly channeling his inner Davide. "Okay then, I've decided! Since you two are physically out of commission, let's test your doubles strategy!"

Val brightened up. "Excellent! My dad quizzed me on this all night, so I think I've got it down."

Percival, on the other hand, hung his head. This was where their similarities ended. "Why can't I just hit power shots all the time?" he grumbled, crossing his arms and looking away. "It works in singles."

Donald clucked his tongue, shaking a finger. "That kind of attitude is why you guys lost so horrifically to Stylus yesterday, dude! The same strategies in singles won't get you far here. Remember, singles is fine for the average player, but doubles is for men." Before Percival could open his mouth to protest, Donald clapped his hands together again. "Okay then, Ron, let's go through Situation Alpha."

His brother saluted and proceeded to somersault to the baseline while the other two exchanged confused glances. Donald stayed at the net, bouncing on the balls of his feet in the ready position, as he gave directions.

"Okay, since you guys will die if you make any sudden movements, just stand there for now. Pretend Ronald is serving to Sweeps. Where will you return it?"

"To Ronald's side?" she suggested.

"Well, duh," Donald replied blankly. Val hung her head, feeling somewhat incompetent. "I mean where on the court."

"Somewhere he won't get to it?"

"Are you being stupid on purpose, or did all that training yesterday mess with your head? I thought you studied for this."

"A high lob down the line!" she said at last. In response, Ronald dashed to his left, simulating a return. Donald nodded, still staying on his toes.

"Okay, one possibility. Ron, where do you hit it?"

"Right down the middle. Who'll get it?"

"Me," Val and Percival said simultaneously. They looked at each other, while Donald facepalmed.

"Or he would get it," they both said hastily, trying to rectify the situation. This time, Ronald's face landed in his palm with a *smack*. Finally, they tried again.

"One of us would call it?"

"Thank you!" Donald announced, sweeping his arms out. "And if both or neither of you called it?" Before either could open their mouths, he stopped them. "Wait, I'll tell you now instead of risking giving myself a black eye to match my brother's. There's really not a strict rule, so decide right now what to do. We usually go with whoever's on the forehand side."

"Oh, so I *was* right!" Percival exclaimed. Donald ignored him.

"Okay, so Perce hits it back where?"

"Short down the line?"

Donald took one step, and his long legs placed him directly in the field of fire. "Bam. We win."

"A lob down the line?"

Again, Ronald ran towards the spot indicated, not even trying to hide the boredom on his face. "And back to Val it goes."

Val suddenly widened her eyes. "OH! I'll go to the net this time!" Her initial exuberance was quelled when Donald's jaw dropped. "No? I'm wrong?"

"No, you're right," he said, feigning utter astonishment. He began to tear up. "Sweeps, I'm...I'm so *proud* of you! You've grown so much!" When he sensed the blatant lack of laughter, he coughed, and continued.

"Right. Having someone at net is important in doubles, since it cuts off the number of places your opponent can hit to. Well, assuming your reflexes are good enough. Val, how're your volleys?"

Before she could respond, Donald produced a ball out of thin air and chucked it in her direction. She immediately hit it crosscourt, justifying a nod from the elder twin. Two seconds later, he threw one at Percival. It hit him squarely in the face. Even Val had a tough time suppressing a laugh when his hair bristled up in anger.

"Heh, sorry Per – whoa!"

Donald dodged the point-blank projectile an enraged Percival had hit his way. The ball clanged loudly against the fence behind them. Percival crossed his arms, frowning.

"They're fine," he answered sullenly, avoiding eye contact with his teammates. Val and the twins exchanged looks briefly, but said nothing. Ronald suddenly remembered why they made sure to tease Quincy more than him. While Quincy could get his revenge with a simple computer virus, Percival would *kill* them.

"Riiight. Okay then, so Val's at net, and you hit it – "

"Hopefully crosscourt for a winner."

"Correct! Assuming I get it and it goes down the line – "

"I'll slam it and run up to net as well," Percival answered, still stubbornly evading everyone's eyes.

Donald sighed in relief. *They're not stupid idiots after all!* He thought, raising his face to the heavens. *We may actually stand a chance now!*

Suddenly, thunder rumbled in the distance. The puffy white clouds he had been admiring transformed into an angry gray as abruptly as his mom's Transitions Lenses. He continued to display his impressive flexibility by bending backwards further until he could see his brother, who was staring at the storm like a normal person.

Davide's whistle resounded through the courts, in a duet with Cuyler's voice.

"All right guys, let's call it early," Davide announced once everyone had turned their heads in his direction. "Mother Nature is one woman I will *not* flirt with."

"Aren't you already dating Ms. Miceli?" Ronald announced loudly. Percival immediately cheered up once someone else was being teased, and joined in on the mirth. Davide glared at the speaker, mentally assigning laps to him.

"My social life is mine! Practice is officially over!"

Everyone raced out of the courts, but only two stayed behind. They exchanged glances with each other, then in the direction of the gray clouds, which seemed so far away. Val opened her mouth, but was cut off when Davide called for them to come inside. Her eyes met Percival's again, but this time he shrugged, and they did as they were told.

Alan had stayed behind to wait for Val, but upon noticing how she trudged, he decided against it. He would just e-mail the notes to her later.

~~~

Val sat against the school building, watching the electricity show in front of her. The graying sky would briefly light up with every flash, but would darkle again just as quickly. When thunder boomed from directly overhead, Val barcely blinked. She would have felt more fear had gloominess not been consuming her. Sighing, she hugged her knees closer to her chest. Val had not bothered changing out of her uniform. Instead, she just pulled the team sweatpants over her shorts.

She played out the day's events in her head. *Even after all that training,* she thought glumly, bringing her chin to her knees, *Perce and I still aren't good enough.*

Suddenly, someone sat beside her. She turned her head to see Percival, looking somewhat sheepish. He was dressed the same way, and reeked as much as she suspected she did. Apparently, he too lacked the energy and heart to change clothes.

"Hey," he said, leaning his head against the wall. Val gave a curt nod, and turned back to the courts. They were silent for a while, and finally Percival exhaled and spoke.

"Sorry about the, you know," he muttered. "I get real irritated if things aren't going my way. It's über negative, I know."

Val shook her head and looked back at him. "Nah, it's fine, I understand. I'm the same."

Percival smiled, patting Val softly on the back. His eyes glistened with gratitude. "Thanks, man."

Thunder rumbled again, seemingly louder than a jet engine. Their eyes flickered back to the graying clouds, which loomed ever closer. Percival rose slowly, and offered his hand to Val, who gratefully accepted the help.

"We'd better get out of here," he said, walking to the parking lot. "You need a ride?"

"You have a car?" she asked in surprise. Percival laughed uneasily.

"Yeah, um, no, a bike," he answered, motioning to the last bicycle on the rack. A wire basket in the front held his empty lunch bag, which he had dumped unceremoniously after emptying it of its edible contents.

"You want me to sit in *that*?" she asked incredulously, pointing to the rickety case.

Percival quickly shook his head as he began unlocking the bike. "No, there are spokes attached to the back wheel. You can stand on them. Don't look so scared, man, I did this with my dad when I was younger."

Younger, Val repeated, rubbing the back of her neck. She winced, the pain reminded her if the training she endured yesterday and would no doubt repeat tonight of her own volition. Lightning that struck so closely that she could feel the electrons dancing on her skin made her decision for her.

"Hang on tight!" her teammate shouted, having livened up considerably. Val dug her nails into Percival's shoulders, shutting her eyes. Percival never bothered bringing a helmet during his rides, so Val wondered how much head protection a tweed cap would provide. At least the road was smooth, and the "backseat" was quite comfortable, even with the tire whirring between her knees. As long as her grip was strong enough, she would live to see tomorrow.

"Where do you live?"

"59 Ashe, off the corner of Roddick," she hollered, competing with both the wind and thunder.

"Oh, that's pretty close. Would you mind if I grabbed a burger first?"

"I guess no – ahhh!!"

Val instinctively snatched her hat before it lifted off her head. A few strands of hair had escaped; she would have to redo it when Percival was distracted. She figured that would be easy, though. If the very thought of food had reenergized him so, its actual presence would provide an equally adequate diversion. Once they stopped speeding past cars, of course.

Percival took a sharp right, jerking Val to the left. Her hands had recovered enough to save her life, but she still squeezed Percival's shoulder.

"Hey, could you try not to kill me?" she shouted over the din. Something flew into her mouth and struck her uvula. She gagged and did her best not to think about what it was.

"Oh, sorry," he laughed, easing on the pedals. The scenery stopped blurring together, and Val finally looked at where they were, gasping as she did.

What usually took her a fifteen-minute walk had been covered in less than three. The houses were again familiar, but instead of continuing on, Percival was signaling to turn left. She was about to open her mouth, and say she could walk from here, but Percival cut her off.

"Thanks for coming with me Val," he said calmly. He chanced a quick glance behind him. His eyes had softened, and Val could tell she was staring at the true Percival. "For some reason, being with you clears my head. I'm really glad we can talk like this."

He turned back to concentrate on the road, apparently overlooking the tresses poking out from Val's hat. He began humming nonchalantly, Val's mouth still hanging open. The words rang through her head. Other than Alan, the only other people who ever said words like that to her were her Rejina tennis friends.

She closed her mouth before another bug could enter, and smiled, relaxing her grip on both his shoulder and her hat. She leaned forward, letting the wind whip her face.

"No prob, man. But you're paying."

~~~

"Cheers!" they cried, tapping their sodas together happily. Percival dug into his triple cheeseburger with delighted relish. Val snickered, biting into her own chicken wrap.

"Dude, didn't you eat, like, three sandwiches for lunch?"

"Yeah, I'm starving," he answered, voice muffled by a mouth full of meat. Half his burger was already gone. He grabbed his medium Valley Frost and slurped it noisily. After coming up for air, he belched satisfyingly. "Ah, that hit the spot." He grinned widely at Val, who smiled back.

He might be a hothead sometimes, but he's still a cool guy and good friend. And hopefully doubles partner, Val thought somewhat somberly, losing her appetite. When she lowered her hands, Percival seemed to sense her thoughts, and held out a fist.

"Hey, we'll get this doubles thing down," he said, brimming with conviction. His voice was entirely serious, and he was smiling confidently. "I believe in you, in me, in *us*. One hundred percent."

Val nodded back brightly, and reached over with her arm as well. "Yeah. We *will* win our doubles matches, I can feel it." *And we'll do it together.*

"So…why Porcupine?"

"Long story."

"We've got time."

~~~

The days passed, one after another. The twins, the self-proclaimed masters of doubles, drilled Percival and Val mercilessly every practice, reprimanding them harshly if they did even the slightest thing wrong. They needed it, though. Every day, they improved tenfold, exceeding even Davide's expectations. There was no way the twins were *that* good of teachers.

Finally, they reached the last day of practice before the District tournament. The players assembled before Davide, who had only one thing to say.

"Good practice everyone! Now go home and get some rest, and show up at the Tournament courts bright and early tomorrow at nine!"

A huge cheer erupted, and the players raced to the locker rooms to change. Davide was too distracted to realize two Regulars had hung back, hidden in the foliage. In fact, they did not reveal themselves until Davide had at last driven away.

Percival finally stepped out of the bushes, and signaled to his partner that the coast was clear. Val emerged behind him, tightening her hat for one last round. They simultaneously held out their fists.

"Let's do it."

~~~

The last rays of sunlight disappeared behind the Yole High school building. The parking lot was completely vacant; only a light blue bike remained chained to the rack, waiting for its master and passenger to ride it home. Within moments, the streetlights flickered on, immediately attracting a cult of moths.

Two figures were still on the nova tennis courts, breathing heavily. They stood at opposite baselines, chests heaving, but they both clutched their racquets tightly.

"Again! Situation beta!" the younger player repeated, her face smudged by sweat and dirt. Percival nodded, and thrust his racquet upwards.

"EXPLOSION!"

Val dashed to the left and hit a return on the rise, aiming it for the doubles alley. Percival had already began racing there after serving, and skillfully returned it to the right side of Val's court.

Practice had ended three hours ago, but the night was young; the previous days they had lingered until mosquitoes emerged and purloined several pints of AB- and B+. They still felt they were far from done, though. The first day of their secret practice, they vowed not to stop until a thirty-hit rally was played by doubles strategies, since with the twins they could barely get past three. The next day, they rashly increased it to fifty. Almost two weeks later, their record was forty-seven.

Val instinctively ran directly to the path of the ball. She cried out and managed to get the tip of her racquet onto the ball with enough power behind it to aim for the doubles alley once again, this time down the line. Pure willpower was the only thing that drove her; she had lost all feeling in her arms after returning so many of Percival's shots.

Within seconds, Percival was at the ready, this time hitting a backhand return. Again, he forced Val to keep her legs pumping, and she did the same for him.

The ten-hit benchmark was passed, as was the twenty, thirty, and forty. Eventually the two stopped counting aloud, and their bodies moved on their own. Both were at their limits, but Percival managed to gather enough energy to swing his racquet one more time. The moment he did, though, he noticed something was off.

His hit sped forward, but the ball struck the top part of the net. While it did go over, it was jostled upwards a fraction of an inch before beginning its descent to the ground. Percival collapsed onto his hands and knees; this was one drop shot he did *not* want. With the last of his strength, he howled, "HIT IT VAL!!!"

His partner had already reached the service line by the time he finished shouting. Her muscles begged her to stop, and even her brain warned her it was futile. But her heart, and the feelings contained within, told every part of her body not to give up.

I can do this!

At the last moment, when her eyes registered just how little distance was left, she leapt.

"Ahhhhhhh!" she cried as she dove forward, thrusting her racquet as far as her arm would allow it. Although her eyes had shut upon impact, by some miracle, she felt a small vibration; the ball had landed! She commanded her limbs to do one more thing for her, and weakly flicked the ball upwards.

Neither Percival nor Val dared to look, but they did anyway, and watched with combined horror and fascination as the ball landed on the top of the net, trembled, and slid down onto Percival's side of the court. Once it touched the ground it had missed for so long, it rolled away.

Percival and Val locked tear-filled eyes, and simultaneously said the same thing.

"One hundred."

de_macho has entered the chatroom.
de_macho: hey everyone, I finished the lineups
thing1tweedledum: its just us, Davide
de_macho has exited the chatroom.
tweedledeething2: the young grasshopper, he has learned well
thing1tweedledum: i do want to know the lineup, though
tweedledeething2: me 2, i hope im not stuck playing doubles with that jerk twin of mine
thing1tweedledum: yeah, hed dazzle the audience with his blinding good looks
tweedledeething2: and huge ego

powerknight has entered the chatroom.
tweedledeething2: speaking of...
powerknight: what?
thing1tweedledum: nothing. he said nothing.
tweedledeething2: your late, man. it took you this long 2 bike home?
powerknight: haha, no.
powerknight: just wanted 2 say val and i have a few secrets up our sleeves.
powerknight: we'll mop the floor with every1 2morrow
powerknight: ain't that right val?
powerknight: val?
capnsword has entered the chatroom.
capnsword: I'm sorry
capnsword: my fingers just recovered
capnsword: they were so sore
powerknight: ...
thing1tweedledum: LA~~~
tweedledeething2: ~~~ME
thing1tweedledum has exited the chatroom.
tweedledeething2 has exited the chatroom.
powerknight: u ruined it Val.
powerknight has exited the chatroom.
capnsword: I'm sorry...

"Hey bro, what kinda eggs do ya want?" Donald asked, as his twin shuffled into the kitchen. It was a miracle he had survived the trek down the stairs with his eyes shut so firmly. Their two pet Siamese cats, both of whom were sprawled out on the rein-forced Novara table, looked up blankly, and then went back to napping. Ronald was still in the holey plaid pajamas that he had outgrown two years ago, his hair as disheveled and repulsive as if he had not washed it in a month, but his record was two. Com-pared to his brother, already showered and garbed in his nova tennis jersey, Ronald looked like a slob. Nevertheless, in response to the question, he yawned widely, made some awkward hand motions, snapped his fingers twice, and seated himself at the ta-ble. With both eyes still closed, he shoved both the older Milly and the fatter Lilly out of the way. After one more earth-shattering yawn, he laid his head down to rest a bit more. Twin telepathy worked its magic, and Donald nodded knowingly.

"Omelet with tomatoes and cheese? You got it!" he said, cracking open a few eggs and pouring their contents in a bowl. He proceeded to beat the egg with a fork, and opened the refrig-erator door with his toes to get the other ingredients.

The Dwyryd kitchen was rather small, but for their larger meals, they would eat in the dining room, the one room in which the twins had sworn never to fool around. Inside the kitchen, however, the tile floor had a distinct pattern of footprints, and a pile of unwashed dishes sat untouched in the sink, along with broken promises to clean them. Their mother had stopped being Mrs. Nice Dwyryd, and decided to let the males fend for them-selves when they had to eat cereal out of the box. However, that lesson was far from learned. Once Donald was done whisking, he added to the mound by throwing the Novara bowl on the top of the heap. Luckily, mass-produced Novara porcelain was not as fragile as the real thing.

"Here, bro," Donald said, placing the steaming plate in front of his sleeping sibling, along with a fork. "Eat it while it's still hot!"

Ronald did not look up, but groped around the table with his right hand to try to find the utensil. Donald snickered.

"Dude, you're gonna hafta open your eyes eventually!" he said with a smile. His little brother paid him no heed, and continued to move his hand about to locate the fork. Once he succeeded, he stabbed around the table (the cats were sure to hiss threateningly if the tines came too close to them) until finally piercing his breakfast. The melted cheese oozed out of the sides as he broke off a piece, then tried and failed to direct it towards his open mouth. He succeeded at last, but not before smearing his face with hot grease. Donald just looked away, laughing. It was good to have a younger brother.

"And for me, how about sunny-side up?" he decided, breaking another egg in the pan. When he saw the contents spill out, he grinned again. "Sweet! Two yolks!" He took the pan off the stove just as the egg whites began to coagulate and shoved them in front of his brother's face. "Look, bro! Twin yolks!"

Ronald did not hear him. He was once again in a deep slumber, with the fork sticking out of his mouth. Donald shook his head, and picked up his brother's empty plate to toss into the sink.

<p style="text-align:center">~~~</p>

Scrambled eggs, sizzling bacon, and mounds of buttered toast were piled upon a plate in the center of the Parrish dining table. It was enough to feed a family of seven. The eldest son gladly shoved a large fistful of it down his throat the moment his mother placed it on the table.

"Percival!" she scolded, slapping his right wrist with the hot, oily, spatula. The youngest Parrish, Sammy, guffawed in mirth. He looked like a miniature version of Percival, but shared one simple hobby with the person his brother often complained about; Quincy and Sammy both loved to drive Percival mad. The elder brother whined, pulling his hand away.

"Ow! Mom!" he complained, rubbing his smarting wrist with his left hand. "I need this hand to do my Overhead Smashes and Explosions!"

Emma Parrish was approaching middle age, and had the graying hair to prove it, though she did her best to hide it under a white bonnet. She sniffed and turned her nose in the air, returning to the stove. "Hmph! I'll apologize once you actually chew the food I cook for you. I might as well give you raw eggs if you won't taste them."

Percival lowered his head repentantly, while Sammy laughed accordingly.

The Parrish kitchen was much cleaner than the Dwyryd's, since there was a stricter list of chores, as well as a firm mother with cookware weapons. Her son may fight with a racquet, but *she* had a foot-long cheese grater. The dishes were stacked neatly behind solid wood cabinets, and the porcelain floor was spotless. Several documents were uploaded onto the refrigerator, from school pictures to crude drawings of orange dinosaurs Percival yearned to delete, especially when friends came over. However, one thing was similar between the two breakfast tables; one person was missing, and from the Parrish's residence, it was the father, Mark. He had already left for work half an hour ago, and would not return until Sammy had to go to bed. Even when a battered and bruised Percival had come home at ten at night in the past weeks, his father had not been there to greet him. Everyone at the contracting company had seen longer hours since the mayor had handed their president plans for a new wing for Town Hall. While Percival was slightly upset his father would not be able to watch him "positively dominate" the District competition, he cheered up knowing he could tell him every detail on Sunday.

"Hey PORKY, are ya gonna get beat up again today?" Sammy sneered from across the table, although the gap between his front teeth gave it a rather comical effect. Percival's hair perked up, but he kept his anger in check.

"*I'm* going to win as usual," he said, as his mother smiled from the sink. "No one can beat me. Besides," he continued, smirking as he stared out the kitchen window to the sunny street. "Someone very important is depending on me. I can't let him down."

"Wow, he must be really stupid to rely on you, Porky!" his brother snickered. A vein on Percival's forehead bulged.

"Shut your trap, brat!"

"Percival!"

"OW!"

~ ~ ~

"Elizabeth, please pass the pepper," Quincy said politely to his sister. She was on break from medical school, but still toiled well into the late hours, much to her father's approval. In one fluid motion, Elizabeth quickly put down her silverware, picked up the shaker, and gracefully passed it to her younger brother across from her. "Thank you," he said, accepting it.

He carefully tapped the stethoscope-shaped shaker over the mixed vegetable omelet his mother had prepared. One, two, done. He set it down in front of him, and tasted his meal again. Perfect.

Unlike Quincy's teammates, his family ate all meals in the dining room. The kitchen was in the next room, and was kept spotless by Quincy's mother alone. She preferred her children to spend as much time studying as possible.

All of the members of the Harris family were doctors, or training to be. Quincy's parents were already in their spotless white coats, with matching stethoscopes hanging from their necks. His sister, on the other hand, wore a conservative turtle-neck and dress pants. There was no way her father would allow her out of the house in anything else.

Quincy was already dressed in his tennis uniform, and his father made it clear how much he disliked it, despite the fact that his mother was quite proud. For better or for worse, it was the first time a sports uniform had ever graced the Harris household.

The eldest Harris son, Alfonso, was finishing his hospital internship in city across the country. By the end of the year, he would be a full-fledged doctor, and join their father's clinic. Eventually, Elizabeth and Quincy would do the same, following the fates set out for them since they were blastocysts in their mother's womb. Despite family friends extolling him and his siblings, Quincy found it hard to feel as proud as his parents did.

If there was one other thing people said about the Harris family, it was how strikingly similar the family looked. Each one of them was borderline identical, with the same rectangular glasses frame, the same slender figure, and the same straight black hair. Quincy's was the longest, though, which did play a factor in his father's clear revulsion. However, this was another position on which Quincy would not budge. Short hair suited the other Harrises perfectly. Long hair made Quincy look cool. As long as his mother approved, his father was forced to comply. Due to this one-sided compromise, though, he took every opportunity to belittle his youngest child.

"So, I see you will be playing nova tennis again today," his father began after a sip of coffee, his voice carrying across the room much like a man Quincy knew and respected to a much greater extent. Quincy looked up, staring at his father's angled face (which also wore a constant look of disapproval, like the man preferred to idolize), prepared for the question. "Are you going to win?"

Quincy finished chewing and swallowed before answering. "Of course, father."

His father nodded. "Good. I know I raised my son to be the best."

While some would pause to think, and finally decide it was a compliment, Quincy knew better. His father was not finished lecturing just yet. "However, I hope you are still keeping up with all of your studies, and not frivolously wasting all your time with meritless extra-curriculars. Not just anyone gets into medical school nowadays. Right, Elizabeth?"

Elizabeth had sensed a question was heading her way before it had been asked, and answered instinctively. "Yes, father. You are absolutely correct."

In truth, she had absolutely no idea what her father had said, and passed a sly grin at her little brother, who acknowledged the message with his eyes. *You'll be free one day, Quince. Hang in there for three more years.*

Dr. John Harris missed the silent message, just like many before. To end the conversation, he cleared his throat and adjusted his glasses by his temple. Everyone else in the family followed suit.

Quincy was quite surprised he got off so easily. Usually his father would have brought up Alfonso's 4.0 undergraduate degree, one of his favorite pastimes. Then again, that ended when he disgraced the family with his board examination grade. While a score of 235 was usually nothing to sneeze at, it was when someone else got 236. Quincy's breakfast suddenly took the flavor of ash.

"Don't forget to stretch, dear," Dr. Marianne Harris reminded with an affectionate smile. "Especially the hamstrings." Quincy nodded, glad that he could depend on his mother. It seemed having two X chromosomes made someone a better person. At least *she* treated her children equally.

"Yes, mother, I will not forget," he answered. How could he, anyway? Such information had already been bored into his brain by repetition; he would be a fool to overlook such habits.

Breakfast continued as usual. Whenever the father adjusted his frames, his family would do the same.

~~~

Cuyler was not tired. He had woken up early to jog around the family inn's property after fixing himself breakfast, and he was far from done. He did this every morning, so it was not much of a challenge. He had been running since the first ray of sunlight warmed his face that morning. After the first hour of training, he decided to call his parents with his atomic phone to tell them that they did not have to give him a ride; he would run there himself. His parents were only too happy to oblige. Things were rough at the Cuyler residence since his grandmother's injury; the slightest reprieve was like heaven. After he made the call, he took a deep, calming breath and resumed running towards the courts where the District tournament would be held.

Cuyler himself was halfway to the courts by the time his teammates had begun breakfast. Two sesame bagels were stowed in his jersey pocket just in case he got hungry before he played. While he felt fine at the moment, fatigue could strike at any moment, and he had trained himself to be well aware of his body's needs.

The streets were rather busy for a Saturday morning. Hover cars whizzed by at the speed limit of their zones. The zone closest to the ground obeyed the signs of thirty miles per hour, while the middle zone was allotted a maximum highway speed of eighty miles per hour. The top zone was for cross-country travel only; up to two hundred miles per hour was permissible.

Cuyler stopped and stared at the three layers, shaking his head. Humans were so concerned with their advancing technology that they completely ignored the nature around them. He turned to see a sturdy oak tree with brown leaves so shriveled that Cuyler could already hear them crunching underfoot. A deserted bird nest rested on the top bough, slightly obscured by the foliage. It had been a long time since eggs hatched in that grass home, but in a few months, new chicks would live there, chirping for their mother to feed them the freshly caught, juicy, worm. Cuyler gave one of his rare smiles. Nature was a wonderful thing to imagine, and even better to behold.

All right, Christian, he thought, and turning his attention to the sidewalk. *Proceed to the courts to lead your team to victory!*

He began to run towards the District courts once again, feet pounding on the pavement. The trek to the courts was only another half-mile, but the road ahead of him stretched much farther than one street alone.

~~~

Val stood in her bedroom, once again immersing herself in her imagination as sunlight poured into her room.

Today, those fans would not be silent. They would be deafening, cheering for her.

Today, that scorecard would not read 2-2. It would be 6-0, and she would score the winning point.

Today, Kawamura would not be her opponent. It would be some random high school guy she had never met, and would never again meet. The sole reason he existed was as a stepping stone. A stone for her, her team, and their dreams. Val smirked. *How pleasantly sadistic.*

Suddenly, a nova tennis ball flew towards her forehead. She caught it swiftly, not intending to experience a concussion before she played. She walked over to the clock and locked it back in place, reading the face. 8:00. It was time to go.

Necklace in place, hat securely fastened with extra pins, and jersey prominently displayed on her back, she hovered a finger over the blinds' controls to close them. At the last second, she thought better of it. Smiling, she left the room as it was.

Her father was in the living room, watching the news. He tore his eyes away from the screen to recognize Val's departure, as his daughter bent down to tie her shoes. Tightly.

"Got everything?"

"Yup."

"Hat, racquet?"

"Yup."

"Okay then. Good luck."

"Thanks. Bye."

"Bye."

After rising, she walked to the door and placed one hand on the knob. She exhaled slowly as she turned the handle.

"Valley."

Val turned to see Richard leaning against the wall with his arms crossed, staring into her eyes seriously. She waited for his mouth to open again, her right hand seconds away from pushing the door open.

"Your mother would be proud."

Val nodded just as solemnly. "I know."

And with that, she exited the house. Richard watched her go, and once the door closed, he sighed. So far, his daughter was having fun. As long as that continued, he would regret nothing in his life.

~~~

Val casually made her way to the courts. Though she hid it well, she was thrilled for the day's events. It was her first official high school tournament, an event she had dreamt of since youth. The sweat, tears, and blood of past weeks all culminated to this one day. It would all be meaningless if they lost; not only their team training, but her own reason for coming here.

Val shook her head, resuming her trek. She could not afford to imagine such things. When she was depressed, her playing was horrible, and it would be *her* fault if thinking of losing made it so. Instead, she imagined lifting a giant, golden trophy over her head, and a smile immediately crept onto her lips.

Within the first twenty-four hours of moving to Yole, it was a given that the first thing Val located were all the public courts in the area. She memorized the directions to the closest ones like the back of her racquet, and was glad to find out the tournaments would be a mere ten minute walk. (If she lived where Cuyler did, she would probably request a taxi. Sure, she was fast, and she did not mind running that much, but once distance went over a mile, her true laziness revealed itself.)

Suddenly, a familiar person pulled up beside her, holding out a fist. Percival smirked, waiting for her response. With a grin plastered over her face, she slammed her fist against his, and jumped on the back of his bike, instinctively holding on to both his shoulder and her hat. Up ahead, the twins were already soliciting around the courts, waving them down.

As Percival sped up to reach them, all her worries slipped away. As long as the Yole High Nova Tennis team was together, nothing would go wrong.

~~~

Seven people in Yole High uniforms made their way to the registration desk.

The tallest two led five more, all walking slowly and in unison, as if choreographed. Everyone around them stopped and stared, pointing and whispering conspiracy theories. Most of them circulated around the last member in line, who was noticeably shorter than the others. At last, opposing teams concluded that the Yole High Nova Tennis team must have been getting desperate, if they were recruiting such a *shorty*.

Behind the desk stood a hologram of the single elimination tournament schedule. Names and match times were displayed for all to see. Yole High was the one on top, with a bold "BYE" written prominently beside it.

The coach walked up to the man standing at the registration desk, James Orvid, and handed him the HoloStick with his team's information.

"Davide Ercole, coach of the Yole High School Nova Tennis team," he said proudly, jerking a thumb in the direction of his students. They stood together, united, and ready to make a lasting impression.

Orvid nodded, and took the HoloStick, plugging it into his desk to pull up the lineup. He had been in charge of the tournament for many years, and always looked forward to new players. As Davide led the returning champions, he held high hopes for his lineup. He cast a critical eye over all the students in front of him, and announced, "Welcome back to the District tournament, Yole High. I hope you'll have good matches in store for us. The tournament will start in a few minutes, so in that time, let me tell you the main rules.

"There are six teams competing today, but both you and East High have byes, so you won't play until next round," he continued, while motioning to the screen behind him. "Don't get cocky, though, you still have to make it to the top! The winner will be decided by the best three out of five matches: two doubles and two singles, with each match being one set. The fifth match is a singles match to be played by either the coaches or, if both teams agree, a reserve player. This is the same format used in the rest of the tournaments until States, when matches will be comprised of best two out of three sets. Does everyone understand?"

"Yes, sir," they chirped. Davide had already told them the rules, but it never hurt to review. Besides, both the twins and Percival had not been listening the first time. And judging by the way Percival was practicing his Overhead Smash without his racquet, he was not listening this time either. An unaware Orvid smiled, and glanced at the coach.

"I remember this team, Davide. Let's see, Bruins, Collim and — what's his name? – Sierna. They graduated right? Still, you've got Cuyler as usual. The twins, too. Guys, please don't trap people in the bathroom this time."

"It wasn't us!"

"Parrish, I remember you from the crowd. I hear you've got quite the power serve. Harris, too, you looked like the most accurate player out there. And finally…"

His eyes rested on the last player. She stared back, a winning game face on. Orvid hid his surprise at seeing such a short player, and looked down at the list.

"So, your name must be Valen Haus…"

The word died on his lips when he noticed that specific player's age. He did some mental math, surveyed Val up and down, and looked at Davide quizzically.

"A freshman? Really?"

Val's smile disintegrated while Davide was caught by surprise. True, it was a rare occurrence, but not THAT much of a bombshell. Both he and Cuyler had been first year rookies, after all, although they were admittedly much taller and a smidgeon more threatening.

Suddenly, he noticed Val march up to Orvid, and stare him squarely in the eyes. Silence followed as she gazed intensely at the uncomfortably shifting skeptic.

"Is there a *problem* with me?" she asked, such gumption surprising even herself. It seemed like acid was dripping from her voice.

"W-well," Orvid stammered, unsure how this sequence of events had come about. "I-it's just – "

A shadow was cast over both of them. Val turned to see Cuyler standing behind her in more than one way.

"Mr. Orvid," he began as levelly as usual. Val's eyes shone with admiration and elation. "Do you find Hauser out of the ordinary?" Orvid shrunk back, promptly shaking his head.

"Not at all, I'm sure he's a very fine player," he squeaked quickly, avoiding both Cuyler's and Val's gazes. He transferred the HoloStick's file, and a large, red "OK" appeared next to Yole's name on the roster. Orvid rubbed his temples, and then gave a strained smile to Val and Val alone.

"Yole High, you are now able to compete in the District Tournament. Good luck and play well. Valen, I hope yo – I mean, I *know* you'll make your team proud."

"Thank you!" They chorused back, Val grinning the widest of them all. She hopped away, while Cuyler merely nodded curtly, still frowning. Davide finally allowed himself to breathe, gave Orvid an apologetic smile, and joined his players in yet another march away. This time, no one dared speak, in fear of attracting the unwanted gaze of the stoic captain.

Val stared at the captain who led them, deep feelings of admiration welling up from within. She would follow that man, chasing his back, until the time came for her to face him. She just hoped that when that fated day arrived, Cuyler would respect her as much as she did him.

~~~

"We are starting the match between Yole High and Poole Private!" the umpire called from the high chair stationed beside the net. Like the other officials, he wore an argyle sweater vest, long pants, and a white visor.

The Yole Regulars stood on one side of the net, facing their opponents, who mirrored them. Poole's uniform was, as the twins so aptly put it, less flashy than their own: a faded green with dots of brown. Each Regular was slightly taller than Val, yet their faces were red, and the entire team was fidgeting. Anyone could tell that they did not want to play against the famous Yole High, even if they *did* have a freshman on the team.

A wire fence and a crowd surrounded the courts, onlookers intently looking forward to the match ahead. The twenty remaining Yole players scrambled for a place to watch the face-off, competing with both themselves and Poole's team of half the size. Alan and Heath struggled to snag a spot front and center, ready to watch all the matches in all their glory. And first up...

"We will begin with second doubles!" the umpire shouted again. Cuyler and the rest of the non-playing members retreated to the sidelines where Davide sat, nervously rubbing his hands. While he did admit that Percival and Val had improved extremely quickly in a short amount of time, he could not shake the unease. Judging by how tightly Cuyler was crossing his legs, neither could he.

The other team followed suit at their team bench, directly across from their opponents. Foot-tall water bottles for each player were set up beside each bench, so their respective coaches could offer advice during breaks. Davide honestly hoped he would only have to tell his players to "keep on winning."

Percival and Val offered their hands to their opponents, the junior Lucas Ferrell, and the sophomore Corey Hicks. While Lucas took up Percival's hand in his own firmly, Corey's trembled when he shook Val's. His arm felt like a jackhammer. Val felt nervous just looking at the guy. But before she let Corey release her grip, she squeezed his hand loosely. He shot her a perplexed look, but she simply smiled.

"Good luck," she said brightly, before finally letting him free. "Let's do our best, okay?" Corey found himself nodding, and quizzically watched her return to her partner until Lucas brought him back to reality with a quick tap on the head.

"Get your head in the game, Hicks!" he commanded, scowling at his partner. "I won't let you ruin this for me!"

The confidence Val had unintentionally implanted in Corey began to fade. "W-well, I'll do my best," he stuttered, trying to sound as strong as his opponents seemed. Lucas raised an eyebrow, and tapped Corey's head sharply again.

"Your best's not good enough unless you win, idiot," he snapped, leaving his partner at the net, as he walked to the baseline. Corey slumped, letting the words sink in, before turning to face his opponents. He wondered if Percival was as harsh with Valen as Lucas was with him. The surprise showed on his face when, instead of flicking his partner's forehead, they slammed fists with determined smiles. Was that how doubles partners were supposed to act?

"I'll take this side," Val announced, positioning herself on the left side of the court. Corey attempted to make eye contact again, but she seemed to be ignoring him, too intensely focused on the match at hand. Eventually he stopped, and just got ready when Lucas held the nova tennis ball in front of him.

"Red or blue?" he asked, being surprisingly civil to the other team. Val did not even look up when Percival answered with their team color. When Lucas threw it to the ground, it came up red. Percival gave a low whistle.

"Hey, über positive," he said, catching the tennis ball with one hand when Lucas hit it over the net, as well as two more brand new balls. Percival stuck two in his pocket, while Lucas then got ready to receive. Corey prepared himself as well, feeling his partner's eyes boring into the back of his head. The words "don't screw up" resonated in his ears. He swallowed. All he could do was hope that his best *was* good enough.

Percival gave a curt nod to Val at the net, who then proceeded to inch a little farther to her left. The umpire called out the score, and the match officially began.

"Here we go!" Percival yelled, thrusting the ball into the air, and then used his entire arm to do his famed Explosion. It flew past an unfazed Val by inches, and landed in; Lucas was not even able to get to it. He simply froze in position, nervous sweat running down his face already. He definitely had *not* seen that coming.

Corey had blinked, and missed it completely. At least Lucas could not blame *that* on him.

The rest of the Poole Regulars, and their meager members, stared in disbelief. What kind of monster *was* he? On the other hand, the Yole Regulars jumped up, shouting cheers of encouragement, as did the rest of their crew.

"All right, Percival's Explosion!" Alan exclaimed, jumping up in the air, while many of the other members showed their support in similar ways. High fives and backslaps were traded all around, and even Heath threw an arm around Alan's shoulders. "An ace right off the bat!"

Percival and Val exchanged smug looks. So far, so good.

The rest of his serves were just as powerful; Percival and Val won the first game with ease. As their team continued to root for them, the pair took a quick sip from their bottles, ready to keep going. Davide said a few words of encouragement, and then let them walk to the other side for the next game. Alan was proud that he knew why they were changing courts, even though it was only because Val had told him. After every odd game, whether in singles doubles, the players must switch sides. This happens so each person has an equal amount of time looking into the sun while playing outside. (At least, that was the rational reason players gave when people asked. No one quite knew the real answer.)

Lucas and Corey, after taking their drinks, held a short conference with their coach before returning to the court.

"It's obvious the older boy is the driving force behind the team," the man said, running one hand through his balding hair, and then twirling the brown mustache above his lip with the other. "Try hitting to only the freshman. I doubt that racquet is good for anything besides decoration." He paused to laugh, though none of his students did. He coughed, and continued. "They probably only have him for show. Just relax and keep playing."

The rest of the team nodded in unison, goading the pair. Corey nodded, and held his hand out to Lucas. Though they may not be on fist bump terms, surely a handclasp was okay?

Lucas simply ignored it, and Corey himself, heading onto the court alone in preparation to serve. Again, Corey's shoulders drooped, and he shot a pleading look at their captain. Johnson simply smiled apologetically, which made Corey even more depressed. He trudged onto the court, heart and mind in a happier place.

"Remember Hicks. Just hit to the freshman," Lucas reminded him, as if he had not been standing inches away from him. Still, Corey nodded obediently. Anything to stop Lucas from flicking his head again.

"Love-1!" the umpire called out. "Ferrell to serve!"

"Here goes!" he exclaimed, thrusting the ball into the air. He let it drop, and then swung his racquet up. As expected, the ball landed in, but nowhere near as quickly or powerfully as Percival's Explosion had. The Yole sophomore rushed up, and hit a simple return over Corey's head. Distress showed clearly on his face when he failed to reach it.

Lucas ran towards the ball with no problem, mentally blaming Corey for being too short. First, though, he had this problem to deal with. He quickly slammed a forehand right at Val, who was ready at the net.

"Eat THIS!" Lucas screamed, as it sped over the net. He expected Val to fall in the fetal position. Instead, after a blur of motion, the ball landed within the doubles boundaries on Poole's side.

Val had hit a drive volley right down the line, where no one was standing to return it, much like Cuyler had done to them before. By the time the Poole Regulars rubbed their eyes and realized what had happened, the umpire already called out the score.

"Love-15!" he said, amongst cheers from the Yole side.

"All right, Val!" Alan shouted, hoping his words would reach her ears, and give her the confidence she did not need. Val did hear them, and took them to heart. But she was playing, and that was the only thing she would allow herself to focus on. The only things that mattered were the match and the people playing it. She promptly turned around to retreat to the baseline, briefly slamming fists with her partner as they passed. Donald and Ronald glanced at each other, and grinned. PorcuSweep's telepathy was definitely doubles-grade. But theirs was still better.

The next points of the game had the same outcome. Val either received, or was hit to after Percival received, and every time she would aim for the doubles alley, where they did not expect. Finally, just to mess with them, she landed a perfect drop shot over the net, something else she had picked up from the captain. That won the game, as well as filled up the last bits of white on her racquet face.

"Game to Parrish-Hauser pair!" the umpire shouted once again to the cheers of the crowd. "Two games to love!"

Percival and Val slammed their fists together, and instead of staying silent, cried, "YES!" So far, things were going well. Now they would have to make sure it stayed that way.

"Keep it up, you two!" Davide said from the sidelines, no longer worried. After a few moments' pause, though, he added, "Don't screw up!"

While Val and Percival promised not to, Lucas grabbed Corey by the shoulders before the third game began.

"Hicks, seriously, get it together!" Lucas snarled, tapping his partner smartly on the head again. Corey rubbed his forehead. More than just heat was getting to him. "If word gets out that I got beat by this freshman poser – !"

"We," Corey muttered under his breath. Lucas blinked, and cupped a hand to his ear.

"I'm sorry, did you say something?" Words already formed in Corey's brain, but when he looked at how fierce Lucas' eyes were, his mind went blank. He looked down, and shook his head.

"No. Never mind, it's nothing," he muttered, shutting his eyes in shame. "I'm sorry, I'll do my bes – err, win."

"Yeah, yeah, that's what I thought," Lucas scowled, heading to the baseline to receive. Corey waited until Lucas was out of earshot before sighing. He was getting a migraine.

Once Val decided her opponents were as ready as they would ever be, she took a deep breath. "Ready Perce?" she asked, preparing to serve. Percival looked back and gave a thumbs-up.

"Go for it."

"Here we go!" she said, thrusting the tennis ball into the air. She bent her knees and, right as the ball reached its zenith, heaved her arm up and struck it with her racquet. Corey's mouth curved to a smile, as he watched the ball leave the racquet and shoot towards the net. This guy's serve was not all that great after all! In fact, it was pretty lame!

"It's all yours, Lucas!" he shouted.

"That's Ferrell to you!" His partner answered irately. Lucas ran up to hit it directly at Val, and then dashed up to the net, so both he and Corey were ready in front.

"Double poach!" their teammates exclaimed, jumping up in excitement. "We've got it now!"

However, Val had other ideas.

"Don't you dare take me lightly!" she warned, holding her left hand out, as if to catch the ball. She slid her finger into the neck groove of her racquet, which excited many of her teammates. They had not yet seen Val's special ability, and this would be their chance. Heath literally pushed his face against the wire fence to get a better look.

The face of her racquet glowed as brightly as the gemstone after which it was named. Right before the ball passed her, she struck, and everyone waited with bated breath.

"Take *this*!"

"Don't you dare take me lightly!" she warned, holding her left hand out, as if to catch the ball. She slid her finger into the neck groove of her racquet, which excited many of her teammates.

At the moment of impact, the ball turned neither red nor blue, but *violet*. She swung her racquet upward for a forehead lob, sending the ball soaring high above Percival's head, and way above their opponents at the net. Both Poole players began running to the baseline in preparation for the incoming lob, but Lucas shoved Corey out of the way.

"Outta my way!" he barked, eyeing the strangely colored ball as it approached its zenith. "This one's mine!"

Just as it reached the peak of its trajectory, though, the violet ball plummeted straight to the ground and, defying any possible law of physics, *rolled* towards the astounded Poole duo.

Agape mouths from all directions asked questions to the smirking freshman as she pointed her racquet to her opponents.

"Nice, huh? I call it my Lead Balloon technique. Whatever type of shot I hit, the ball will drop like a stone once it reaches its highest point. It'll stop bouncing too, so there's absolutely no way to return it."

"Believe me," Percival interjected, as he slammed a fist into Val's, grinning gleefully. "I've tried." Then, he inclined his head to the umpire. "Yo, ump! What's the score?"

"O-oh, right!" the man said, slowly regaining his senses. "15-Love!"

The official call snapped everyone else out of their trances as well, and the Yole side erupted into applause.

"That was AMAZING!"

"I've never seen anything like it!"

"Man, wish I could afford one of those babies!"

Heath had to lean against the fence to stop himself from collapsing, and Alan was still too dumbstruck to utter coherent phrases, but both watched Val let the compliments wash over her before returning to the baseline. She cocked her head towards their opponents and smirked. "Not bad for a poser, eh Lucas?"

Lucas growled, furrowing his brows. Manners were officially gone; these guys were going down.

"Let's go!" Val shouted again, slamming the tennis ball, and then recovering behind the baseline. Corey was receiving this time, and, while very disheartened, would not give up without a fight. He let the ball bounce, then hit it somewhere neither of them had tried before; at the net, but on Val's side.

In his head, the strategy made sense. It would force Val to come in, but make Percival want to hit it. He and Lucas always screwed up when their first doubles pulled this stunt. Unfortunately for him, Yole High was nothing like Poole Private.

"Situation Gamma?" Percival called out, dashing to the left. Before Val could answer, he scored a volley right at Lucas' feet. He was unable to react, and stood gaping, mouth as wide as it had been a minute ago. Percival straightened up, and cast a critical eye at that opponent.

"You know," he said loudly, as Val skipped jauntily to the right side for another serve. He positioned himself as well, but while still facing Lucas. "You offend my partner, you offend me. And trust me. You do *not* want to get on my bad side."

Val expected one of two things to happen. The first included Lucas' face paling and his immediate change of heart by apologizing to both her and her partner. The second was that he would ignore everything Percival just said and take his anger out on Corey. In the end, she was half-right.

"You look a lot like a porcupine, you know that?"

Every single Yole player tensed up. Val's blood turned to ice. In the span of days she had practiced with Percival, he had revealed why he hated that nickname so. She reluctantly turned her head to see what Percival's reaction would be, and her suspicious were confirmed.

"What was that?" He asked quietly, the very tips of his hair twitching dangerously. Val debated with herself, wondering if intervening would hurt or help. With every second that passed, though, Lucas repeated the forbidden word. By the time she decided to calm her partner, it was too late. Lucas had unwittingly tipped all the scales in his favor.

"No, you know what? You're definitely a hedgehog."

Val immediately ran between Percival and the net, already horrified. By now, she knew calling him "Porcupine" was one thing, but calling him "Hedgehog" brought up painful childhood memories. When she looked at Percival's eyes, she was not surprised – yet extremely worried - that they looked *blind.*

"Perce, dude, deep breaths," she said, choosing her words carefully. The umpire issued a warning to Lucas, and while that was good news to hear, it would mean nothing if her partner did not calm down. Unfortunately, it seemed like she was the last person he would listen to.

"I'm fine, Val, just serve," he said gently, avoiding eye contact with his partner. "I'll show him just what this dirty animal can do."

Val creased her forehead, looking to Davide for advice. He currently had his face buried in his hands, mouthing an orison. She sighed. *How helpful.*

Cuyler had plenty of words for her, but held his tongue as well, frowning deeply. If these two could not get through the first match of the first tournament, he would have no regrets in leaving them behind. Their goal was the National tournament, and that was no place for people who acted in such a manner.

The twins were quite disappointed in their students. Had they learned *nothing?* Even Quincy, who usually found joy in every instance that Percival was mocked, had a hard time feeling anything but perplexity. The rival he knew was much more composed.

Eventually, Val decided Percival was *not* going to listen to her, no matter what she said, and returned to her spot on the court, bitterly wondering how in the world things had taken such an ugly turn.

Perce, she thought bitterly, tossing the ball up. *Don't lose yourself. Please.*

"Ugn!" She cried, pouring out her frustrations in that one point. Lucas ran to it nonchalantly; the warning had done nothing to quash his arrogance. In another second, he returned it straight to Percival. Val prayed for the best, but anticipated the worse, especially when Percival activated his own special ability.

He swung his glowing racquet forward with all his might. His mind was racing, but one thought prevailed: he was going to beat the crap out of Lucas, no matter what it took.

The impact sounded like a clap of thunder, but Val knew better than to get her hopes up. True to her expectations, what should have been an amazing use of his special ability smashed against the net. Groans of disappointment could be heard all around, and each one was amplified in the sophomore's ears. The inner Percival beat himself up, but his exterior was just as unfeeling as before.

"Percival!" Davide finally shouted, hoping it would break through. Judging by the cold shoulder his player was giving absolutely everyone, it had fallen on deaf ears. Davide shouted his name again, but instead of responding to his coach, Percival just told Val to serve again. She shot Davide another helpless look, and returned to the baseline. There was nothing she could do but oblige. Right now, Percival was just a broken marionette, and Lucas was the puppeteer.

Lucas was having the time of his life. It was the most fun he had had the entire match. At every opportunity, he would irk Percival further, and the idiot just took the bait, like a wild animal.

Corey, though, felt immense pity for both opponents. When an enraged Percival slammed yet another ball into the back fence, he could not share in Lucas' joy at winning such an easy game. He could only try to catch Valen's eyes one more time, and maybe – through pure coincidence – say that he knew the feeling. It was pointless to do anything at this point; their partners were better off left alone. He sighed, walking to the court sidelines where his delighted coach and partner were waiting. It would be over soon.

Alan exchanged worried looks with Heath, wishing more than anything that he could do *something*, because at that moment, Val looked helpless, staring futilely at Percival's back.

"Yole High, please proceed to the opposite side of the court," the umpire warned.

Val suddenly took a deep breath. They had just lost three games in a row, and if she did not stop it now, it would be too late. There was only one option left for her, other than "lose miserably," and she did not get onto the Yole High Nova Tennis Team to do *that*.

She set her sights on Percival once again, and stepped forward.

"Hey Val?"

"Hmm?"

"Why do you play nova tennis?"

"That's a weird question."

"Ahh, sorry!"

"Oh, no, I'll answer it."

Val and Alan were sitting together at the lunch table a few days before the District tournament. The normal lunchroom chatter echoed through the crowd, especially from the tennis Regular table, where Quincy and Percival were engaged in yet another heated discussion about whether power or precision was better.

"Tell me, Porcupine, what's the point of putting all your energy into a shot if it goes out?"

"Well, it's better than an accurate ball with no power, Stylus! A gust of wind could return it!"

The two freshmen continued their conversation, while trying their best to ignore the squabble. It required a few seconds of thought for Val to find the right words to use, but she eventually formed a decent answer.

"Well, you know how I didn't really listen to you when you warned me about Josh?"

How could I forget? *Alan thought, recalling the incident.*

"I sorta have that kind of thinking in tennis too; I don't really care what other people say or think about me, as long as I can do what I want. My old team back in Rejina felt the same way." Val snickered as she reminisced. "We're a bunch of rebels. So I guess to answer your question, I play nova tennis because I can."

Val looked at Alan with a cheesy smile. "I bet you think that's sort of weird, huh?"

"Oh, not at all!" Alan said, shaking his head. "In fact, I admire that. I'd never go against the rulebook, even if I wanted to. And it's for something you really love too."

Val nodded, eyes gleaming. "Yeah. You know, when I'm on the court, I'm not Valen Hauser, not a student, not anyone. I'm just me."

~~~

Alan bit his lip, her final words ringing through his ears. *You're you when you play?* He repeated as his friend approached the intimidating Percival. *Then…then what in the world are you doing* now?

Percival was still standing at the net, fully aware that he had just ruined their lead, but unwilling to admit it. It *was* his fault and every time he tried to calm down, Lucas sneered yet again, making his blood boil, continuing the cycle. He had a sinking feeling that both the match and his nova tennis career would end with this devastating loss.

He felt something at his shoulder. A familiar grip, one he was used to after many days of riding home together. He turned his head slightly. Maybe he could apologize now before he screwed up his partner's life forever.

"Val, I — "

Suddenly, Val seized the sides of Percival's head and *pulled*.

A sickening *thud* reached everyone's ears.

Davide jumped to his feet. This behavior was *unacceptable*. He was about to step onto the courts when Cuyler grabbed his sleeve. Davide exhaled loudly.

"Let go of my arm, Christian."

"No," he answered, staring straight ahead. The captain seemed blissfully unaware of the chatter around them, which drove Davide mad. Those were *his* students they were talking about.

"Christian, as your superior, I command you to release me."

Once again, Cuyler refused. Davide was nearing his wits end; first Percival, then Val, and now even *Cuyler* was acting up? What was the world coming to?

But Cuyler knew. The senior had seen the fierce expression Val wore. It took a while for it to emerge, but it was what Percival needed to regain his senses. Cuyler looked at Davide with such intensity that the man was forced to sit and watch the events unfold.

One way or another, Percival realized Val's eyes were mere inches from his own. They glared at him, daring him to defy them. They made him feel seven again, when throwing tantrums was his specialty. Val was saying something, too, something other than just his name. He unblocked his ears, and Val's message rang, loud and clear.

"Wake *UP*, Perce!" she cried. "You're telling me those long hours meant *NOTHING*? Training with Davide, the twins, *me*! That's all been a waste of time?!"

Percival felt the urge to defend himself, so he opened his mouth. His weak words lost to his partner's, though, and Val continued on her hysterical tirade without letting him get in even a syllable. This was just another match, and her only opponent was Percival's ego.

"The Percival *I* know wouldn't act like this. He'd pull himself together, he'd snap out of it, and he'd work *with* me to get the job done! Where's *that* Perce? That Perce who'd eat hamburgers with me, ride his bike without a care in the world, and above all never give up! My friend, my doubles partner!"

"I – "

Val could take it no more. She pushed Percival's head back, arms shuddering, tears falling down her cheeks. Her words had come out in a rush, and now came the finale. It was now or never.

"I WANT MY PARTNER BACK!"

For the second time, Val slammed Percival's forehead into her own. They both staggered backwards due to recoil, groaning. The audience's whispers intensified. This was undoubtedly the most entertaining match ever to be played on these courts. Alan nearly fainted, and Heath instinctively grabbed his own forehead, wincing.

Val found the energy to feel her forehead, and was not surprised when her fingers were stained red.

May have taken that a bit too far, she thought, amazed she was still standing, and even more impressed that her brain was still working. She glanced over to Percival, who had stumbled into the net. *Well, Perce?* Val asked, staring straight at him. *Was it worth it?*

Percival rubbed his forehead, and brought his fingers before his eyes. Dark red fluid stuck to them, revealing his fingerprints and getting under his nails. He blinked a few times, and looked at his partner, staring back at him expectantly with those big brown eyes.

Memories flashed through his mind.

The intra-school ranking tournament.

Lunch.

Burgers.

Lightning.

Bike rides.

More burgers.

The vertiginous recollections spun around him, sending his mind into tumult but, when he regained his senses, Percival felt more levelheaded than ever before.

He walked forward until he was directly in front of Val, who was watching him intently. The sophomore pulled his arm back, and punched himself in the face, inducing another round of fervent whispering. Then, with the utmost sincerity, he stood straight in front of Val, his vision finally clear.

"I'm back."

Val broke into a victorious smile, and once again held out her fist. Percival took a deep breath, and touched it with his own. Once again, he stared into his partners eyes, this time to relay a single word.

Thanks.

The pair slowly walked over to the bench where Davide stood, his face contorted in rage. It seemed like his baby-face had aged 30 years. Percival gulped, and met his coach's eyes while his teammates sat and watched. Val, meanwhile, took the opportunity to wash some of the blood from her forehead.

"I'm sorry."

Davide continued breathing through his nose, unsmiling.

"You are an idiot. But I'll save the lecture for later. If Valen is willing to forgive you, so am I."

He pointed back at the courts, still dour, and commanded, "Now go. Go out there and win. Remind me why I made you a Regular. Remind me why you wear a team jersey."

Percival simply nodded and joined Val on the courts. When his back was turned, Davide collapsed next to Cuyler, massaging his temples. He was getting too old for this.

Cuyler looked approvingly at not only Val but Percival too. As long as he never again lost his cool, he would one day be a formidable opponent.

Corey was open-mouthed. Two strikes to the head was all it took? He clutched his racquet and the tennis ball tightly, shivering with jealousy. "How?" he whispered, holding back angry tears. "How do they get along so easily?"

"Sorry for the wait!" Val joked, while Percival just smiled ruefully behind her. He had done enough acting up; Val deserved to be the hero of this match.

Lucas immediately soured once he realized his "strategy" had fallen to pieces. He whipped his head around and glared at Corey.

"Don't. Mess. This. Up," he seethed before turning around again. Corey bit his lip, and threw the ball into the air. Although he served with all his might, his opponents were renewed. At their level, there was no way to stop them.

*Val broke into a victorious smile, and once again held out
her fist. Percival took a deep breath, and slammed it with
his own. Once again, he stared into his partners eyes, this
time to relay a single word.*
Thanks.

Point after point, game after game, once Percival got over his anger there was no looking back. The only thing that tied him to the memory was the blood drying on his and Val's foreheads, but that link just made him more passionate.

Val, too, was enjoying herself, judging by the smile that appeared on her lips every now and then. The twins were right. Singles was for anyone. Doubles was for men.

At last, it was 5-3, and Percival was serving again. Everyone on the Yole side could taste victory, despite the bitter events that led to it. Lucas, on the other hand, would not give up without a fight, or at least big talk.

"Dammit!" he cursed, kicking at the court as if that would stifle his anger. Percival was already poised to serve, but after the ruckus he had caused everyone, he was willing to wait as long as necessary for Lucas to calm down. Corey gazed at his coach and teammates in distress, but all they could do was give him pitying looks. When Lucas was like this, no one could stop him.

"Ferrell, if you do not stop that, you will be penalized!" The umpire warned again. Lucas glared at him and was about to retaliate when someone took hold of his ears and pulled.

Jaws dropped from all sides of the court, from spectators to teammates. Val and Percival cringed, feeling their own injuries. Watching someone else imitate them just made the pain worse. (The umpire was the second most dumbstruck, though. Twice in one match? Was he lucky or cursed?)

Lucas was speechless, for once, but quickly regained his voice to curse wrathfully at his partner.

"Dammit Hicks! What the hell do you think you're doing?" He tried to push himself free, but Corey would not allow it. After enduring eight games of hostility, enough was enough.

"*I'm* trying to play as a team!" Corey argued, finding his voice at last. "This is *doubles*, we're supposed to work together to win!"

Lucas eventually broke free, and shoved his partner away, retreating to his position. "Just saying that won't change anything," he muttered darkly, stubbornly refusing to give up the last word. Corey stared at him, determined. He had witnessed one miracle today; he would make sure another worked in his favor.

You're right. It won't change a thing. Corey thought, striding to the net. *But it sure as hell is better than this. And I swear I'll make you see it.*

Percival winced at Lucas' harsh words. Though they lashed out in different ways, he saw a part of himself in his opponent, a part that he hoped was gone forever. It pained him knowing that he had hurt Val, the person who trusted him enough to call him "partner." He tossed the ball into the air, focusing intently. For all the trouble he caused his entire team, he would end it all this game!

"UGHN!"

Lucas was again unable to return the Explosion. He scowled, but Percival did well in ignoring it. The Yole sophomore faced Corey, and while he did sympathize with him, now was not the time to let it show.

For Val's sake, he told himself. He once again threw his arm up, and served his specialty.

He was about to walk to the right side to serve – again – when he noticed Corey had actually made contact with the ball. In fact, his racquet was glowing, and he was *following through*.

"What the – "

"OPEN YOUR EYES!" Corey exclaimed, sending the ball soaring over the net. Val jumped up to intercept, surprised at the additional power. It was just as hard as Percival's Explosion, and it took every ounce of her strength to hit a drive volley in Lucas' direction. Corey grit his teeth and dove to the right, managing to hit yet another return, since Lucas had become immobile. When Corey somehow returned another one of Percival's shots, even Cuyler had to show him the proper respect.

Eventually, the boy ran out of steam, and collapsed on the court after Val hit a forehand winner. He gasped for air, and heard members of the Poole crowd whisper his name. Still, it meant nothing unless Lucas could follow Percival's lead and see the light.

"I...I am your partner," he repeated, gazing at his teammate. Lucas was still stationary, stunned by what Corey had just accomplished. "I agreed to play with you, to take your old partner's place when he moved away. You don't have to like me. Hell, you can *hate* me for all I care. I just ask that for the time we're on the court, you'll treat me like an equal. Like a teammate. Like a friend."

The two stared at each other for less than ten seconds, but to Lucas, it felt like an eternity. And Corey was not finished, either.

"There's more to nova tennis than winning. It's about doing your best and loving every moment of it, like any other sport. And in doubles, it means sticking with your partner through thick and thin."

He finally hung his head to continue panting crazily, but a hand was suddenly held out to him. He looked up, breathing heavily.

"You're right. I don't have to like you," Lucas said bluntly. "But you're also right that this is doubles, and you're my partner. I'm sorry for my actions. You gave it your all, and now it's time for me to do the same."

"Poole Private, please prepare for the next point," the umpire stated again. Corey looked at the extended hand, blinking through his sweat.

"Well, it's not ideal," he admitted, clasping it within his own. "But it's good enough."

Lucas did not smile, but neither did he scowl. Instead, he nodded, and pat Corey awkwardly on the back. "Let's do this then. Together."

Corey let himself smile as he and his partner got into position. *A pat to the back beats a flick to the forehead any day.*

Once both his opponents were ready, Percival resumed bouncing the ball on the ground, mind racing.

What the heck is happening today? Were we, like, destined *to play to-gether?* He brought the ball in front of him, and smirked at the determined look in Lucas' eyes.

Yeah. We were.

"Huah!" he grunted, heaving the ball towards Lucas, looking for an ace. Lucas defied the odds, and sprinted up as fast as he could to hit a backhand return at the net on Percival's side. Everybody was shocked, except for the players on the court.

I'm glad he realizes the importance of partners, Val contemplated as she ran forward to hit a drive volley crosscourt. *But nova tennis is much more fun…*

She looked up to see Percival leap up to hit another exceptional Overhead Smash, and marveled at how passionate his shout was.

When you play with a friend.

Corey tried to return the smash, but missed and hit the air, and the ball landed in the doubles alley. He immediately turned to Lucas, afraid of his reaction. A hand was placed on his shoulder, and he looked up to see Lucas shrugging.

"Nice try, man," Lucas said. "Keep it up."

Corey grinned, clasping their hands together. Now, doubles with Lucas did not seem that bad after all.

The last point went to the Yole High team, and they won with a score of 6-3. The four players went to the net and shook hands once more. Each one was sweaty, and Val had to admit this was one of the most difficult matches she had ever played in, and not just because it was doubles. But she would never trade this experience for anything.

"Good playing, you guys," Corey said, beaming, as he took Percival's hand. Percival nodded, shaking firmly.

"If you ever want to play doubles again, just call us up at the Poole courts," Lucas cut in. Corey turned to him with a surprised look on his face.

"You…you still want to play with me?"

"Of course," Lucas responded flatly, turning to his teammate. "'Cause you're my partner." He then shocked everyone by grinning and flicking his own forehead. "I just needed a knock to my head."

He pointed to his opponents, smirking. "Next year, we'll definitely beat you guys!"

"I'll look forward to that," the freshman replied cockily. Percival said nothing, only smiled.

Finally, they returned to their respective teams, though the Yole sophomore was reluctant to match Davide's disapproving stare. Still, he had to. It was only right.

His coach was waiting for him, arms crossed. The usual happy-go-lucky smile was replaced with a frown that matched Cuyler's. Playtime was over. The coaching began.

"I already said you're an idiot," Davide began, while Percival bowed his head in remorse. "And I already said I forgave you. But your actions were shameful. A disgrace to this team, to your partner, and to that Regular jersey on your back."

Percival cringed. Saying he was unworthy of the cloth he treasured so dearly was the greatest of insults, but it was so true.

"Still, you did win, so I can't be too stern with you. But if you ever – EVER – lose it like you did today – "

Suddenly, Percival clenched a fist, nodding. Passion burned in his eyes as he made a vow that would stick with him for the rest of his life.

"I understand, Davide! If I fall out of line again, I swear, I'll hang up my jersey for good!"

Davide's mouth was still formed to say, "you WILL get three weeks of detention," but he decided that Percival's punishment was much more meaningful. He clamped his mouth shut, and finally broke into a smile, thumping his student heartily on the shoulder.

"Good to have you back. And Val," he said, glancing at the freshman. She was still trying to wash the blood from her forehead, and had enlisted Quincy's reluctant help. The freshman eventually looked in Davide's direction, as her teammate held gauze to her head. "Thanks."

She nodded, smiling, until Quincy pushed her face towards him and said, "Porcupine, please don't make a fool of yourself like that again. As your rival, it makes me look bad too."

Snickering, Davide turned to the twins, and jerked a thumb towards the courts. "Guys, you're up."

They jumped off the bench, but instead of heading to the net, they stood on either side of Percival.

"Pay attention, Porcupine," they chorused, fully intending to abuse the nickname until the end of time. "This is how a *real* doubles team plays!"

They bounded towards their opponents, leaving Percival with one final test: Captain Cuyler. He sat next to the senior, whose eyes were transfixed forward, and gulped. Did he dare speak? When he opened his mouth, Cuyler cut him off.

"Wash the blood off of your face, Parrish, and observe the Dwyryds' match. I will not think ill of you as long as you are able to take something away from these events."

His words sent a chill through the sophomore's spine, but he did as he was told. Cuyler was letting him off easy. And Percival knew it.

~~~

"Game and set to Dwyryd-Dwyryd pair, 6-0!" the umpire exclaimed to the delight of the Yole team. Donald spun his racquet around his wrists expertly while his brother did the same in complete unison. When they were done, they stood back-to-back and pointed their racquets at their sweating opponents.

"Don't think that both our doubles teams are like those dolts," they said in perfect harmony. Val and Percival hung their heads in embarrassment, but knew their teammates were right. Even with Percival in his right mind, both of them would have to work extra hard if they were to play doubles again. They definitely would have to play doubles again if Yole was to stand a chance in future tournaments.

~~~

"Game and set to Harris, 6-0!"

"Hn, do not underestimate me," Quincy said, adjusting his glasses. "I may have astigmatism, but accuracy is still my forte."

"That's how you do it, Harris!" Val cheered from the sidelines. "Wow, he's pretty awesome!" Percival looked away, trying to hide his jealousy.

"Yeah, I suppose so," he replied uninterestedly. He did get up along with the rest of the team to stand at the net as they did at the beginning of the match, so they could shake hands one last time.

"The winner is Yole High School, with three wins out of three matches," the umpire announced. "They will go onto the final round. Please shake hands!"

"Thank you for the match," each side chorused. Even the captains who did not get a chance to activate their racquets exchanged words.

"Perhaps we can play together some other time," Cuyler suggested to the Poole captain, Johnson. Johnson chuckled uncertainly.

"If you play half as good as the players on your team, I'm going to have to decline," he said. Cuyler nodded his head in respect.

"I see. I would be no match for you, I suppose."

"No, that's not what I meant!" Johnson corrected, but it was too late. Cuyler and his team had already begun walking away. Johnson shook his head. There was no way he was playing against Cuyler *now*.

The second doubles pair clasped hands for much longer. Both Corey and Lucas had expressed their thankfulness to the Yole pair for everything. The day's events could have played out much differently if Val had not been present, and she knew it. Moving away from Rejina was the best thing that could have happened to her.

~~~

"So about how long do we have to wait until the finals?" Ronald asked. Everything from his posture to his face to his voice exuded boredom. "That match didn't even faze me."

Davide checked his watch. "Ah, about thirty minutes or so. If you want, you can eat something. They have food stands set up at the front desk. I've got to go there anyway to report the score."

The team decided to go along with Davide, and maybe leech some food or money off of him. Cuyler, though, was looking forward to regaining some energy with the carbohydrates in his pocket.

"Ercole to report Yole High is the victor, 6-3, 6-0, 6-0," Davide told Orvid. He took down the scores, shaking his head.

"I knew you guys could do it," he laughed, turning around and typing something into the keyboard behind him. The team watched as the numbers appeared above their name, which now was written in one of the slots for finals. Val glanced at the two schools that would be competing for the other slot, and saw that it would be either East High or Outterridge.

"We'll probably play against East again," Donald said, answering her question before she could ask it. "They lost miserably against us last year, but there's no way East would lose to a no-name school like Outte – "

"Beckham to report Outterridge is the victor, 6-0, 6-0, 6-0," said a voice from beside them. All turned to see a lanky senior with freckles and short blond hair leading the rest of his team. He spoke with a slight drone to his voice, and without any r's. He was not even paying attention to whom he was speaking, for he was too busy keeping a soccer ball in the air, bouncing it with his right knee. Each time it went up two feet in the air, neither too high nor too low. His blue eyes were focused upon it intensely, and even the entire Yole team gawking at him could not disrupt his concentration.

The boy was surprising not only because he was playing with a soccer ball at a nova tennis competition, but because he was not wearing a nova tennis jersey. In fact, none of the team members, standing behind the captain in an unorganized mass, wore tennis uniforms. Each player wore the dress of a different sport. Beckham was garbed in a yellow, vertically striped shirt, white shorts, knee-high black socks and cleats. A soccer ball was neatly stitched onto the back of his shirt below his surname, much like tennis balls were on the Yole Regulars' backs.

Second in line was an Asian boy, with his narrowed eyes staring straight ahead in perfect discipline. Nothing would cause him to avert his gaze, but it seemed as if he was still completely aware of his surroundings. His jet black hair was in a ponytail much longer than Quincy's, and trailed to his waist. He was wearing a black kung-fu uniform, with horizontal yellow buttons going up the torso. White bandages were tied around his hands, and they went all the way up to his elbows. Percival gulped. This guy looked tough.

The rest of the team was comprised of golf, hockey, baseball, and lacrosse players, and each one looked apathetic, as if they had been to more intense matches than these.

"Well?" Beckham drawled, still bouncing the ball on his knee-cap.

"O-oh, right," Orvid said, hastily typing Outterridge's score onto the hologram. They appeared on the line beneath Yole's name as their next opponents.

"Beckham," the Asian player said. "I think we should prepare for the next match against Yole."

A few seconds passed, but Beckham was still absorbed in his soccer ball. The Asian boy cleared his throat, and then finally put a hand on his captain's shoulder. Beckham seemed to jolt back into reality, because he began chuckling.

"Sorry there, mate! You know me! This bloody thing is like my heart; it's got to keep beating!"

At last, he bounced the soccer ball higher into the air than it had been before, so that is soared high above even Cuyler's head. Beckham quickly pivoted with his left foot, and then deftly caught the soccer ball again with his head after he had rotated a complete 180 degrees.

Val's jaw dropped to the ground.

"Well, you're always on the ball anyway, Li, pun fully intended. C'mon chaps, we could do with a proper nosh up. Curtis, you're paying!"

There were murmurs of agreement and one groan from the golf player, but they all began to head for a nearby snack stand. Li seemed to be the only one to have noticed the Yole team.

"So that's Outterridge, huh?" Ronald whispered, suppressing a shiver. "So much for being a no-name; a clean sweep!"

"We will have to be careful when playing them," Cuyler warned, crossing his arms. "Keep your defenses high!"

Everyone nodded. They could not afford to let their guard down, even this early in the tournament. Davide turned to his team, smiling as widely as he could.

"Aw, come on you guys!" he said, trying to cheer them up. "We've already got one win under our belt, it'll be okay! Worrying won't help anything. Besides, we've got a bunch of cheerleaders, and I don't see any from Outterridge."

Their "cheerleaders" were nothing more than the other members of the team, and some girls who decided to show up. The freshmen had been sent away to refill water bottles or watch other matches. These were the only times most of them ever got to do anything worthwhile.

When he realized no one else had smiled, Davide tried again. "How about lunch, on me?"

He immediately saw the severity of his mistake.

"ALL RIGHT!" Percival exclaimed, throwing a fist into the air. His forehead was blood-free, and the very mention of victuals erased horrible memories from his mind. "Free food leads to a free victory!"

"Bet I can eat more than you," Donald goaded, winking at the excited sophomore to the anguish of Davide. Three seconds later, Percival was halfway to a hamburger stand. Val reached up to put a hand on Davide's slumping shoulder, trying her hardest to stifle a laugh.

"Don't worry, coach. I'll pay for my own food."

"But it'll be over for me the moment Perce opens his mouth," Davide whined, staggering away, as if there was no shred of hope for him or his bank account. "So much for taking Rose out to a victory dinner tonight…"

Val chuckled uncertainly. This team was full of interesting characters.

"Augh, I don't feel so good," Percival whined, holding both his hands to this stomach. No one gave him any pitying looks.

"After all that talk, you could only eat four chili burgers!" Ronald continued to gloat, as his brother snickered into his hand.

"I did not eat four!" Percival argued, holding up his right hand and wiggling all the fingers. "I had five! Plus a large soda!"

"Hn, what an idiot," Quincy muttered, adjusting his glasses. "Such a drink contributes absolutely nothing constructive to the body." Val tugged her hat down further, whispering almost the same thing. Percival was about to reply angrily, but a sharp pain shot through his stomach, and he was forced to keep silent. Davide sighed from the lead, shaking his head in despair.

"Perce, I put you in singles two!" he said, holding up his HoloPad and pointing to the lineup. "So unless you want to be replaced by another freshman, you'd better win!"

"Ugh, I think I'm going to barf…"

"Well, at least you've got a few minutes before the singles matches, dude," Donald tried to console. "We might even give in a few games to stall!"

"Gee. Thanks," the sophomore retorted, holding a fist to his mouth.

The team kept walking, and finally reached the courts, where Alan and the rest of the non-Regular members stood with six newly filled water bottles and an extra tankard of water. They quickly distributed the filled containers, careful to make sure the liquid was still cold. Even though they had just filled them from the free fountains near the registration desk, one could never be too cautious.

"Will the Yole and Outterridge teams please make their way Court B?" Orvid's voice resounded from the hovering intercom stereos. "The match will begin shortly. Yole and Outterridge to Court B."

"All right, everyone," Davide said, turning to his Regulars. "We'll just wait here until our opponents arrive. The lineup will be the same as before, except Quince, you'll play doubles with Valen, and Perce, you're in singles two. And Perce," Davide said, casting a tired look at the spiky-haired sophomore. "Try not to mess up."

"Don't worry Davide," Percival began, activating his racquet, and balancing it over his shoulders. "I never screw up twice in one day."

Quincy smirked, adjusting his glasses. "Hn, I highly doubt that."

A vein bulged on Percival's forehead, and he turned to Quincy with narrowed eyes. Val felt an odd sense of déjà vu, but trusted Percival had not forgotten their painful lesson. It seemed he had not, as his anger was somewhat controlled.

"What. Was. That?" he seethed.

"You. Heard. Me." Quincy replied, a provoking grin plastered on his face. Percival had enough time to recuperate from Lucas' insults; it was *his* turn now.

Percival let the racquet drop to the ground, and leaned upon it with his elbow. The two stared at each other, neither one dropping a gaze. Val withheld a sigh while absentmindedly tightening her hat. This was getting banal, and she had only met them a few weeks ago.

While the two rivals continued their glaring contest, Cuyler turned to her. "Are you prepared to play again, Hauser?"

Val nodded firmly, looking up at her upperclassman with a determined grin. "Of course, captain! We want to go to Nationals, right? So, I'll give it my all so our dream can become a reality!"

"Gee, that was pretty deep," a voice said from behind them. All turned, and even Percival and Quincy ceased their silent argument to see Beckham standing in front of his team, the soccer ball still bouncing up in the air. But now, he was not concentrating so much on the ball as he was on other humans. His teammates behind him were less outgoing, and instead decided to chitchat amongst themselves.

"So you're the infamous freshman ace, hey?" Beckham stated more than asked, surveying her up and down. His eyes stared at Val in curiosity, seemingly analyzing every inch. She returned the gaze boldly, refusing to reveal any weakness. He smiled, and then turned his face away.

"Heh! I'm lookin' forward to seeing you play, chap!"

Val blinked stupidly. She had been expecting an insult.

"Oh. You're, uh, not surprised by a first-year?"

With another quick bounce, Beckham caught the ball in his hands. He smiled brightly, eyes on only Val. "Why would I be? I'm looking forward to any secrets you've got in store for us."

"However, there's another school out there now: Outterridge High. It's not because they're powerful that they're a threat. We've never faced them before, since they just made a nova tennis team out of the blue. We have no info on them, so we've got to be prepared for anything.

Val fiddled with her hat idly, and opened her mouth to reply, but by then Beckham had turned his attention to Cuyler, irking her slightly. It was as if he suddenly decided that the Captain existed, while she was no longer around.

"The renowned Cuyler too, you guys have a full lineup. We're quite buggered at this rate, ha!"

"I am honored you know me," Cuyler nodded. "However, I'm afraid I cannot return the gesture."

"Beckham's the name," he said, extending a hand. But just as Cuyler went to take it, he pulled back. "Oops, I guess it's a bit early, hey? We can save it for our match."

Cuyler nodded, somewhat affronted. "Right, I suppose. Let us go, then."

Both teams filed into the courts, but for some reason, Cuyler was uneasy. Never before had he met a captain so *amiable* to his opponents. He cast a wary glance at the blithe Beckham, whose stride matched his own, although height-wise, Cuyler still dominated. Their match would indeed be interesting.

Before Val could follow her team, Alan prodded her shoulder, causing her to turn about.

"Y-you're doing well, but g-good luck anyway, Val," he stammered, pushing his glasses back up his steaming face. Val smiled, and thanked him before disappearing into the fenced area.

He took a deep breath to calm himself, before running to join Heath watch the match. *Why am I so worried? It's not like I'm playing, but I can't help but get nervous when it's Val standing on the court!*

Other teams, and several adults unrelated to either team surrounded the courts, as this was the deciding match for first and second place at Districts. Both schools would go to the County tournament, however, only number one would be seeded. The third and fourth place match between Poole Private and East High was taking place at the same time on another court. The winner would be the last to go onto the next tournament level. There was likely a substantial crowd there as well, since it was an "all or nothing" match.

"We are starting the match between Yole High and Outterridge!" another umpire exclaimed from his high chair. His voice screeched and cracked like a man dying of thirst. Apparently, he had been calling shots since the morning.

He drank noisily from the lemonade jug in his cup holder as each team shook hands with one another, Beckham's soccer ball now safely tucked beneath his team's bench.

Davide was the sole person who stood at the net without a counterpart. He looked around the entire court, looking for someone who resembled the coach. He had not seen an adult supervising the Outterridge team, as opposed to all the others. Usually there was some person herding the students like sheep or Kindergarten children, responsible for preventing utter bedlam. In fact, he did not even see any Outterridge non-Regulars watching them.

Interesting, he thought, pocketing his hands until his students had finished their formalities.

"Hey Beckham, you know Val and the captain," Percival blurted out excitedly, pointing a finger at himself. "Know me too?"

"Nope!" the soccer player said simply, returning to the team bench without even glancing in the sophomore's direction. Percival let that sink in before he retreated to the bench to slump beside his snickering teammates.

Finally, after the umpire finished quenching his thirst, he bellowed his next line.

"We will begin with the second doubles match!" he shrieked, throat only slightly soothed. It sounded painful just listening to him. "All four players please meet at the net!"

They all did as they were told, so only Quincy, Val, and their opponents stood on the field.

When the lineup had been released, Quincy was less than thrilled to be teamed up with Val. Yes, the improvement was astounding, but he preferred partners of higher caliber. If Val wanted his respect, the freshman would have to earn it with astounding plays. Being a freshman rookie meant nothing without the skill to back it up. Val noticed him looking in her direction, and smiled brightly, oblivious to his thoughts.

"Let's win this together!"

The sophomore did not smile back, but instead adjusted his glasses by the frames. "Of course. Leave it to me."

Their first opponent introduced himself as Ray Curtis, and wore a yellow polo with two crossed golf clubs embroidered at the back. Curtis had an average build, with short brown hair and bangs hanging low over his eyes, so he constantly had to throw his head to one side to clear his view. He held his dark orange racquet over his shoulder like many players, but he acted as if the tool was awkward to hold, grumbling about it being "too big."

His partner was Tony Rumyantsev (who clearly enunciated his surname as "rue-*mian*-sev"), a tall player with blue eyes, short hair so blond it seemed white, and a skinny stature. He had extremely long legs and a straight carriage – he moved with all the grace of an elegant dancer, but his shirt proclaiming him as number 6 of his hockey team showed he had other tricks up his long-sleeved shirt. His blue racquet looked somewhat similar to Quincy's, but the white grip was covered in gray smudge marks. Apparently, he handled it as roughly as Percival did his. While he carried his racquet more comfortably than his teammate, he too agreed it had an incorrect feel.

Quincy surveyed both of them quietly, and then gave a thumbs-down for blue. After Curtis bounced it, it did indeed turn blue. The sophomore gave an inner sigh of relief while accepting the balls. If he was able to serve first, the probability of victory was slightly higher. And slightly was all he needed. With that out of the way, each player walked to their respective positions, and prepared for the game.

All right, Quincy, it's up to you, the sophomore thought to himself, bouncing the ball as per his routine. *Hauser's probably tired from the Percival fiasco, so I shouldn't depend on him too much. Now, theoretically speaking, golf players must not be as fast as hockey players, for in golf all you need to do is hit a ball and take a cart to your next destination, while in hockey you must run to both get the puck and avoid bone-shattering impact. Thus, Curtis will most likely stay in the front, while Rue-my – no, Ray-mia, er –* Tony *runs around in the back, getting all the shots Curtis missed.* Quincy closed his eyes, as if double-checking his work, and then opened them again to thrust the ball into the air. *But for now, figure out their weak spots!*

"Ungh!" he grunted, striking the ball directly on its sweet spot. The ball sped to the center mark, as always, and caught Rumyantsev off guard. Rumyantsev swung and missed, while many of the Yole members chanted "Super Sonic Serve."

"Awesome, Harris!" Val yelled back, clenching a fist to present it to Quincy for a victory fist bump that she and Percival had equated with victory. But when she turned around, her partner was already stationed at the baseline preparing for the next point, showing no signs of having heard her. She shrugged it off and positioned herself at the right side of the net.

Quincy had heard her, though, and smugly thought, *I assure you, you haven't seen anything yet.* He hit another Super Sonic Serve, but Curtis was ready to receive. The Outterridge player managed to hit it right back at Quincy, while Rumyantsev backed up to join his partner. Quincy noticed the movement, and wondered why the hockey player chose not to poach. Still, that would not change his initial strategy, and he aimed for a short angle shot to the alley on Curtis' side. Curtis ran but could not get to the shot in time; his return bounced harmlessly off the net and rolled away to cheers from the Yole side, and quiet groans from the Outterridge Regulars.

The rest of the game played out similarly, and soon the umpire shrieked, "Game to Harris-Hauser pair!" Quincy had commandeered the game, keeping the ball short on all his shots while aiming for the middle or the alleys and testing forehands and backhands. As such, Val had not once hit the ball, much to her chagrin. Nevertheless, when the pair approached the team bench, she offered her fist to Quincy, but he ignored the invitation.

"It seems like they are both relatively new to the sport," he said offhandedly, picking up his water bottle. "Both of them stay near the baseline, as if they're afraid to come up. Anyway, just try hitting short, low balls, if possible."

"Okay," Val responded after a sip of water. Davide snickered, directing a thumbs-up in the sophomore's direction.

"As usual, you do my job for me, Quince. Keep up the good work."

Quincy adjusted his glasses before walking onto the courts again. "Of course."

"And fist bump Val once in a while, will ya?"

Val almost spit water over their captain as she caught Davide's winking eye. "Tha – !"

"I would rather not engage in such an action with Hauser, coach," Quincy said, turning back to face not Val, but Percival. "It feels so *primitive*."

The twins burst out laughing while Percival's hair bristled with controlled rage. Val felt her face blushing, but at the same time tried to stifle the feeling of annoyance towards her partner.

"If not fist bumps, are high fives okay?" she asked flatly, holding her hand up as she joined him. When Quincy made no movement, she added, "Studies show doubles partners who do small things like this after winning points are more likely to win the match in the end."

His eyes widened briefly, but he quickly narrowed his brows in suspicion. "Really?"

No. "Yes," Val lied, hoping the poker face her dad mocked would not give her away this time. She could see Quincy musing over the tidbit, and grudgingly lift his hand up as well.

"If science says so, let's see," he said as a grinning Val slapped her palm into his. "If we win this match, then I'll continue this silly gesture after every victorious point. If not, though, you'll agree fist bumping is juvenile."

"Deal," his partner laughed, as Percival's retort reached their ears. "I'll take the first return, then. It's my turn to hit something now."

Quincy let her do as she wished, and turned his attention to analyzing Rumyantsev's serve. He was unsurprised to see Curtis had joined his partner at the baseline. *That's quite a fatal strategy,* he mused, straddling the service line as his opponent tossed the ball up. *But I guess they haven't been playing long enough to trust themselves in front.*

"UGHN!" the hockey player bellowed, almost losing balance from such power. Quincy resisted the urge to quiver, and kept his eyes firmly planted on the right service box to call it if it was out. The heavy shot landed well within the boundaries, though, and sped towards Val.

Luckily Perce's Explosion is twice as hard as this guy's, Val thought, smirking. She caught the ball on the rise and managed to get her strings' meter to increase a sixth. Her return landed in the alley (a little too deep, for Quincy's taste), forcing Curtis to run to the left to hit a backhand. However, his return buried itself in the net, winning the Yole side another point.

Quincy briefly met Val's eyes as they passed each other, merely to ensure she understood the backhand weakness. While she nodded, she also stubbornly held out her hand again, which he reluctantly high-fived before taking his place at the baseline to return. He glanced at his racquet face, fully aware that it glowed a pale blue.

Not yet, though, he thought, backing up a couple feet for the coming power serve. *When the time is right.*

"UGHN!" Rumyantsev grunted again, heaving a forehand in his direction. Quincy smirked, planning the trajectory of his return down the middle to exploit the golf player's weak spot. His stroke was flawless as usual, but like Val's, the ball landed slightly deep, instead of short as he had intended. *It's only Tony's power,* Quincy assured himself, as the hockey player shouted he would get it. *My stroke was perfect.*

"UGHN!" came the repetitive roar, as Rumyantsev hit a return down the line. Quincy was about to dash to the right when he saw Val intercept and hit a volley crosscourt, into Curtis' alley. *I guess he's not that bad either*, he admitted, as more claps filled the area. *Or our opponents are just weak.*

"Love-30!" the umpire screeched, as Val made Quincy high-five her again. Suddenly, they heard bickering from the opposite side of the court.

"You're sucking!" Rumyantsev complained to his partner. Curtis looked away, annoyed.

"So golf isn't as similar to tennis as hockey is, sue me! I don't see you scoring any winners either, Ru-my-ant-sev!"

"Rue-*mian*-sev! At least my backhands go over the ne – ow!"

"C'mon chaps," their captain interjected jovially as Rumyantsev gaped at the soccer ball he had just thrown at his head. "Stop having a row and start playing your sports! Remember our promise!"

That statement seemed to do it, since their opponents' eyes widened just in time for the umpire to rasp a time warning. The pair spoke briefly before taking their positions, but Rumyantsev first kicked the ball back to his captain.

"Next time, tell us without giving me a concussion," he hollered, rubbing the back of his head. His captain merely laughed a cheerful apology.

Quincy and Val exchanged brief glances as Rumyantsev finally began bouncing the ball to serve. *A change in tactics?*

"UGHN!" the hockey player shrieked, with what seemed like more power than before. It zoomed to Val, who returned it with slightly more effort. The extra strength surprised her, though, so her return sped to the middle of the court, instead of down the line. Rumyantsev took advantage of the momentary shock, and slammed a backhand straight at Quincy, grunting all the while.

Quincy barely had time to pull his racquet in front of his face, shocked at how much force was behind the return. It felt even *stronger* than Percival's!

Without enough time to prepare, his volley regrettably landed in the middle as well, but this time, Curtis brought his racquet back. He waited until the ball was below his knees, and swung a return in Val's direction.

"I've got it!" she cried, pulling both her hands back for a full stroke with all her strength. *I'll return whatever power shot they hit to me!*

But after she hit the ball, it zoomed against the fence on the opposite side, the impact sending an echoing *clang* through the courts. Her mouth opened soundlessly. *That wasn't supposed to happen!*

"Hauser, exactly what was that?" Quincy asked, trying to keep as civil as possible. He would overlook mistakes, yes, but not ones so *glaring*. The freshman shrugged confusedly, bewilderment plastered on her face.

"I don't know! All the other balls were so strong, so I got ready for another one!" she said, waving her hands around in an attempt to explain. "I don't know why it went out, I tried to hit it to Curtis' backhand like usual."

Quincy sighed, adjusting his glasses again. First years were so unreliable, and she was starting to speak like a certain annoying jock. "Well, try not to let it happen again. They can still turn this around, you know. We can't let our guard down after winning one game."

"I *know*," Val muttered sullenly, suddenly irritated. *No wonder Perce can't stand this guy! It's not like I hit it out on purpose!* When his back was turned, she was overcome by a strong impulse to blow a raspberry.

Quincy stationed himself at the baseline, mind whirring. Rumyantsev had become incredibly strong in a short amount of time, and he had still been recovering from the would-be hit to the face when Curtis hit his return, so he had no time to analyze the shot.

No matter, you can make up for Val's mistake, he told himself as Rumyantsev tossed the ball into the air. *Retake the point!*

Rumyantsev's serve touched the service line, and Quincy inhaled sharply before straining through the stroke. It was *definitely* harder than Percival's Explosion, but he finally managed to hit it where he wanted: in the crosscourt alley, at a sharp 45-degree angle, as per the original plan. *Tony won't get it there!* Quincy thought smugly. *It's impossible to hit it before it reaches the fence!*

Unbelievably, the hockey player charged forward, roaring all the while, his long legs enabling him to reach the ball before it even bounced. Quincy was shocked to see him hit another return right at Val. She was quicker in getting her racquet ready, and slammed a drive volley towards Curtis. Shaking the sequence of events out of his head, Quincy concentrated on the next shot, watching the golf player's every move.

Curtis did nothing special, though, and brought his racquet back just as before, hitting the ball just as it descended for a second bounce. In all, it seemed like a normal stroke of amateur form, which Quincy ran forward to get. *There's nothing wrong strange with this sho —*

"30 all!"

The sophomore's eye twitched as Rumyantsev and Curtis high-fived. *That's utterly* illogical*!*

"D-did Harris just hit it into the *net?*" Roz exclaimed in disbelief.

There were murmurs of astonished agreement, and Val turned to him, fighting back the urge to say, "HA."

"See what I mean?" she asked instead, as Quincy re-preformed the stroke. "Curtis' hits are *different* from Rummy, er, Tony's!"

"But they're just forehands," he muttered back, half to himself. "And his form is utter garbage. Theoretically, my forehand should have gone crosscourt. Something's not adding up…"

Val waited for Quincy to finish his mental calculations before saying, "So what's your plan?"

"Stop hitting to Rum — er, Tony for now," he decided, still frowning. "And also get ready for his special ability. The racquet face looks full now."

Val nodded, tugging her hat lower. "Got it."

The two parted ways, Val not bothering to extend her hand to Quincy. The distressed look on his face told her this was not the time.

Davide felt equally anguished, and bit his lip trying to keep his words of wisdom down. Legally, he was not able to say anything until changeovers, and the next one would not be for another two games. *If Val and Quincy don't self-destruct before then, though,* he thought in distaste. *Val's acting a little too Percival-y. And Quincy's arrogance isn't helping.*

He glanced at Cuyler beside him. As usual, the senior was as easy to read as the blueprints for a Novara reactor, but Davide knew Cuyler had seen through the opposing team's strategy as well. Even though Regulars on the bench were unrestricted in giving advice, the terse captain was quite the firm believer in "learning the hard way," which was probably one of the reasons they lost during the previous year's State tournament.

Well, Davide thought, turning back to the match. *Two games shouldn't be that long to wait.*

"40-30!"

Crap.

Quincy had erred again, his shot landing a mere three inches too long. He redid his stroke again, doing his best to ignore the baffled questions his teammates asked outside the court.

"Don't worry, it's just two points," Val said cheerfully. "We can win the next one."

"We'd better," he muttered quietly. "And the next two for the game."

The partners retreated to their appropriate positions, and Quincy focused on Rumyantsev's every movement. Suddenly, the hockey player began chuckling.

"You want the next point?" he shouted, a small grin on his face. "You'll have to take it by force!"

Quincy's brow furrowed further as Rumyantsev tossed the ball up. *He's trying to anger me,* he thought, gritting his teeth. *But I'm above that...*

"UGHN!" rang loud and clear again, breaking into Quincy's thoughts. Quincy shuffled to the right, quickly bringing his racquet back for a backhand. *This should give me a little more accuracy!*

"Ugn!" he grunted, feeling his wrists groan under the pressure. He returned it crosscourt in the alley once again, and was unsurprised to see Rumyantsev dart towards it. However, this time the hockey player held his racquet in both hands, but at a low angle with the head almost scraping the ground. And its strings were glowing bluer. Upon realization, Quincy's heart skipped a beat, and he prepared himself for the worst Rumyantsev's special ability had to offer.

Will it be like Percival's? Or something far more difficult to counter?

He watched Rumyantsev hit the ball a mere inch above the ground with the very tip of his racquet, just catching the frame. For half a second, Quincy felt relief; usually hitting it with an area other than the sweet spot caused the shot to be out or hit the net. Sadly, the smirk on the hockey player's lips quashed his hopes.

"Hup," Rumyantsev said simply, following through over his shoulder. The lack of decibels confused Quincy, but the shot was just as fast as before. The ball seemed to fly over the net in a low arc, and narrowly evade Val's outstretched racquet before landing a foot behind her. Quincy ran up and brought his hands back before realizing the ball was no longer bouncing. It was *gliding,* but at the same high velocity. Val looked back in disbelief as Quincy stared dumbly at the phenomenon for a millisecond before trying to return it in the same fashion as Rumyantsev had hit it. Unfortunately, his endeavor proved fruitless, as the ball struck the net to groans from the audience.

Rumyantsev exhaled noisily, and cocked a head in the other pair's direction. "I was the star attacker on our hockey team, and that Flick Shot was my best move. Hit the puck so it flies just above the opposing sticks, and starts soaring on the ice again, right into the goal. Of course, it works fine in nova tennis too!" He started laughing, and high-fived his partner, before tossing the other two balls to Val.

"Game to Curtis-Rum-yant-sev pair!" the umpire croaked painfully. "One game all!"

"It's Rue-*mian*-sev," the hockey player corrected irritably, taking his place at the baseline.

Val bobbed her head in apology for missing the volley as she met Quincy in the center of the court. "It's sorta similar to mine," she whispered. "So I guess one way to beat it is to hit it before it bounces."

Which you failed to do, Quincy thought, but held his tongue. He did not want to have another enemy on the team just yet. "How long until your racquet is full?"

"Another hit, I think," she replied. "I should get it on my serve. Um, when do you plan on using yours?"

"When the time is right," Quincy answered offhandedly, walking to the baseline to signal the conversation was over. Val sighed audibly and went to her own position. She knew they would have to get along eventually. She just hoped losing her service game was not a requirement.

She stared at her opponents again to calm herself. Rumyantsev was keeping on his toes, ready to receive, and looking quite menacing. Curtis, though, seemed more relaxed...

Suddenly, her eyes widened, and a huge grin spread across her face. Davide and Cuyler both observed the sudden amusement, and while the coach beamed at his freshman rookie, the captain's lips stayed dutifully unmoved. Nevertheless, coach and senior thought the same two words.

She knows.

CHANGE THE RHYTHM!

Val's serve was neither as sharp as her partner's, nor as powerful as her opponent's, but it landed well within the box, and was easily returned with double the speed by Rumyantsev. Still smiling, she hit a forehand towards Curtis.

Then she shut her eyes.

Once she heard the sound of impact, she snapped them open again, and she gave a little hop they pinpointed the ball's location, soaring towards her left. With fresh eyes, she noticed it was slower than Rumyantsev's. *Much* slower.

"That's it!" Davide could not help but exclaim when Val hit an equally soft ball in Rumyantsev's service box. The hockey player easily raced to it, but instead of heading towards Quincy's face, the ball buried itself in the net.

"15-Love!"

Quincy's mouth dropped, and he whirled around to Val, who had clenched a fist in victory.

"It's the *pace!*" she explained, running up to him in glee. Ignoring his blank stare, she babbled on. "Tony hits it so hard, so we're used to that when Curtis hits his slow balls. Since they're so much slower, we're not used to the pace and just hit it back hard, as if Tony is hitting it!"

"And since we're expecting a fast shot," he continued slowly, realization dawning on his face, "we hit the slow one incorrectly! Hauser, that's genius!" When he realized how much that statement sounded like a complement, he cleared his throat forcibly. "Ah, I mean, good job. Let's apply this strategy for now."

He turned to walk back to the net, but Val stopped him by extending a hand. For some reason, he felt his cheek muscles smile, and he slapped his hand into his partner's.

Davide let out a sigh of relief. *Yes! As long as you don't let them set the pace, and as long as you don't play to their speed, you can win! Hit fast balls when Curtis makes it slow, and hit slow balls to screw up the other guy's pace! Prove yourself to Quincy. And to Cuyler.*

Rumyantsev and Curtis shot apprehensive looks at Beckham, which all but confirmed Val's theory. Their captain merely clapped and shouted, "C'mon chaps! Keep trying!"

Sorry to burst your bubble, Beckham, Val thought, tossing the ball up. *But I'm fully prepared to win this point!*

She aimed for Curtis' backhand again, but the golf player would not give up so easily, and pressed the button his racquet.

He turned to walk back to the net, but Val stopped him by extend-
ing a hand. For some reason, he felt his cheek muscles smile, and
he slapped his hand into his partner's.

"Might as well," he said, running around into a forehand position. He held his racquet as if it was a golf club, and swung at the ball with both hands, following through over his shoulder.

Both Yole players kept their eyes peeled on the ball as it flew in a high arc over Quincy, heading towards the right alley. Quincy ducked down, and dashed to the left, leaving it for Val to prove her worth.

The freshman ran directly to her right, trying not to blink. Though she did want to know what Curtis' special power was, this was not the time for curiosity. Before the ball even reached the ground, she brought her racquet to meet it, hitting a forehand into the opposite alley for Curtis to jump for and miss.

"D'aww, that was my super power thingy," Curtis complained sullenly, blowing hair out of his face. "But I guess it doesn't work if you don't let it bounce first…"

"That's the weakness, then!" Val half-shouted when she and Quincy met in the center. She stopped herself before adding it was a way to beat her ability as well, but she figured Quincy was bright enough to figure it out himself. "Anyway, as long as they don't come out with any more tricks, we should be fine!"

"Yes," Quincy agreed, holding up his hand. "Let's win this, Hauser!"

Val stared at his outstretched palm and grinned before clasping it. "Hey, this is the first time *you* offered the high-five, Harris."

His cheek muscles disobeyed him again, forcing Quincy to break into an awkward smile. "I, uh, suppose so. I'll try not to make a habit of it."

Both players returned to their respective positions with up-turned lips. Donald leaned to Percival, and jokingly whispered, "Better watch it, Porcupine, or Stylus'll take your doubles partner away."

"Psh, as if," he smirked back, as Val took control of the pace to win both points in a row. After the umpire choked out the score, they returned to the bench for a well-deserved water break.

Davide shook his head, unable to contain his joy now that his players were right in front of him. "Great job guys! Val, you managed to figure it out!"

Val beamed as she took a drink. "It actually wasn't that hard. I mean, hockey is really fast paced, but golf isn't. So I figured Curtis wouldn't be able to follow a fast-moving ball, and a star attacker like Tony might have trouble with such slow speeds."

Davide snickered. "Nice! You guys are doing great, just keep it up and victory is in the bag."

His players nodded, renewed, and stepped onto the courts once again.

"Hauser, I have to apologize," Quincy said, as their anxious opponents finished their water break. "I didn't think you would be a very good partner at the start, but you've proven me wrong. I admit my mistake."

While Val longed to burst out laughing, she instead grinned at him, a hand on her hat.

"I'm glad you accept me now. Just try to remember that I'm your teammate, whether you like it or not. And your partner too, or else I'll have to give you a bruise that matches mine." She jerked a thumb at the ugly wound on her forehead, which looked even worse when she was making a point.

Quincy smirked, adjusting his glasses. "I'll keep that in mind, Hauser."

"Val," she corrected, as she turned to walk to the baseline. "Just Val."

~~~

"It's finally match point," Alan said excitedly, curling his fingers around the links in the fence that separated him from the action. "They've almost won 6-2!"

"Val's got this in the bag," Heath agreed, grinning proudly. "And we can say we knew him when!"

Quincy took a deep breath and faced Curtis, who was bouncing the ball calmly at the baseline. The golf and hockey players had fought well, not giving up even when Curtis' serve had been broken in the fourth game. Rumyantsev had kept his service game with spectacular aces by increasing his power, but during the other games Quincy and Val had set the pace, and eventually tired out those unused to nova tennis. Curtis' fatigue was clearest; he was panting heavily, and the darker yellow spots near his underarms and neck pointed out copious amounts of sweat. Quincy glanced down to his racquet head as Curtis tossed the ball up.

We can easily win this match without me revealing this ability, he thought. Once the ball came towards his backhand, though, Quincy ran forward and pressed the button in the groove.

But where's the fun in that?

Davide shook his head, suppressing a grin. That student just *loved* flashy endings.

Quincy took both hands back and the ball made impact with his racquet's blue sweet spot. He followed through, and closed his eyes to savor the resulting applause.

Alan watched with rapt attention as the ball twirled in the air in what he could only later describe as a tornado motion. The blue tennis ball spiraled between his paralyzed opponents, and landed at the baseline hashmark, before jumping up and hurtling towards the right, narrowly missing Rumyantsev's face.

Val rubbed her eyes and turned to Quincy, who had straightened up and adjusted his glasses one more time. "Sir, would you please announce the score?" he asked the umpire casually. The man made to get off his chair, but Rumyantsev unsteadily shook his head.

"I-it was in," he stammered, staring at the blue smudge in disbelief. "It's impossible, but it was in. Loud and clear."

"T-then game, set, and match to Harris-Hauser pair!" the judge croaked. "Six games to two!"

A cheer arose from the crowd, as the opponents approached the net to shake hands again.

"If you don't mind me asking, what exactly was that?" Curtis ventured hesitantly. Quincy smirked, more than willing to explain his perfect technique.

"That was my Gyro shot. The theory behind it is simple. The torque applied to the ball by my racquet creates an angular momentum that causes it to move in a cyclonic fashion to a pinpoint location on the court."

"I know my English is spotty, but could you please repeat that?" Rumyantsev asked, puzzlement written all over his face. Quincy fingered the frames near his temples, recalling that he was among the less scientifically minded.

"It causes the ball to shoot off and follow a spiral path."

"Ohhh," the three around him replied in complete unison.

"Well, I guess we were lucky enough to get two games off you," Curtis sighed, shoving his hands in his pockets. "But I'll have to train harder so I don't let Rumyantsev down again."

His partner smirked as the pairs returned to their team benches. "Hey, you actually said my name correctly this time!"

"Oops, I meant to say Rummy-ant-sieve."

Davide clapped his hands on his students' shoulders proudly. "Good job you two! Glad you can work as a team now. This'll make lineups easier."

Suddenly, Val's face fell. "Wait, does this mean I'll be stuck in doubles all the time?" she pressed, voice panicked.

"Hey, what's wrong with that?" the twins simultaneously inquired, faking hurt feelings.

As Davide quelled Val's fears, Quincy smirked, and turned his nose up at Percival before dismissively saying, "Hn, as long as I never have to work with Porcupine, I will be pleased with anything."

"Right back at you, Stylus," his rival grumbled in response.

"We will now begin first doubles!" the referee screeched. "The four players please step onto the court!"

"Ready, bro?" Donald asked, pressing the emerald button on the butt of his racquet. The orange arms swung out, glinting in the sunlight, before forming the frame.

Ronald did not answer; he simply got up, and massaged his right shoulder while moving his arm. Donald shook his head, suppressing his mirth. That question was not even necessary — both of them were always prepared to win.

Quincy had already taken a seat, eager to watch the Diamond Duo play against the baseball player and the lacrosse player. He motioned for Val to take a seat beside him, so there would be some sort of barrier between him and Percival. However, she declined, deciding it was a much better idea to use the bathroom before sitting down.

Percival watched her run out from the corner of his eye, and before he knew it, he had stood up as well. Right after Ronald scored the first point, he followed her out, knowing he would not miss anything. Besides, they were the Diamond Duo. If they lived up to their reputation, it would be a clean 6-0.

"Yo Val!" Percival shouted after her. She turned her head back, and upon seeing who was calling her, merely continued running faster.

"Not now, dude, it's an emergency!"

"But you just passed it! It's on your left!"

Val stopped short and backed up a few paces to see an outhouse with the door wide open. While the outside was shiny and looked as high-tech as any, the inside made Val want to gag.

"Seriously?!" she whined, as Percival peered within. Tracks of what he severely hoped were mud decorated the floor, and some dark yellow fluid was dripping from the ceiling.

He whistled, trying his best not to snicker at his partner's expense. "Man, do I feel sorry for you."

Val hung her head and trudged inside. "If I die, you can have my hat."

"Cool!"

Percival watched as she slammed the door. The word *OCCU-PIED* was displayed on all sides of the box, which he had always found funny. It pretty much screamed, "Donald and Ronald Dwyryd, please do something unsavory to the person inside!" While Ronald originally wanted to topple the entire structure over as payback to the opponent who had loudly mocked them during their match, Donald – as well as the several nails that kept it firmly grounded – had stopped him. Instead, they had just trapped the blissfully ignorant junior inside by duct taping the door shut. Why exactly they *had* duct tape was a commonly asked question, which the twins always successfully dodged.

Percival began whistling some melody as he paced up and down in front of the outhouse. He had wanted to take advantage of the privacy to thank Val, once again, for everything. But words could barely describe his emotions, and every time he tried, his carefully created script would vanish from his mind. He sighed audibly. Val was quite an interesting guy. He hoped he could return the favor one day.

Finally, the door opened, and his annoyed-looking partner exited the outhouse, her hands outstretched in front of her.

"And of course the faucet was broken. Wanna shake my hand?" she asked, shoving it in his face. Percival laughed, backing away.

"Heh, I'll pass, but come on, you can wash them at the fountain."

"Ah, good idea," Val agreed. The pair ran off together, with the freshman holding her hands out at arm's length.

~~~

"Ahh, I no longer feel like a toxic waste hazard," Val sighed, swinging her hands by her wrists to dry them. When that proved ineffective, she just wiped them on her pants.

Percival cupped his hands under the faucet, and brought them to his lips, drinking deeply. After he had taken his fill, he turned the handle clockwise to shut it off and watched the excess water run down the drain below.

"And I'm rested and refreshed for my match!" Percival smiled back, as they began their trek back to the courts. "Hey, do you wanna see how the Poole versus East match is go – oof!"

Percival instinctively stepped backwards after he ran into Val, who was standing still, now hiding behind a tree. She turned around and put a finger to her lips, then pointed to three figures in the distance. Percival looked to where she was motioning, and quickly concealed himself behind the tree as well.

Upon further investigation, it turned out to be Li, Curtis, and Rumyantsev. Their vice-captain was re-wrapping the bandages around his arms while reprimanding the doubles pair. Even though his eyes were closed and his back was turned on his teammates, it still seemed as if an aura emitted from his being.

"Look, we're sorry we lost, but there's still a chance!" Curtis began, staring at Li. "If McKenzie and Maynard win doubles, with you and the captain in singles, then the next three matches –"

"The score for first doubles now stands at 4-0, Dwyryd-Dwyryd leading," Li replied, tightening his knots. Curtis seemed taken aback, Rumyantsev concerned. The vice-captain continued. "As for Beckham, well, even if we won the next two matches, victory would be hard to come by in regards to the tiebreaker. We have no coach, nor any substitutes, so one of us would have to play again. While I cannot speak for the captain, my own endurance is still lacking when it comes to this sport."

"So, you're going to forfeit your match?" Rumyantsev suggested uncertainly. Li's eyes opened, albeit narrowed, and he spun around to look the hockey player squarely in the eyes. Even without being victim to his penetrating gaze, both Val and Percival gulped simultaneously with Rumyantsev.

"Rumyantsev, do you remember why we are on this team?" he asked softly, advancing on him. Even though his voice was not raised, it still had the same effect as Cuyler's words. Curtis watched fearfully as his doubles partner backed up against a tree. "Do you remember why you are not captain of the hockey team, Curtis captain of the golf team, and I captain of the martial arts team?"

Rumyantsev nodded, as if hypnotized by Li's penetrating black eyes. Moments later, Li backed off, walking in the opposite direction, leaving Rumyantsev to catch his breath, and look at his worn sneakers. Curtis eyes were downcast as well. Li stopped in front of a tree and crossed his arms.

"It is important – nay, imperative that we do not forget our collective pasts. That is the force that drives us. *That* is the reason we play nova tennis."

Curtis shuddered involuntarily. "After everything that happened that day, how *could* we forget?"

"That day," Rumyantsev repeated, staring at his tennis racquet handle. Something in his eyes told Val that it was a hockey stick he was imagining, though. "That day changed me. It changed us all."

Percival and Val exchanged confused glances. They mouthed conspiracies to each other, unsure whether they should keep eavesdropping, or get back to the game before it finished. In the end, they decided to stay put. They could discover something interesting, after all, and spying on Li before his match with Percival was bound to be fruitful.

Curtis held his racquet handle in both hands and brought it to his face tenderly, also seeing a different piece of equipment before him. "I remember the days before then. Man, it felt so good to finally be called captain!" He closed his eyes, as if reliving the moment. He tightened his grip, and then released it after a while.

"Mm," Rumyantsev grunted in reply, swinging the racquet handle as if it was a hockey stick. "To be called number one, it was simply amazing."

Li had nodded at everything his teammates had said, and finally stared at his own clenched fist. Eventually he relaxed it, gazing at his bandaged palm. His eyes were soft, almost vulnerable.

"I, too, had dreams of bringing our martial arts team to glory. We were unbeatable, at the top of our form. And then…and then…"

"The principal cut off our funding," Curtis and Rumyantsev replied in practiced harmony.

Li's eyes hardened instantaneously, and he brought his right fist back. With a roar that could pierce the heavens, he struck the tree trunk. There was an ear-splitting *CRACK*, followed by a small dust cloud that appeared around his hand. Val instinctively shut her eyes, but Percival lost control of his jaw. Curtis and Rumyantsev held their hands over their faces to shield themselves from any of the flying debris.

After the veil dissipated, they saw Li retract his hand from the bark, and walk away. Both Yole Regulars struggled to get a closer look, while still keeping a good distance between them. They quickly wished they had not bothered.

The imprint left on the tree was nearly an inch deep, and about double the size of Li's fist. A few more shards of bark fell away, revealing a perfectly shaped impression, an indent impossible to repeat by even the most pinpoint of equipment. Val glanced nervously at Li's right hand. It seemed unfazed. Curtis and Rumyantsev were both unimpressed, or perhaps they were inured to Li's explosive power. Percival stared uneasily at his future opponent. He would have to get used to it as well, if he wanted to get even one point from him.

"That man cut off our funding!" Li spat out irately, transforming into the antithesis of what he was only moments before. His eyes were in frenzy; it was as if he had become berserk. "He cut it off and put it into a new office for him! Buying new furniture, having portraits painted! Even splurging on a golden-gilded desk!"

The doubles players looked down, equally as furious.

"Not even a cent went to academics or any other extra-curricular activities," Curtis added quietly, leaning on his stick. "All our teams fell apart due to lack of interest. Even our coaches left, since they weren't being paid. No one wants to play if you have to pay for your own tee time."

"The hockey team as well," Rumyantsev agreed sadly. "Our field was overrun with weeds and tall grass, it was a total hazard. Ice rinks don't take care of themselves, either."

Li said nothing in detail about how the martial arts club disbanded, but Val could tell that it hurt. Instead, the boy told the second half of the story, pacing up and down the path to release his pent up frustration. His friends knew this tale all too well, but paid attention regardless. When Li wanted to rant, they let him rant.

"The principal said the only thing we could do if we still wanted to participate in sports was join the one sport he approved of: wrestling. Some betrayed and enrolled to our dismay, but I would not. To do so would be unforgivable.

"Instead, I searched for an alternative to my kung fu, outside of school. Unfortunately, no such thing exists around here. Not since my father died.

"However, by a stroke of luck, I happened upon a nova tennis court, and was intrigued by the activity. And to add to my awe, one of the players was the ex-captain of the soccer team — none other than Beckham himself!"

Curtis smirked, giving a slight laugh. "Yep. I saw that too, and so did everyone else on the team. He had picked up a sport that our school didn't have, and wanted to create one with or without the principal's permission. *That* was awe-inspiring."

"Truly a trendsetter," Rumyantsev concurred. "And after he beat that college guy, the rest of us pledged to follow him. We were going to bring glory to our sports, even if we couldn't officially play them. If we apply our personal skills to nova tennis, it's possible! With or without funding, we would – no, we *will* succeed."

"That is why...that is why we cannot lose again!" Li exclaimed, punching his fist into the air, and turning to his teammates. "We will each bring our sport to Nationals! None shall get in our way!"

"YES!" the doubles team agreed, thrusting their hands upwards as well. Val and Percival stayed hidden, keeping quiet, both still deciding what to make of the situation. Suddenly, they heard a hoarse voice over the floating speakers.

"Game and set to Dwyryd-Dwyryd pair, 6-0!"

The Outterridge team lowered their hands, spirit unaffected by their second loss. They began to jog back to the courts, luckily in the opposite direction of where the Yole pair was hiding. The duo waited until the threesome was out of sight, and came out from behind the tree.

"Well?" Val asked nervously, glancing up at her upperclassman. "Are you ready to play?"

Percival said nothing, just journeyed forward. Val noticed his paces were unsteady, breathing labored. Finally, he stopped by the tree Li had punched, and spoke.

"I guess...I guess I'll have to see," he said shakily, staring at the trunk. Bark was still falling away, and the mark seemed even more threatening from a foot away. He resumed walking, and opened and closed his mouth several times, but intelligible words never escaped. Val joined his side, worried but hoping for the best.

Percival knew himself, that he had reached both ends of his spectrum today. While he had eliminated his rage, what could he do with this cowardice? Never before had he felt so afraid for his life. His singles match would truly be a test of strength, and it was a challenge that only Porcupine Powerhouse Percival could undergo.

~~~

"We are now starting singles two!" a replacement umpire bellowed. The previous one had been rushed away when he began an uncontrollable coughing fit. His hacking could still be heard, even from the courts.

Percival started stretching out his limbs, trying to keep his face calm. Though it was a good thing he had first seen his opponent's power before being subjected to it, it was at the same time a curse. His mind was a wreck – sure, if he lost this match, Cuyler would most likely dominate singles one, but what if Beckham was as good as the others had said? It was like Poole Doubles all over again, and he did not want Val to have to knock some sense into him for the second – or rather, third – time. It would be all his fault if Yole got second place. They would still go to the County tournament, of course, but the only ones who matter are the winners!

Apparently, the agitation was clear on his face, because Davide began shouting encouraging words from the sidelines, as only a coach could do.

"DON'T SCREW UP!"

Percival laughed nervously, tightening his racquet grip. He pressed the button and watched as the red arms emerged and formed the frame and strings. It suddenly felt much too heavy for him to hold up, and even his legs objected to the weight of his own body. Val shot him an anxious look, and clasped her hands together in her lap.

C'mon, Perce, I know you can do it, Val prayed, biting her bottom lip. *You're my friend, my doubles partner. You can beat this guy!*

"Li from Outterridge, please make your way to the court now!" the referee exclaimed. Li had been searching through the things below their bench, and got up, holding something in his grasp. The Yole sophomore's eyes grew wide while Li apologized.

G-gloves? Percival thought, fear increasing exponentially as he watched Li pull the thin, leather gauntlet over his bandaged hand. Although the logical part of Percival's brain said gloves would contribute little to the overall power, every other part of him cowered in fear.

Li then took out his racquet, and engaged it during his trek to the net. Crimson arms emerged from the pure black handle, but instead of a logo on the racquet strings, a black Chinese character adorned the sweet spot. That just made it even more threatening.

When Li cast his eyes over him at last, Percival felt more paralyzed than before. He could not shake the feeling that Li was analyzing him like a science experiment, finding the fastest and easiest way to completion. After the span of a lifetime, Li held his hand out for Percival to grasp. The sophomore eyed it warily.

The gauntlet's overall appearance was not very impressive — there was considerable wear and tear. The leather had weakened over time, no longer strong and taut, and the golden studs that once decorated the knuckles had worn away to reveal the naked brass underneath. It was fairly clear that this was a family heirloom, or was that just Percival's overactive imagination? The racquet was likewise well used when looked at up close, with small scratches on the frame and a grip that needed replacing. However, both tools emanated with the same overwhelming aura that their owner did. Percival gulped; this would be a tough match.

After several moments, he clasped Li's hand firmly in his. Li's grip was equally as strong. He would not be beaten, even in the act of shaking hands.

"Good luck," Percival offered, as he broke away. Li gave a light grunt of acknowledgement.

"Thank you, but I have no need for luck," he replied, beginning his walk to the baseline. "If one cannot win without luck, one does not deserve to win at all."

Percival blinked, suppressing a shudder. He turned around as well, as Li caught tennis balls from the referee.

No, this won't be a game of luck, Percival thought, shaking his head and confidently taking his place at the baseline. He flashed a thumbs-up for red. Li nodded, and then threw it against the ground. *This will be a game of power!*

A moment later, it came up red. Percival blinked, and then could not help but smile.

Well, Percival thought, catching the ball deftly. *A little luck never hurt anybody either.*

"Game to Li! 5-0!"

Li landed deftly on the ground from his winning overhead smash, racquet still at the ready. Upon hearing the score, he lowered his arms, and walked coolly toward his team bench for another drink.

Percival staggered to the Yole side, but Davide's encouraging advice was only white noise to him.

His teammates looked on, disheartened. He was losing so horribly, even though it felt like he had served the first point just five seconds ago. It had been an ace too, an Explosion right off the bat. So were the next two serves. Li had just stood there at the baseline, with his seemingly closed eyes taking in his surroundings. When the first game score was 40-0, the entire Yole team had been jumping for joy, especially Val. This guy was not as tough as he had first appeared!

Then, the unthinkable had happened.

Just as Percival had brought his racquet up for the serve, Li had vanished from his spot. In the next second, he had been at the service line, and struck the tennis ball with his racquet's sweet spot just as the ball bounced up. The ball was sent speeding to the other side for a return ace down the line, mere inches to Percival's right. Even if the Yole player had recovered from the shock, and even if he was able to move his arm to hit the ball, there was no guarantee his return would make it over the net, let alone be within the boundaries. Li's return merely skimmed the court before hurtling towards the fence, frightening the bystanders in that area. A small black smudge near Percival's foot was the only solid proof of his outstanding shot.

After Li recovered, he had opened his eyes and asked the umpire to call out the score. After a slight pause, the man did so with a trembling voice. "F-forty-fifteen!"

Everyone watching the match, with the exception of the Outterridge team, had rubbed their eyes in disbelief; no one was left unimpressed. Li had been standing like a statue for the last three points, but when he chose to move, he had a killer shot under his sleeve. On top of that, it was only a normal shot, not even his special ability.

"One who strikes blindly, and without thought, will end up defeating himself in the end," Li began, punching out a fist from his baseline position. "However, one who sacrifices in order to gain knowledge will most definitely emerge victorious."

At first, Percival disregarded the statement, and continued playing normally, deciding that last score was a fluke.

Li won the next four points, each time leaving a dark spot on the court, as well as in Percival's courage.

The sophomore had gravely walked to his teammates, who were just as taken aback as he was. Li looked like he had moved in half an instant, from all the way at the baseline, to hovering above the service line. He was almost superhuman.

"Just keep playing, Perce, I know you'll find a weakness," Davide had reassured him, though he himself did not believe it. One game alone did not supply enough information to find a weakness, and so far, he found no Achilles Heel on this boy. Still, he was not about to let his students know that. "No one is un-beatable. For now, try concentrating on the return. I know we'll find something."

His teammates encouraged him as well, and even Quincy wished him well-needed luck. Percival nodded, getting onto the courts with slightly renewed vigor. Perhaps Li's serve was not that good. After all, he had only been playing for a month or two.

How good could it be...right?

A full game of aces answered the question for him, loud and clear. At first, it seemed as normal as any other serve, with a simple toss in front. But the next second, the ball had whizzed between Percival's legs, leaving behind only a black mark in the service box as evidence of its path. Percival did all he could to stop himself from stumbling backwards, and shakily walked to his next position. Every inch of his body felt clammy and numb. The next point was an ace, and the one after that. Every time, it was too fast, too strong, too hard for Percival to get to it. It took a mere minute and a half for the umpire to call out, "G-game to Li! 2-0!"

Percival scored no points during his second service game; apparently, Li had done all the reconnaissance he needed. His speedy returns down the line were untouched aces. At 0-30, Percival tried hitting a normal serve instead of his famed Explosion to see if that would somehow catch Li off guard. It had the opposite effect, and a return was sent straight at Percival's body. He could not bring his racquet in front fast enough, and the tennis ball slammed against his stomach, knocking the wind out of his lungs, bruising both his body and his dignity.

"My apologies," Li had said solemnly. Though it was clear that it had been an accidental shot with no malicious intent behind it, his eyes seemed far from apologetic.

Percival had screwed up his next toss, and the one after that, hitting both in the net. That double fault gave yet another game to Li. Val cringed. Unforced errors were pretty bad, but a double fault was the worst of the worst, and when your spirits were low, such novice mistakes could deliver a crushing blow to self-esteem.

And Perce needs all the self-esteem he can get, she thought, as her teammate ambled to the bench, looking somewhat disoriented.

"Perce, I know you're doing what you can," Davide said softly, as Percival took miniscule sips from his water bottle. "I also know you can do better! Li always hits down the line, so back up behind the baseline to buy some time. You might not have the same speed of his returns, but you'll always have your power!"

"My power," he repeated dully, avoiding everyone's eyes. He returned to the courts, and positioned himself about three feet behind the baseline, something he had not done in a long time. He was used to charging serves head-on, and buying time was never his preferred tactic. Even *thinking* during a match was not his forte, and he had used up every brain cell trying to find a strategy. *But times are changing,* Percival admitted, narrowing his eyes to study Li's almost flawless form. *And I need to get used to them, if I want to win.*

Davide was right in terms of Li's trajectory; Percival managed to catch the ball with a fraction of his racquet face. It was far from the sweet spot, but he was incredibly excited; with the score at 3-0, he still had a chance for a comeback! Unfortunately, his racquet was almost immediately blown away. He watched in disbelief as it fell yards away, in the opposite direction of where the ball rolled away lazily. Li slowly recovered, and walked to his next position. That was the last point, at least in Percival's mind. His spirit had faded completely. Even Davide knew it was too late; the color drained from his face as he muttered for Cuyler to prepare for a match.

Val clasped her hands together, and pressed the thumbs against the injury on her forehead, as Li aced Percival another three times to win the fourth game. Davide was staring at Li intensely, trying to find something, *anything* that could be used as a weakness, but he found nothing. It was as if Christopher Li was as unreadable as the man sitting next to him. He frowned, massaging his eyes.

This was so much easier when I was younger.

The twins were getting jittery, legs fidgeting with every point that passed. Quincy was torn between enjoying Porcupine lose, and despising their team losing. Cuyler's face was masked, as always, but harried thoughts ran through his mind. If Percival lost this badly this *early* in the competition, well, it was not unheard of for a player to become psychologically scarred, and unable to play for the rest of his life. Cuyler licked his lips. It was too soon for Percival to fall.

Much too soon.

The fifth game passed quickly, and Percival had failed to score even one point, hit even one ball over the net. Points came and went, but Percival never felt a thing, even when Davide had thumped his back encouragingly at the 5-0 changeover. At last, match point came.

They had only been playing for ten minutes.

"40-0!" the referee shouted. "Match point!" Yells of support rang from the Yole side to their player, but they fell upon deaf ears. Percival's will, like his hair, had wilted. He almost did not attempt to prepare himself for Li's incoming serve. The Outterridge team cheered for their soon-to-be victory. Li simply opened his eyes to serve, and held the ball out in front of him with his left hand.

"C'mon, Parrish, don't give up now!" Roz screamed alongside Percival's fellow classmates.

"Don't go out like a loser!" the junior Hamilton shouted, hoping there would be some sort of reaction.

I am trying! Percival thought bitterly to himself, tightening the grip on his racquet, as if that would somehow give him the energy to defeat his opponent. *But you're not the one getting killed by his shots! Once he wins this one, victory is his! Even if I started a miraculous comeback now, there would be* no freakin' way *I could win!*

He chanced a look at Val, his doubles partner Val, hoping that telepathy would instill something into him. But no matter how hard Val shouted for him to do his best, nothing changed. He was going to lose.

And he knew it.

When Li began his serve, Percival screwed his eyes shut in defeat. It was all over. His dream to make it to Nationals with the team was shattered.

And it was entirely his fault.

Only his breathing, the steady beating of his heart, the pounding of blood in his ears. Then...

"...Percival is not playing his game, I wonder why?"

Percival opened his eyes a crack to see the twins conversing in loud, overly enunciated tones. Both of them seemed bored by the match, barely concentrating on the court.

"Yes, brother, he used to be so hyped up and eager, ready to take on any opponent. What happened?"

"It is almost like he has given up, due to who he is playing."

"Maybe he should have stayed in doubles..."

"Number..."

"Two."

"UNGH!" Li grunted, jumping up into the air and punching the ball downwards, fully prepared for another service ace. It would be his eleventh.

It never happened.

"What?" Li muttered, eyes widening in incredulity.

Percival had brought his racquet backwards with both hands for a two-handed forehand at the last moment, and growled as he struggled to repel the ball away with every ounce of his power. His arms were shuddering, and his forehead creased at the pain his wrists were enduring. He fought to keep his feet steady on the ground, knowing very well that if he gave in for even a nanosecond of the shot, he would be blown away like a leaf.

Sweat poured in gallons down Percival's face, stinging his forehead wound, which just made him fight even harder. He closed his eyes to keep the salt out of his eyes. As he did so, he recalled the twin's words. They played in his mind, repeatedly.

They're right, I wasn't playing normally before, he thought, feeling the pain momentarily subside. *I was scared to play, but why? Shouldn't I just play my game? Just because he hits hard doesn't mean I need to be afraid. And besides, I...I, too, am...*

A guttural cry emerged from Percival's diaphragm, and his eyes flashed open, as he pushed his racquet as far forwards as it could go, and then followed through over his shoulder.

"I. Am. STRONG!"

The ball sped over the net. Li watched in helpless awe as it streaked down the line, barely skimming the court before coming back up and hitting the chain link fence. He was shocked further upon seeing the ball spin continuously against the barrier, then finally stop and sit in the small niche it had created for itself. It was still red.

Percival looked up to see the result of his forehand, open-mouthed. His lips slowly came together and formed a satisfied grin. This match was not over. Not by a long shot.

"A-amazing!" Alan mouthed, his throat suddenly very dry. Everyone else was equally bowled over, except for the twins, who had knowing smirks on their faces. Without warning, the entire Yole team threw their hands into the air, cheering as if Percival had just brought home gold. Davide even tried slapping Cuyler on the back, though he received a vexed glare in response. Val jumped to her feet, victoriously shouting, "PERCE!" Even Quincy allowed himself a smirk, which disappeared in a flash. Only the Outterridge team looked bothered by the event.

After a few moments' hiatus, the bewildered referee remembered he still had a job.

"Fo-forty-fifteen!"

"Unh!"

The joviality of the Yole team was ceased as heads turned to see Li, who had red, throbbing marks on both his cheeks. His hands were held out in front of him, palms facing up. He brought them to his face again, and again, never flinching, never slowing. The Outterridge team looked away, as if ashamed their own player was this regimented. Finally, he stopped, and let his arms fall to his sides. His cheeks now looked tender and puffy. However, his eyes were fiercer than ever.

Percival was taken aback.

"Dude, it was only one point," he said, smiling nervously. "It's not good to get worked up over just tha – "

"One small leak can cause the death of many sailors," Li interrupted. "Such weaknesses should be dealt with immediately to avert further damage."

"It was one point!" Percival repeated, raising his voice, more annoyed than ever with Li's method of speaking. This rage was similar to what he experienced with Lucas, but this time he was not angry with someone else, but *for* him. "You don't have a right to be mad unless you're in my position, and you don't see me hitting myself!"

The umpire nervously looked back and forth between the two players standing on the court, who were currently glaring daggers at each other. He could risk intervention, of course; however, after witnessing the strength they possessed, the very thought of being pelted with nova tennis balls from either one of them forced him to hold his tongue.

Li turned around, walking towards the fence to tug the ball free. "One as undisciplined as you could hardly understand my methods," he replied. "Flexibility depicts weakness. I once relented, and for that, our club suffered."

Percival was silent as Li pried the ball from the fence. However, when Li walked to the left side of the court to serve, the sophomore spoke up.

"What exactly *did* happen to your martial arts club?"

Li paused for a few moments, and then brought his hands to his sides. All eyes were upon him as he lowered his head. His teammates, with the exception of the captain, looked at each other in bewildered realization. None of them really knew exactly what happened to his team either; since he never went into great detail, they simply assumed it was extremely bad. Now, however, they could find out what made their vice captain so strict, so hardened, so *cold*.

"You heard about how we lost our funding, correct?" Li asked.

"Ehh?" Percival exclaimed, almost taking a step backwards in surprise. "You knew?"

"A warrior must always be wary of his opponents, even from afar," Li countered, pulling another fortune cookie phrase from his brain. "I knew you and Hauser were in hiding. However, I am glad that saves me a few minutes explanation."

The Yole players glanced curiously at their freshman. She shrank down in her seat, tugging her hat down with her. Although the 20-second limit for between-point breaks had already been passed, the umpire allowed Li to continue undeterred.

"This year was going to mark the season of champions, in our eyes," he began his tale, tilting his head to observe the clouds. They were floating in the sky lazily, without a care. "Everyone was prepared to finally earn that National trophy. I was a young captain, a mere junior, but I upheld that honor proudly. All the members followed me without question, both seniors and lowerclassmen. I felt on top of the world.

"When they stopped giving us money, we felt unaffected. We could fight as true warriors. Who needs expensive, brand new possessions, when all you need for martial arts are your fists, character, and determination? That is what we thought at first.

"But then…"

~~~

"What are you saying?" Li protested, as the principal lit a cigarette in the training room. There was no answer, only the clicking of the lighter.

Those behind Li kept their temper in check. Kung fu, karate, taekwondo; all styles of barehanded Asian fighting were more than welcome. Unfortunately, not for long.

Finally, there was a flame, and he brought the white cylinder to his lips, taking a deep drag before speaking again.

"This crap is pointless, kid," the man said coolly, blowing away a cloud of smoke. "At least to reporters. Face it, your 'old way' style of fighting is utter shit in this day and age."

Li's face contorted with rage while his club members protested loudly. But to strike would be against his mandate, his father's mandate. Control your breathing, *he told himself, holding his arm out to calm his teammates, and inhaling deeply for emphasis.* Be a role model for your men...

The principal took one final puff. "This club closes down tomorrow morning, there's nothing you brats can do about it. If you still wanna punch things, join the Wrestling team." He looked back at Li, smirking vilely, and then dropped the still-lit cigarette onto one of the mats, extinguishing it with his Italian heel.

"If not, go back to China, you useless worm."

He had done it. Li did nothing as his disciples lividly charged the man. There was no mercy as he was severely beaten by the admirers of the pupil he had just insulted. Li simply watched, with admittedly sickening glee, as blood shed on their white uniforms.

The next day, the entire club was officially disbanded, and all were brought in for questioning by the police. The e-newspaper's headline read Innocent Principal Mortally Wounded by Ungrateful Students. *Though none of them were sentenced to more than community service, nearly all of them moved away, or transferred schools, to escape painful memories.*

All except Li. He watched helplessly, as his once-perfect team slowly fell apart to only one: him. He kept to himself, isolated from the others, enduring punishments the principal unjustly delivered to him.

He searched unremittingly for another place suited to his style of martial arts, to his kung fu. None existed in the city, and he no longer had his father to spar with. Day after day, week after week, he searched for something, anything.

One cloudy Sunday in mid-September, he chanced upon the local college nova tennis courts. They had been empty during his previous visit, but this time there were two figures playing a match. According to one player's uniform, he was a member of the Yole College nova tennis team. At first, Li was uninterested. But then, he recognized the boy — no, the man — standing on the other side of the court. It was Beckham, from the recently disbanded soccer team.

And he was winning.

Li was so engrossed that did not notice others had slowly joined him. Curtis, Rumyantsev, McKenzie, Maynard: they unwittingly had converged. Finally, Beckham dealt the final winning blow, causing his opponent to collapse, prostrate before him. Beckham, though, left his adversary, and walked up to the crowd.

"You're Li, right?" he asked, pointing with his racquet, and looking him straight in the eyes. Li was at a loss for words, when Beckham suddenly grinned. "I've heard a lot about you. Say, how'd you lot like to join a nova tennis team?"

~~~

"…That was the start of it all. We trained for long hours in this past week, making up for lost time. Later, Captain Beckham asked me if I wanted to be his vice-captain," Li concluded, a lone tear descending his cheek to his lips, which was, amazingly, curved into a small smile. "It was the happiest day of my life. I was once again useful to someone else, to another group. I was content."

Percival was speechless at first, as was everyone else present. There his opponent was, punching himself in the face a mere two minutes ago, now showing human emotion. It was almost heartbreaking for him. Val, too, was amazed, and found she was crying as well. She quickly wiped her tears away, but new ones soon replaced them.

The Outterridge team looked at their vice-captain, eyes shimmering in renewed respect, then at their captain. Beckham was uncharacteristically solemn, and nodded, answering the unasked question.

It's no wonder he's so cold and demanding of himself, Alan thought, seemingly sniffing louder than anyone. His round glasses were already fogged up, and snot dripped from his chin before he finally blew his nose into his shirt. Heath held his composure slightly better, but still rubbed at his eyes with the back of his hand. *After seeing his friends defeated by such an evil man, not to mention their own pure rage, it's no wonder he wants to bring kung fu to the National level, even if it is on a tennis court. It's his dream. It's his team's dream.*

Percival had thought along the same lines, and smiled. "To bring your kung fu style of tennis to the National level, is that your dream?" he said aloud, pointing his racquet at Li. Li repositioned his head back to face Percival, tear now completely gone from view, smile replaced with his default impassive line.

"My dream?" he repeated. After a second of thought, he slowly nodded. "Yes, I suppose it is."

"It's a good dream. And you know what?" Percival continued. "I've got a dream as well, to go to Nationals with *my* team. And we won't stop there! We're gonna *win* the National Tournament. But in order to do that, I have to beat any players in my way! And right now, that means you."

Li's eyes narrowed and closed. He stood stock still for a few moments. Everyone's eyes were on him. Suddenly…

"Heheheh," he began, shoulders trembling slightly. His light laughter evolved into chest-heaving joviality, echoing throughout the courts. Curtis and Rumyantsev pointed and whispered with each other, as did the other Doubles team. Was it really happening? Was their vice-captain actually *laughing*? Even the Yole team, who had known him for less than an hour, was taken aback.

His mirth eventually subsided, and he punched out a fist towards Percival, much like someone else he knew.

"Your dream is a grand dream as well, Parrish," he began, the faintest presence of a grin on his face. "I would like to see it fulfilled. However, every journey has its obstacle, and for now, your roadblock is this match! Let us continue!"

Li held the tennis ball out again, as if asking Percival for permission to recommence the game. Percival replied by bending his knees, ready to receive. Just as Li threw the ball up, time seemed to stand still for both players. Though Li dared not say it, Percival knew exactly what he was thinking. They were familiar words that he had mentally told his doubles partner countless times today alone.

Thank you.

"Haaaa…" Percival began, once again making contact. "UNGH!"

~~~

"Game and set to Li! 6-1!" the umpire called out after a harrowing thirty minutes. Neither player approached the net to shake hands, though. Neither was able to. Both were on their backs on the ground, lying in a pool of their own sweat, letting the late afternoon rays beat on their bodies.

Percival's palms were close to bleeding, blisters already formed. His shirt and shorts were sticking to his skin – even a cold shower would not feel like enough. Only his hair stood at its neutral position. The sun was a little lower; it shone directly in his eyes. He shielded them with a grimy hand.

"Hey, Parrish."

Percival rolled his head in the direction the voice had come. Li lay at the other service line as well, a fist raised towards the net. He was in no better condition than the Yole player was, with gloves so saturated that they dripped sweat onto the courts.

"Nice playing."

Percival smirked, and held out a fist as well.

"You too."

The onlookers, who had remained silent until then, could not bear it anymore. A unified cheer erupted from all of them. They cheered for Li, they cheered for Parrish. They cheered so loudly that Val thought her ears were bleeding but she shouted the loudest of all. No one within a one-kilometer diameter would stay quiet, and with good reason. Percival had been killed in the first half of the match, and then pulled through enough to get one miraculous game. Then they played one more game, until Percival was finally overcome with fatigue. Though he did not keep his service game, each of their rallies lasted longer than imaginable. He deserved to be considered a winner, regardless of the score. And he was sure he would be treated as such.

Suddenly, his coach appeared in front of him, right hand outstretched. Percival found the energy to extend his arm, and Davide helped him get to his feet. When he began to topple over, the twins caught him, helping him keep his balance.

"Heh, thanks you two," he muttered in embarrassment. "It's 'cause of you that I was able to pull through this time. It seems like I can't get through anything alone."

"It is no problem, Percival," they responded in unison, still keeping up the monotonous clarity. The sophomore laughed uneasily, getting somewhat creeped out.

"Seriously, you don't have to keep doing that."

"I do not think we can stop so easily," they twittered on. Percival eyed them, nodding in mock understanding.

"That was seriously an awesome match, Perce," Davide exclaimed, leading him towards the bench, where a beaming Val, Quincy, and the captain awaited. "Don't sweat the small details — you played great."

"Way to go!" Val cheered, jumping up from the bench. She was about to congratulate her doubles partner further, when Cuyler interrupted simply by towering over the two of them. Percival looked up, and bowed his head to his superior, while Val backed away.

"Hey, Parrish."
Percival rolled his head in the direction the voice had come. Li
lay at the other service line as well, a fist raised towards the net.
He was in no better condition than the Yole player was, with
gloves so saturated that they dripped sweat onto the courts.
"Nice playing."
Percival smirked, and held out a fist as well.
"You too."

"Sorry I acted so bad in the first half, captain," he muttered shame written all over his face. "That's twice now. I swear it won't hap – "

"Parrish," Cuyler's voice boomed. The Outterridge team paused from trying to make Li laugh again to see what was going on.

"If you continue to play as you did just now," he continued, as Quincy withheld his delight caused from seeing his rival reprimanded by their captain. Percival braced himself for verbal punishment.

"Yes?" he asked, almost reluctantly.

"You may find yourself captain of this team when I leave."

Quincy ceased his inner joy.

"I understa..." Percival paused to blink, and then jerked his head up faster than a bungee cord. "What?"

He received no answer from Cuyler, as he was walking onto the courts, racquet held loosely in his left hand. No one could see, but his mouth slowly wavered into a smile.

Percival looked from his captain to his coach, who shrugged, then back to the captain, eyes wide with anticipation.

Captain Parrish, huh? he thought to himself, watching Beckham hastily race onto the courts with Cuyler. He grinned. *Yeah. It's got a nice ring to it.*

"Hey Parrish, I think I know who you are now," Beckham called from the net. Percival looked up to see the jovial captain jerk a thumb back to Li. He was resting on the bench, head tilted back, with moist towels over his face and hands. "You're the bloke who'll one day take over Li's spot as the number one power player in the District."

He smiled, nodding his thanks, as Beckham finally turned to an appreciative Cuyler and shook his hand at last. Li, too, had the slightest upward curve to his lips. (Later on, he firmly declared that it was a muscle spasm.)

Percival sat between Val and the twins, who acted as buffers between him and a fuming Quincy.

That *moron, become* captain? he thought lividly, seething through his teeth. *What a complete joke! How dare they ignore me, ignore my superior abilities? Next time, next time I will play singles, and Porcupine will be stuck in doubles two again, let's see him grin like an idiot then!*

Quincy continued to fume in silence, barely paying attention to the match that was being played out in front of them.

"We will now begin singles one! Cuyler versus Beckham!"

"Let's give it our best, hey?" the Outterridge captain grinned, jogging backwards to his position. Cuyler nodded his head, and walked to the baseline normally.

"Certainly."

The two seniors, both old enough to be called men, took their places. Beckham guessed red, but it was blue, so Cuyler got into his preparation stance. Beckham, meanwhile, jumped around a bit to stretch his legs, and then activated his racquet. Red arms came out of the dark blue handle, and white strings crisscrossed at the head. According to the logo on the front, it was a Ravolat, but something told Val that Beckham possessed much more skill than Josh White ever would.

"Ready when you are!" Beckham announced cheerfully.

After receiving a polite nod from Cuyler, the umpire cleared his throat and officially began the match. "Start!"

"Ungh!"

"F-fifteen-love!"

Val blinked and missed it, as did all the rest of the freshmen. The second years were getting better, and could at least see the point of impact. The juniors present had become used to it and by now saw the flawless mechanism of Cuyler's One Stroke Serve. Clearly, all Regulars save Val too understood. Even Quincy had put aside his silent odium to train his eyes further.

"Um. What?" Val ventured. Percival snickered, playing with a blister on his hand.

"Heheh, ow. You'll see."

Beckham gave a low whistle as he watched the ball roll back to him. He stepped on it, then rolled it back onto his foot, and lifted his leg. "That was quite impressive, hey? Let's see you do that again."

With a fluid motion, he kicked it over, and Cuyler deftly caught it.

"Gladly."

Val and the rest of the first years strained their eyes, vowing to catch it the second time around. Out of them, only Val succeeded when Cuyler demonstrated his prowess. Unfortunately, so did Beckham.

"Gotcha!" he declared proudly, as he ran up to it. "Try this one!"

He pulled his arm back before it bounced, then hit the ball on the rise. It was launched in a high arc towards the left side, but Cuyler was near it in an instant, and hit a magnificent forehand.

What happened next caused both Davide and Cuyler to narrow their eyes.

Even though Beckham could have reached the ball with ease, he let it pass by him, standing erect. He stared at where the ball bounced, hands on his hips, and cocked his head as the umpire shouted out the score.

"No, that doesn't seem right," he said aloud, before suddenly turning around to get into position for the third point. "Maybe this one!"

Cuyler eyed his opponent warily, troubled by both his words and actions, but he did not let worried thoughts affect his One Stroke Serve, the serve he had perfected since before high school. Val watched him attentively, mentally taking notes.

He brought his racquet down with both hands as usual, and the ball toss with his right hand was normal too. His left arm, though, followed a very careful path in one fluid movement, without even a nanosecond hiatus. The moment his right hand released the racquet, his left arm guided it in an elegant course behind his back and over his head to meet the ball, without the pause Val herself usually took when her hand touched her back. The full stroke took less than a second in its entirety, and sent the ball flying towards Beckham's box. The soccer player dashed to it quickly, but when Cuyler hit a backhand return, Beckham once again let the shot pass him untouched.

"Come now," he muttered, shaking his head, though exactly to whom he was speaking was unclear. "That wasn't right either!"

At that point, Beckham's teammates had begun whispering to themselves, but Li's voice suddenly cut through the babbling.

"He knows what he's doing," their vice-captain muttered assuredly, his face still covered with a towel. "Let him be."

Cuyler's ears picked up the words, and the Yole captain creased his forehead, staring intently at his opponent. Now he was *sure* that Beckham was up to something unsavory, and he did not like it one bit.

His teammates, though, seemed to find nothing wrong with his winning streak.

"This'll be a cinch," Donald grinned, putting both hands behind his neck and leaning back on the bench. "Who wants to bet it'll be another bagel?"

"And that it'll last less than ten minutes?" his brother suggested, conjuring a dollar bill from thin air and slapping it into his brother's hand. Ronald smirked victoriously as Beckham let yet another return bypass him, winning Cuyler the game.

Cuyler returned to the bench with a frown that carried meaning. Before he could unscrew the cap to his water bottle, though, a loud voice from the opposite side of the court piped up.

"When are you planning on playing seriously, hey?"

The Yole captain froze in position, then ever so slowly turned his head around. Beckham was drinking from his own bottle, his back facing Cuyler, but it was clear he was waiting for a response. When none came, he continued during his walk to the baseline, Cuyler's eyes following him every step of the way.

"Not much of a talker, are ya? Well, if you won't start playing your proper best," Beckham paused to point his racquet towards the Yole bench, voice eerily serious. "I'll *make* you."

Davide caught his breath as Cuyler's eyes widened. When his student looked to him for advice, he gave his head a quick shake.

"Ignore him," he replied firmly, causing Val to exchange clueless glances with her teammates. "Play as you normally would."

Cuyler nodded, and proceeded to the opposite baseline, but he still gripped his racquet more tightly than usual.

"Love games to one! Beckham to serve!"

"Right then, mate," the senior shouted cheerfully, bouncing the ball a few times. "Lemme show you my *real* skills, hey?"

Although most everyone had expected a remarkable serve to back up his words, the subsequent stroke did not leave a firm impression in people's minds. It was his next action that inspired fervent whispers.

After his serve, he ran straight towards the net in what Davide considered to be too risky a serve and volley play. Cuyler's ensuing passing shot seemed to consolidate his belief, but Beckham quickly dashed to the left, his arm extended, and hit a stunning volley down the line. Cuyler wasted no time in running to it, this time countering with a high lob for the back right corner. Beckham broke into a grin.

"Ah, *there's* the play style I want, hey!" he called out triumphantly as he spun around to race to its supposed landing site. "Now I can relax!"

Before anyone could ponder the meaning behind those words, he jumped up, twisted his body about, and hit the incoming ball squarely in his sweet spot, sending it towards the service boxes. Cuyler had recovered to the center hashmark after his previous return, and now sped forward, hitting an approach shot to the far left corner, away from Beckham. His opponent did not give up, though, and darted to his left, beaming all the while. And so the rally continued.

And continued.

And continued.

Davide grew concerned, biting his thumbnail. He literally could not recall a point that Cuyler had allowed to last this long.

Val watched each stroke of the rally breathlessly. Back and forth they ran, but neither let up his pace, neither gave an inch. Instead of leaving balls to pass by him, Beckham chased down each one as impressively as a pet retriever, and gave no sign of fatigue.

"It's the soccer," she overheard Hamilton explain to inquisitive freshmen. "Lots of tennis pros say soccer teaches you good footwork. My guess is Beckham's crazy soccer skills are helping him reach every ball."

Cuyler, too, hit through every stroke fluidly and flawlessly, as if every step he took, every part of his stroke, was necessary; there were no extraneous movements. But even though Val watched the pair with vapid awe, she eventually sensed something was amiss. She glanced at her teammates, as absorbed in the rally as she was. Just as she leaned over to consult the twins, Cuyler hit such a nimble drop shot that Beckham finally could not return. Instead of groaning in disappointment, he leaned over to catch his breath, a foolish grin still plastered on his face. Cuyler could not help but glower at Beckham's smugness as he wiped his chin with his wrist. Davide watched his mind whirring, and he shook his head when Cuyler straightened up, his icy eye narrowed.

"You wish me to play seriously?" he asked, his usually level voice bordering on edgy. "Then I shall, when you do the same."

Davide rubbed his face tiredly as the buzz of gossip reached his ears. *Don't do it, Christian…*

Alan exchanged shocked glances with Heath and his fellow teammates. *I-if that last point was "for fun,"* he thought, gaping mouth large enough to fit an entire can of tennis balls. *Th-then how long will a "serious" rally last?!*

After hearing his opponent's words, Beckham smirked victoriously and walked to the baseline. "Ah, that's what I wanna hear, chap! Let's both play like proper men, hey?"

Cuyler did not nod, but merely bent his knees, scowling at Beckham all the while. "Then be prepared for the consequences," he said softly, though his mesmerizing voice reached the ears of everyone in the area.

Oh, don't you worry, old bean, the Outterridge captain thought, matching Cuyler's intense look with a fixed stare of his own.

I am.

~~~

"Game and set to Cuyler! 6-0!"

Cuyler did not smile at his success, nor did he when Beckham extended a sweaty palm. From the way they carried themselves, a latecomer would assume Beckham had won. Cuyler's lips remained downturned as the two shook hands, but Beckham's jollity seemed insuppressible.

"Thanks for the match, hey?" he chortled more heartily than possible, especially after a match of such intensity. "I'm utterly *knackered!* Told you we were buggered, hey?"

Cuyler returned the kind words with a steely gaze and said nothing. For some reason, this made Beckham laugh even harder.

"The winner is Yole High School, with three wins out of four matches. They are the first place winners of the District Tournament!" the umpire's voice rang out through the courts, for all in the area to hear.

Unaware of the thick tension engulfing them, the Yole students raised a huge cheer as all the players rose to shake hands with their opponents one last time, though Cuyler continued his unyielding grimace. Davide feigned a smile as he stood behind his team, though he continued analyzing Beckham just as rigorously.

Like their captain, Curtis and Rumyantsev were grinning widely, promising that Yole would be defeated by the combined power of golf and hockey next time. Donald and Ronald's opponents had nothing to say, but all four knew they would not play together again. With such scores, the Outterridge doubles teams would surely switch places. However, they were in high spirits nonetheless. Perhaps they would do better if they stepped down for now.

Mutual respect exuded from both Li's and Percival's eyes during their handshake, but Percival suddenly piped up a question that had been badgering him since their match had ended. "If you don't mind telling me, why didn't you use your special ability?"

Li stared at him for a second or two before closing his eyes and upturning his lips a fraction.

"Why didn't you?"

Percival opened his mouth to give his answer but stopped himself when they released their grips.

"Remember, Parrish, that power comes in many forms," Li continued, stepping back. "Whether, why, and how you choose to use it is up to you. Good luck in the County tournament."

Percival pondered that as Orvid stepped inside the courts, leading an exhausted-looking East High team. The coordinator briefly conversed with the umpire, East High's coach, and Davide as the three teams assembled before him. The East High players were sure to stay as far away from the Outterridge team as possible, avoiding eye contact all the while.

"Congratulations to Yole High School, for winning first place in the District tournaments!" Orvid shouted at last, triggering more hoots from outside the court. "Second place goes to Outterridge High School, and third place goes to East High School! All three schools will proceed to the next tournament next month, the County tournament in October.

"Once again, thank you for putting on such a splendid display today, and good luck in your next tournaments!"

"Yole will win!" the students outside roared as the teams dispersed. "Phoenixes will win! YOLE PHOENIXES WILL WIN!"

Alan watched in immense glee as all the players exited the courts. One by one they left, until Val stepped outside of the courts at last. *You're doing great, Val,* he thought proudly as she strolled casually behind Cuyler and Davide, who were conversing in lowered tones. *You're gonna rise in the nova tennis world, I just know it!* He closed his eyes, already imagining Val acting in racquet commercials, signing movie deals, and advertising deodorant sticks.

And when that happens, I hope you'll remember me.

"C'mon, Alan," Heath called out to him. "We're leaving now, stop daydreaming."

"Ah," Alan called out, eyes snapping open. "Y-yeah!"

"Alan!"

"Huh?"

He turned to see Val grinning at him. The wound from the Poole match had healed somewhat, but his heart still skipped a beat when he saw it.

"How'd you like the matches?"

Alan nodded vigorously as they both began running to catch up with the upperclassmen. "You were awesome! Everyone was, especially Percival!"

"Heh, yeah, I sort of paled in comparison, huh?" Val laughed, slowing down to a trot behind Hamilton and Roz. Alan waved his hands in front of him.

"N-no, that's not what I meant! I mean – !"

Davide cut him off, announcing that practice would be the usual time once school resumed. The very mention of the s-word brought about groans from all the students.

"Why'd you have to go and ruin a perfect moment?" Hamilton complained loudly. Davide shrugged, chuckling nervously, as the entire team dispersed, going their separate ways.

"Catch you later, guys!" Heath called out from within the crowd, running down the street.

"Bro, house is *this* way?" a laughing twin offered, pulling the other in the correct direction.

"See you in English, Alan?" Val asked, putting one foot on the sidewalk home. Alan returned to reality in time to nod.

"Uh, y-yeah! See ya tomo – uh, Monday!"

Both freshmen parted, Val sprinting down the road, and Alan jogging lightly. He was smiling very widely, almost unable to contain himself. Yes, Val would most *definitely* stay his friend in five, ten years.

And, judging by the smell, probably advertise deodorant sticks too.

Val had run about three steps before Percival pulled up next to her, a bashful look on his face. With a grin, she hopped on, claiming the spot she had come to love. As Percival began pedaling again, he took a deep breath. This was his only chance.

"Va – "

"If I buy you a quadruple cheeseburger with extra pickles," she said, giving his shoulder a tight squeeze. "Will you stop trying to thank me already?"

Percival could not help but laugh, and immediately picked up speed.

"Done!"

~~~

"Great job, Captain!" Donald congratulated, clapping him on his shoulder as the three walked home. It took a few seconds for him to react, but eventually Cuyler nodded his head slightly.

"Ah, thank you," he said, walking on without even looking back. The twin wore a puzzled expression and exchanged it with his equally confused brother.

"Is it just me," Donald began, as they watched Cuyler's receding figure. "Or was the captain *frowning* a lot more?"

"I wanna say it's just you," Ronald replied slowly. "But something tells me it's just that soccer dude."

They continued staring at their captain's stoic back, until Donald suddenly whipped out his HoloStick.

"Ron, make a note. We're digging up dirt on that guy when we get home."

His brother turned to him and saluted.

"Aye aye!"

Ahead, Cuyler tried not to show how worried he was, but it was difficult for him to lay it aside as if it was nothing. He hid it well, but Beckham definitely had an ulterior motive. The fact that Davide himself thought so all but confirmed his suspicions. He nibbled at his lower lip, a habit he thought he had left behind in grade school. This year would hold many challenges, for him *and* his team.

~~~

"Hey, Li."

Li kept his mouth closed, but glanced over in his Captain's direction. The two rarely walked home with such a distinct dearth of communication between them, so Li was secretly glad to hear Beckham's voice.

"Sorry about all this. I know this goes against your mandate thing."

"Not exactly, Captain," Li replied, watching the traffic speed by at the crosswalk. "I *did* say that one who sacrifices in order to gain knowledge will most definitely emerge victorious, after all. You simply took it to a much greater extent than I ever will."

Beckham studied his vice-captain carefully. Under the scrutiny, Li kept his eyes forward, showing no sign of discomfort. Eventually, the soccer player thumped him gently on the back.

"Thanks, mate. See you at practice Monday, hey?"

With that, the soccer player rolled his ball onto the ground, and dribbled it down the sidewalk. Li turned to watch him go, once again proud to hold such an esteemed position. As much as it pained him to admit, his martial arts team was a thing of the past. For now, he would earnestly follow Beckham until the end, wherever that road would take them and their team.

~~~

"Beckham, I feel we should strategize for our match against Yole," Li began, setting his chopsticks aside. "East was a weak team, but defeating Yole will not be nearly as easy."

The soccer player bit into his pizza slice and chewed thoughtfully. "Yeah, about that. You lot seem to be doing fine without me, so there's no need for me to worry."

Li paused from picking up some egg noodles and raised an eyebrow. "There's more, isn't there?"

Beckham grinned. Li knew well. But not well enough.

"You caught me, Li. If I do get a chance to play – thanks for winning in bloody straight sets, by the way – I'm going to make that Cuyler chap show me his true self, hey."

Li's forehead furrowed. "That would be an unwise decision, Beckham. Cuyler has never lost a match in his entire high school career. I am afraid to say this, but you would lose."

"Aw, I'm offended you think so little of me!" Beckham laughed, but before Li could explain himself, he continued. "But you're right. I know I'll lose. And I'm looking forward to that."

The strip of beef Li was bringing to his mouth slipped out of his chopsticks and dropped onto the ground, but the boy barely noticed. Instead, his jaw dropped in quite an unflattering way.

"B-but, Beckham!" he stuttered, staring at his captain like a startled dog. "You can't mean we're to lose?"

"How'd that saying go? Lose the battle, win the war, hey? It's only the Districts, we're already set for the County tournament anyway. Instead of going all-out to win today, I'm gonna drag out my match as long as possible, and make sure I see every move he has. I'm also thinkin' of not unleashing my racquet's special power, a'course I don't believe for a second that chap will either. I want to see this Cuyler play his proper best before we meet later on, in matches that count. Then…"

Beckham cut off his sentence, but quickly crumpled the biodegradable plate into a ball and threw it into the air. He brought his leg up, and moments later the makeshift ball flew in a high arc, landing directly in the trash can five yards away. He slowly brought his leg back to the ground, and turned back to Li, grinning. "Doncha think?"

Li kept a level gaze. "I'm afraid I cannot concur with you here."

"Yeah, I knew you wouldn't," Beckham said happily.

"I fail to see the logic behind this strategy."

"Yeah, I knew you wouldn't."

"But, I will not deter you from this – pardon my opinion – idiotic idea."

Beckham settled down beside his friend again. He returned the respectful gaze, and smiled.

"Yeah. I knew you wouldn't."

Li's gaze softened, which surprised both of them, but he furrowed his brow before either could ponder it further. "If we're discussing who to keep an eye on, I would suggest that freshman, Valen Hauser."

"Ah, we're back in agreement now. The chap's quite young, hey?"

Li leaned back and looked at the sky. "That's not my main reason…"

It was Beckham's turn to be curious at the runic smile on his friend's lips. "W-what d'you mean?"

"Beckham, you're not the only one who can keep secrets."

~~~

"Still don't know what the bloody chap meant," Beckham muttered, tapping the ball down the street before his house. Still, he could not help but smile. Today had been fruitful and fun. He had played at full strength and got slaughtered; Cuyler certainly lived up to the rumors. But now that Beckham had seen his 100%, Cuyler would stand no chance if they met again.

If Beckham only knew the effects of the seed he instilled in Cuyler's mind, he would have gotten a kick out of the turmoil he triggered.

~~~

"Hey Dad, I'm home," Val announced, closing the door upon entering the house. Confused at the silence that greeted her, she flicked on the lights before kicking off her shoes and running to the kitchen. "Dad? Where are you? I won both my matches today! And I brought some leftovers from Fast Food Utopia…"

She put the greasy bags onto the table, and noticed there was a memo on the table. Puzzled, she picked up the hologram, and activated it. Richard's voice rang out loud and clear.

"Your dad's heading out for a pick-me-up. I'll be back home late. Leave the keys in the mailbox. Love."

Val snorted, tossing the hologram carelessly on the table. "Whatever old man, you can sleep in the bushes tonight!"

She grabbed the takeout, threw them in the fridge and was about to leave the room when she realized there was writing on the other side of the memo. It was messy, careless script, but easily decipherable.

Congratulations.

Val stared at the lone word for a while, and flipped the memo around, inspecting every square inch of it. Finally, she smiled, and slid it into her pocket before unhooking the spare keys from their loop.

~~~

Cuyler could not sleep, and although he knew the reason, the exact rationale continued to elude him well past midnight. Why? Why had he won? No, that was not the issue here. He could say that winning was second nature to him without seeming conceited to others. So why did this "easy" victory seem so *wrong*?

Cuyler ran a hand over his smooth face, and carefully slid out from beneath the blankets. He tried not to disturb his younger sister, who slept on the above bunk, as he set his bare feet on the carpet. He thought he heard her stir, but she eventually lay still again.

Propping his elbows up on his knees, Cuyler stared at the racquet handle leaning against the wall. Replaying the match, for now that was all he could do to calm his nerves.

I shouldn't have given in to him, Cuyler admitted, ashamed of himself. *Even though I still didn't play seriously, Davide could tell I was contemplating it...*

Cuyler exhaled through his nose and stood up, walking to his racquet handle. He bent down to examine the grip, frowning.

Did Beckham know I was using a weighted grip? It was only five pounds, but did it make that much of a difference? Was I being that obvious? Or was it my outsoles?

He spent close to half an hour scrutinizing every piece of equipment he owned, but reluctantly decided that 1:00 AM was a good time to retire for the night. Halfheartedly, Cuyler arose and returned to his bed, pulling the blankets over his chest. He closed his eyes, still watching the match play on his mental screen. He was too young for insomnia, but definitely mature enough.

belleofthetennisball has entered the chatroom.
somechriskid: OMG its val
somechriskid: how r u?
belleofthetennisball: tired. really tired.
speedangel has entered the chatroom.
speedangel: val! hey! your place had the districts, right?
belleofthetennisball: hey Anna! Yeah, too bad I played doubles both times...
somechriskid: nothin wrong with that
belleofthetennisball: guess not...you guys play yet?
speedangel: next week.
somechriskid: we'll pwn!
belleofthetennisball: you'd better!
belleofthetennisball: sorry guys, I'm off. Just wanted to gloat
speedangel: lol!
speedangel: bye
somechriskid: laters

belleofthetennisball has exited the chatroom

"A victory dinner?" Val repeated over the E-phone on Sunday afternoon, the day after their "intense" win at the District Tournament. "Tonight?"

"Yeah, the entire team's invited," Davide replied, stepping away from the camera to reveal what his apartment looked like. Val peered curiously at the monitor, and was astonished to see it was rather neat, and his chic coffee table was completely devoid of snack crumbs. There were no stains on the beige carpet, and his couch (which had team colors) looked as if it had been ironed.

"Wow, you're surprisingly clean for a bachelor!" Val exclaimed, laughing slightly. She did not notice her coach's eyebrow twitch at being called the b-word, however, he remained silent.

"So everyone's coming, or just the Regulars?" she asked.

"Well, I just now finished calling the Regulars, and I guess now I'll just e-mail the others."

"All right, sounds good," Val said, nodding. "Formal or casual?"

"You can see Perce in a tux?"

"Good point. See you at six, then!"

After she hung up, Davide stared at the blank screen, a half-smile, half-frown on his lips. It did not trouble him that Val was still in purple pajamas with a tennis ball and racquet pattern at one in the afternoon, nor did her long, tangled hair, free from the confines of her hat, faze him. It was the man who answered the E-phone that shocked him. He had been suffering from a splitting headache and mumbled slurred words, but a leaf-shaped birthmark on his cheek was clearly visible.

"He looks familiar for some reason," Davide mused, pressing a button to hang up the E-phone on the wall. "I don't remember where I saw him, though."

With a resigned sigh, he returned to his couch, and turned on the laptop on the coffee table so he could contact the rest of the team.

~~~

"Hey there, Valley, why're you still here?" a fully recovered Richard asked, knocking on Val's open door. As usual, it magically led from a modern house hallway to Center Court. Val was busy typing on the laptop at her desk, music playing from her HoloStick. It was a playlist Percival had shared with her, and the catchy pop lyrics had already firmly embedded themselves in her head.

"Oh! I'll score an ace in your heart, baby!" she sang, nodding her head in tune to the melody. "I'll lob one right over your head, uh-huh!" Richard blinked, then knocked on the door louder, raising his voice tenfold.

"HEY!" he bellowed in the middle of the second chorus. Val snapped out of her sing-along to smile as her father came in and leaned against the umpire's chair. "I thought you were going to a party."

"That's tonight, dad, I've still got two hours," she replied, turning back to her laptop. "I've got lots of homework I didn't do yesterday, and I wanna finish up before the sun goes down."

"Why, so your horde of adoring fans will cheer for you to get an A plus?" he joked.

Val frowned, hurt. "You say that like it's a bad thing."

Richard paused, unsure of how to proceed. His daughter was so volatile at times. He struggled for the right words to say, but luckily, the three-story building across the street hid the sun, blocking its rays from entering the room.

"Oh, no!" she groaned, watching the euphoric faces on the wall fade, leaving her in a plain bedroom.

Richard walked in and pat her on the back consolingly. "It's okay, they'll be here tomorrow." Val still sighed, and continued typing.

"Yeah, I know," she replied, pulling up one particular screen, before turning in her chair. "Hey, can you go over my math for m – "

But her father had already left, his unspoken answer loud and clear. Val muttered darkly, and returned to her work.

She eventually finished everything on time, and leaned back in her seat, taking a deep breath. Her stamina was fine in regards to an all-day tournament, but even an hour of doing homework was too much. *I guess I can let loose tonight, though,* she thought, smiling.

After picking out a blue polo and cargo shorts, she wrapped her hair up and carefully pinned it in place before concealing it under her cap. She made sure to save her homework one last time, and then made her way to the exit of the house.

"I don't know what time I'll be back," she told her dad, as she slipped her sneakers on. "But I can walk from here. His apartment building isn't too far away."

"Don't do anything stupid," Richard called from the kitchen table, half a cold taco in his mouth. "And if you do, don't do something stupid with a guy. And if you do, the least you could do is make sure he's rich."

"Right now, I AM a guy!" Val shouted crossly. And with that, she slammed the door, and activated her HoloStick so it could lead the way to Davide's place.

~~~

"This is the place!" Val said to herself, as she stood in front of a twenty-story apartment building. She cocked her head up to gaze at the immense structure in all its beauty. It was a steel building, and the setting sun's reflection gave off a relaxing orange glow that nearly blinded her. She wondered which balcony was Davide's, and inwardly hoped it was not the one with pink boxers drying by the windowsill.

"Hello!" Val said cheerfully, after she entered through the revolving door. The woman at the counter looked up from her work and smiled back warmly.

"Welcome to Venus Suites. How may I help you?"

Val walked up to the beautifully polished wooden desk. "I need to know the room number of someone."

"Certainly," the worker replied cordially, typing at her computer. "Just tell me the name."

"Mr. Davide Ercole," Val said brightly.

For some reason, the woman's fingers stopped moving, and her facial expression changed from sweet and helpful to sour and infuriated in a heartbeat.

"*That* skirt chaser?" she exploded a second later, slamming her fists on her keyboard and standing up. Val backed away almost instinctively, wishing she had just asked Davide the room number while they were on the phone. "Why do you want to know where that womanizing freakazoid is?" Her eyes suddenly narrowed, brows furrowed. "Is he teaching boys like you to break hearts like him?"

"N-no!" Val exclaimed, shaking her head so hard, she was afraid it would fly off. "No way! He's my nova tennis coach! We're having a victory dinner tonight! With the rest of the team! I swear!"

And even she *can't tell I'm a girl?* she added as an afterthought.

The receptionist glared at Val sweating profusely, and then seated herself with a growl.

"Room 1520," she replied, pointing to the elevator. Val quickly nodded, said "thanks" in a tiny voice, and then scurried over to the bronze double doors.

"Davide, my respect for you has fallen," she muttered, pressing the button to go up. The doors immediately opened, and she entered the compartment lined with lavender-colored velvet. It smelled oddly of perfume.

"Close door. Fifteenth floor," she announced. Within seconds, she was ascending, thankfully unable to hear the heartbroken worker cry bitterly to herself.

~~~

"Hey, Val's here!" Percival exclaimed, opening the door to let her enter. He was wearing a T-shirt that was already stained with snack crumbs, and even his jeans were already streaked with cheese dust fingerprints. Their matching cuts had healed over, but a tiny scar still remained. "Finally, you're two minutes late!"

"Sorry 'bout that," Val replied, grinning, as she walked into the apartment. "Hey everyone!"

The people in the room were too busy eating food and drinking punch to offer Val a proper greeting. Her narrowed eyes gazed around the vicinity blankly, awaiting someone else to say hello to her. After a few seconds, she hung her head, and accepted her invisibility.

The apartment was rather big, as far as she could tell. The living room was spacious; the dozen people who could make it had no problem finding room to fit. The kitchen/dining room table had been converted to a finger food buffet, with cookies, chips, and a giant glass bowl of red punch organized in no particular order. Val made that her first stop, since the long run had made her parched. (She wondered how her coach could afford such a nice place on a teacher's salary, or more specifically, *his* salary.)

"Yo Sweeps!" a duo called out, as she poured herself some drink with the soup ladle. She cast a sidelong glance at the twins beside her. They each had a plate piled high with several layers of snacks. Val smirked.

"Stuffing your faces, I see," she dared, taking a plate for herself.

"No, rewarding ourselves," Donald corrected, taking another handful of chocolate covered popcorn.

"We won both our matches 6-0, 6-0," Ronald added, grabbing more crackers and cheese.

"Unlike you," his twin continued, getting on the other side of Val, "who lost a total of…"

"FIVE GAMES!" the pair teased, both displaying all five fingers of their right hands. Val hung her head, smiling despite herself.

"Those were just pity games!" she defended, taking her punch and plate and walking to the living room. "Unlike *you*, *I* like my opponents to feel good about themselves! Good day!"

To top it off her retort, Val marched away to join most of the others around Davide's HoloVision. The brothers looked at each other for a few seconds, quizzical looks on their faces. Finally, Ronald spoke up.

"Wanna put hair dye in Davide's shampoo?"

"Isn't that why we came here in the first place?"

And with that, the brothers headed off to the bathroom, vials of brilliant blue liquid in their pockets.

Val squeezed in through the crowd to see what was so interesting to look at. It turned out to be nothing on the HoloVision, but the gaming system plugged into it. She almost dropped her food, but managed to keep her grip, sparing her coach's gleaming carpet.

"Davide, you have a Woo?" she gasped, as many of the team members begged Davide on the couch to let them start playing with the shiny metal box. Heath was just taking off the virtual reality helmet controller as Davide looked her way and nodded.

"Hey Valen, and yeah, got it as a gift from one of my relatives a few weeks ago. C'mon, let's make a Yoo for you."

Val squealed in delight. Luckily, her fellow teammates were too engrossed in the impressive contraption to notice her girly exclamation.

"Oh, man! Really?"

But Val did not wait for another word from Davide. She was already reaching for the helm, but Heath still held onto it firmly.

"Not…not done yet," he moaned as she finally pried it from his fingers. She grinned victoriously at her moping friend, and then turned to admire the technology in her hands.

It was made of a lightweight metal, in the shape of a pilot's helmet. However, she knew it was nothing like that. A green screen covered the area where her eyes would be. Without another thought, she plopped it on her head.

Almost immediately, Davide's apartment became an empty void. Then, a mirror popped out of nowhere in front of Val. A computerized voice rang out, and a flash went off. In another instant, the mirror was replaced by an exact 3D replica of Val, right down to the length of her eyelashes. Several screens popped out of nowhere, displaying various clothing options. Val withheld another squeal of glee, and then set to work, customizing her Yoo to match her wildest dreams.

~~~

"You were gone for a long time," Davide scolded jokingly by the time Val took the helmet off. She grinned apologetically, and then handed the helmet off to the next person who wanted to create a virtual version of themselves.

"Heh, sorry about that Davide," she said, going back to her food. "What was that, a minute?"

"Nah, a minute and a half," someone answered from beside her. She turned to see a plate with several dozen layers of food piled onto it. She worked out it was Percival obscured behind the platter, and grabbed a brownie from the top.

"Hey!" he called out, but Val had already wandered into the kitchen, shaking her head in disbelief.

I hope the rest of the team hurries up to make their Yoos, she thought, chewing on the chocolate treat. *What games does Davide have? Woo Nova Tennis would be fu —*

"Gahh!" she exclaimed, tripping over a pair of legs. She caught herself on the kitchen counter, and heaved herself up before anything else happened. She whipped her head around to see the legs were connected to a body that had been digging around in Davide's lower cupboards. The person inside had raised his head to see what the commotion was all about, but bashed it on the ceiling of the storeroom instead.

"Ow! For the love of medicine!" Quincy cursed, bringing his throbbing head out from poking around in Davide's kitchenware. He rubbed the injury gingerly, trying to stop the room from spinning. "After I told myself to be careful!"

"Qui-Quincy? Are you okay?" Val asked uncertainly, squatting down beside him. Quincy stopped massaging the enlarging bump on his head to look at her. He immediately adjusted his glasses frames, and then quickly stood up, taking a mixing bowl with him.

"Yes, I'm fine, thanks Val," he said, keeping his head down, eyes focused on the bowl and the things around it, making sure he had everything he needed. Val looked at the counter, and saw there were many different things scattered on it: eggs, vegetables, fruit, and even a raw salmon fillet were arranged around the bowl.

(If Val had been more aware, she would have noticed they were organized in alphabetical order.) Apparently, the cupboards were not the only thing he had raided. Val tried to stop her eye from twitching.

"What, uh, what are you doing?" she dared to ask. Quincy took this as his cue to start cracking eggs.

"Helping the team go to Nationals!" he answered fiercely, beating the eggs with a whisk. "Porcupine says I can't cook, I'll show him! I'll become the next captain, without a doubt!"

Quincy paused from his monologue to toss two handfuls of chopped carrots into the bowl, as well as an over-ripe, peeled banana. The mixing continued, and as he stirred the concoction, Val slowly backed away.

"Good timing too, they stopped supplying Fract Granola Power Bars! What luck! I'll make the healthiest granola bars known to man, to the world! Protein, carbs, the right amount of unsaturated fat. They shall be called – " he took a deep breath for dramatic effect " – QUINCY BARS!"

By this time, Val had completely left the kitchen and was hiding behind the wall separating the kitchen from the apartment's entrance. His maniacal laughter was slightly disturbing, to say the least.

I wonder if that crash into the cupboards really did a number on his brain, Val thought, watching the frenzied Quincy cut the fish into chunks, then add it into the mixture. *Or was he always like that?*

Suddenly, the door opened, and a familiar voice reached her ears.

"Yo bro! I'm home!" her redheaded classmate shouted, leading three others in her wake. "And I brought two more nova tennis freaks!"

Cuyler and Alan eyed Emile warily, but held their tongues. They definitely did *not* like being called, "nova tennis freaks," and therefore left to join Davide at the couch. Liana, on the other hand, found it rather amusing, and giggled into her hand.

"Ah, so you *can* laugh," Emile said, smiling, and taking Liana by the hand. "C'mon, I'll show you my room. Hey Valen. It's this wa…"

Emile stopped talking, and Liana stopped following. Their heads slowly turned to where Val stood, her mouth wide open and almost backed into the wall in the same surprise they all shared.

"You're Cuyler and Davide's *sisters!*" Val deducted at the top of her lungs. Several of the boys on the couch looked back to see what the hullabaloo was about, but were soon drawn back to the enticing Woo.

"You're the freshman big brother's been telling me about!" Liana whispered in shock, for her voice rarely went over that.

"Holy friggin' CRAP!" Emile shouted so loudly, that Quincy hit his head on the cupboard ceiling again. "*You're* the freshman ace that kicked Josh's hairy butt, aren't you!"

"Err, yeeeessss?" Val answered slowly, as Emile began poking at her arm. "Uh, w-what are you doing?"

"I would have thought the superstar newbie would be a little heavier muscled," she replied, feeling Val's biceps. "And a bit taller too."

Val was now offended at the size comment. "I'm the same height as you," she muttered, as Emile began scrutinizing every inch of her, from her skinny wrists, to her hat, and finally the piece of jewelry that hung from her neck.

"Hey, sweet necklace!" she exclaimed, snatching the chain and bringing it closer for inspection. Val nearly choked, but quickly unhooked it and let Emile examine it without suffocating her. "A charm in the shape of a racquet! Nice! Lia, you've got to see this!"

Liana peeked over her shoulder as well, and both girls admired it. Val smiled, glad they were so impressed. In truth, this was the only piece of jewelry she owned, and nothing would ever compare.

Eventually, Emile finished her inspection, and reluctantly returned it. "It's so pretty! Where'd you get it? Girlfriend?"

"Um, ha, no. Actually, my old tennis team got it for me as a going away present." Val answered, smiling and returning the necklace to its rightful place. "It turns into my racquet. It's a lot easier to carry around then a hilt, I'll tell you that much."

"That's really cool!" Emile laughed, punching Val in the arm. Her "lack of muscle" caused her to wince in pain.

"Um, thanks." *And ow.*

Liana's mouth slowly curved into a timid smile.

Wow, they act really similar to their brothers, Val thought, still rubbing her upper arm. *Well, at least Liana does.*

Suddenly, Davide hollered from the couch, causing all three to jump, and another loud *CRASH* to be heard from the kitchen.

"Hey, sis!" he yelled, motioning for them to come over. "We're playing Woo Nova Tennis! Wanna join us?"

"Ah, heck YEAH!" Emile shouted, grabbing Liana's hand and bounding towards the couch. Liana almost tripped as she was forcefully tugged behind her friend, but luckily caught herself before she fell in front of anyone in the room. Emile released her vicegrip and joined her brother on the couch, while Cuyler made sure Liana's hand was functioning normally. "Who wants to lose first?"

There was a chorus of *yeah right*s, all of which Emile glared at, but she stood up and plopped the helmet on nevertheless. A holographic screen appeared from out of the Woo system, revealing an Emile with a three-foot-long red bandana, a black jumpsuit, and a small katana. She wore a cocky grin that reflected in her green eyes.

"C'mon losers, whad'ya waitin' for?" her ninja counterpart's voice boomed.

Hamilton was the first to swallow his pride, grabbing the second helmet controller from a smirking Davide, and putting it on.

A virtual Hamilton showed up on the screen, much taller and muscular than his actual self did. However, his short, neatly combed, black hair and "self-proclaimed" charming hazel eyes remained. His Yoo self was garbed in a ranger's uniform of brown cloth, and equipped with a three-foot rifle.

"There's no way I'll lose to a *girl*!" he shouted, twirling around the gun, and aiming it directly at Emile.

Val and Davide exchanged knowing glances. *Oh, if only he knew...*

Both Emile and Hamilton outstretched their hands and pressed invisible buttons in front of them, selecting their racquet types, as Davide and the others rearranged furniture so nothing would be knocked over.

"Clay court is good for you, right?" Emile asked in such a way that told Hamilton she had already selected it and had no desire to change it now. The junior had no complaints, and a few seconds later, a larger hologram popped out of the Woo, taking up nearly the entire wall. It showed both players on opposite sides of a red court. Their Yoos had traded their weapons for racquets, but their impractical clothing choices remained.

The two took sides on the imaginary court, Hamilton throwing the ball up and down cockily. Emile took her place at the baseline. Val immediately picked up the flaws in her form. Knees not bent, standing up straight, grip on the racquet too tight, basic mistakes of any novice. But then again, this was the Woo they were talking about, and even the most untrained, accident-prone klutz could become a Woo nova tennis pro. In the immortal words of the CEO of Nindento, "All you have to do is move, and Yoo will Doo." (While the original quote had been in Japanese, this was the loose translation.)

Suddenly a huge booming voice bellowed "START!" and an upbeat rhythm filled the room.

"This reminds me of *Ultimate Utopia*," Val commented mildly.

"Seven was the best," Percival cut in through a mouthful of chips as the match officially began.

"*Take this!*" Hamilton shouted. He threw his hand up into the air, and his Yoo self followed his exact movements, tossing a glowing nova tennis ball that the real Hamilton did not have.

Hamilton's serve was swift and strong, but it was the same as it usually was. The onscreen racquet's strings changed color near the bottom, and the ball itself sped across the net, crashing into a glass pane. A small symbol appeared above Hamilton's head, denoting a power-up.

"A Fire Ball!" Alan told everyone animatedly, though whether he did so on purpose or just out of mere excitement was unclear.

Despite the odds she was up against, Emile smirked. She prepared her backswing (almost whacking her brother in the face in the process) and swung. Though most of the Regulars watching knew her timing was off, her arm was much too stiff, and she missed the sweet spot of the racquet by miles, none of that mattered, and she returned the ball with barely any exertion. A power-up was in her line of fire as well, and a green "2X" popped up above her head, which Alan was happy to announce meant a boost to speed.

The ball raced to the other side, where Hamilton was waiting at the ready. His backswing was much better than his opponent's, but instead of returning normally, the emblem above his head glowed. Val sucked in a breath as flames suddenly appeared around the ball as it touched his racquet.

"*Eat that!*" Hamilton said smugly, as Emile's double struggled to reach it in time.

"*I don't wanna use this power-up just yet,*" she muttered, reaching the ball to hit a return. Suddenly, her hand opened up and her virtual self dropped her racquet. "*Ouch! Hot!*"

"Whoa, there's HP in Woo tennis?" Heath exclaimed in disbelief as a red "-10" flashed over the virtual ninja.

"Didn't you know?" Alan found himself saying, a grin on his face. His friend pressed his lips together firmly, humbly bowing his head at his bespectacled classmate.

"15-LOVE!" the voice declared, along with "PLAYER 1 HAS 30 HEALTH POINTS REMAINING, AND HAS BEEN BURNED!" Emile gritted her teeth and picked her racquet up again.

"*I'll finish you off quickly,*" Hamilton laughed, tossing the ball up. "*Put you out of your misery!*"

With every step Emile's Yoo took to get to the ball, she lost health, according to the "-1" that kept appearing. The real her clenched her jaw with every tingle that she felt, and by the time Hamilton hit a sharp backhand, she was down to 5 health points.

"*This serve oughta do it!*" Hamilton shouted, pressing the trigger in his racquet groove. Emile groaned as it started glowing, and the music shifted to a more intense guitar solo. But instead of his serve being twice as fast as normal, as his real racquet would have, the ball immediately transformed into a fist-sized bullet, and the crack of a gunshot was heard as it sped towards the service box.

"*Speed power-up!*" Emile cried, instantly teleporting directly in front of the speeding projectile. Unfortunately, when she brought her racquet up to hit a return, the bullet crashed through her strings, taking the rest of her health points with her.

The words GAME OVER flashed across the screen and the hologram disappeared back into the system.

Davide grinned as victoriously as Hamilton when a disheartened Emile took her helmet off. "Ha! Seems like your 100-win record was shattered, huh?"

"Shut up, bro!" she snapped defensively, hurling the helmet at him. He caught it deftly, and then tossed it to Roz, who was almost jumping out of his skin to play. "One match doesn't prove anything! I'd rule a rematch!"

Before Hamilton could reply, Emile sniffed the air, grabbed Liana's hand, and marched away. "C'mon, Lia, let's jet."

"R-right," she said, following her friend's footsteps willingly. Both girls turned back to see Val accept the helmet from Hamilton.

"See you later, Val," Emile sang fondly, disappearing into the hallway. Val stared quizzically back at them, confused, until Roz slapped her on the back.

"Looks like the new guy's got a girl!" he laughed, as others joined in.

"Wha?" she exclaimed in a combination of surprise and disgust. Roz said nothing, just snickered some more, as he slipped the helmet on. "N-no! That's so not, I mean, so disgusting!" she argued, shaking her head vigorously to get rid of a mental image. The amusement continued as the virtual Roz, who resembled something like a medieval knight garbed in silver armor, appeared. Val, who was still blushing furiously, jammed the helmet on her head to hide her red face. When her virtual self appeared, the same three words spoken by five different people in the room induced laughter from all around.

"It's a TRAAAAP!"

Val's Yoo blushed as brightly as its real counterpart did. She had tried to mimic her Knightworld cleric as closely as possible, by equipping light red robes with crimson trim that trailed to a little above her ankles. Her long purple hair was worn in two spiraling buns on her head, with two or three tiny strands sticking up at the nape of her neck. She held a simple wooden rod about two inches longer than she was tall by her side. She admitted it made her look feminine, but lighter clothes meant faster speed, and besides: there were male clerics too. While Percival's axe-toting warrior and Alan's bumbling alchemist found nothing out of the ordinary when they did quests, apparently the rest of her teammates were not as mature.

"You make a real pretty girl, Valen!"

"*SHUT UP JEFFERSON!*" both Val and her virtual double snarled. He backed away jokingly, shrugging his shoulders.

Roz looked quizzically at her as he chose the court terrain.

"*Dude. That's not fair,*" he said monotonously. "*I'm a real man; I don't fight girls, unlike Hammy over there.*"

"Screw you, Roz!"

Val sighed aggravatingly as she finished selecting her new racquet's abilities, and then pointed a finger at her opponent. "*Whatever, Roz, I'm gonna serve now.*"

Roz shrugged, and then bent down, ready for her to come. "*A'right then, but I'll win this rematch!*"

After both their weapons transformed into racquets (Val's still seemed to be made out of wood), Val grabbed the nova tennis ball that materialized in front of her on the grass court, and then tossed it higher into the air than she would normally. Her serve crashed through a power-up, awarding her a Water Ball item. Roz dashed to it, his heavy armor clanking as he went.

"*Maybe this wasn't so smart,*" he complained, reaching the serve just in time. Val snickered, ready to exploit the weakness for all its worth.

"*Makes my job easier!*" she laughed, sending another shot crosscourt. Roz charged towards it, but mishit the ball into the net, then doubled over panting.

"*I-I shoulda cross-dressed too,*" he huffed, scrambling over to the other side for the next point. He merely repeated the statement when Val won the eventual love game.

"Well, I *still* never lose duels on Knightworld," he retorted as he handed the helmet to someone else.

"Yeah, well, I've never won, so we're even there," Val admitted, extending a hand. "Good match."

Roz laughed as he gripped her hand firmly. "Dude, next time *I'll* wear a dress and *own* you!"

"I think that'd burn our eyes, man," Hamilton mumbled jokingly, evading a whack to the chest from Roz. Val stepped away, deciding against informing them it was a robe.

"You know, Val," Davide called out. She turned to see Davide meet her gaze.

"Yeah?"

"You *do* make a pretty girl."

Val glowered at him, whirling around.

"Well, *you* make a really *ugly guy.*"

Davide chuckled, turning back to watch two of his lesser-skilled students duke it out.

"Touché, my friend, touché."

~~~

"Bad luck, man, bad luck," Roz said sympathetically, as Percival dropped to his knees. "It's just 'cause you got stuck playing against the captain."

"It…it didn't even bounce," Percival whispered, mouth hanging wide open. "How did he…?"

"My Two Step Dance," Cuyler answered, removing the helmet and swaying his head to get the hair out of his right eye, "is still in its infancy. Had this been a real match, I would have had to run to return your Overhead Smash."

And with that, Cuyler gracefully handed Davide his helmet, and returned to his cup of water. Percival slumped his shoulders, still in awe, as Roz continued to blame it on fate. The captain had already returned his Overhead Smash once when he was playing doubles with Val, but it had never been returned in singles before. Apparently, that record was broken with Woo Nova Tennis.

"Relax, dude, he's the captain for a reason," Donald said, helping him up. Ronald came from behind, and was greeted by a suspicious sidelong glance from Davide.

"Where were you."

It was more of a statement, than a question. Ronald looked at Davide with mock surprise, both hands on his cheeks.

"Why, how could you wrongfully accuse me of doing something, when you have no solid proof I committed such a thing?" he asked, in a falsetto. Davide continued staring at him stonily, but Ronald was as immune and unfazed as ever. He had plenty of practice playing innocent. Davide finally just turned away with an unsatisfied growl, while his student continued masking his glee.

Suddenly, Quincy came up to the couch, carrying a cookie tray, wearing a small white apron and a smirk.

"Hey, Quince, you haven't played yet, right?" Davide asked, offering him the helmet. The sophomore shook his head, but held out the tray, which seemed to have several medium-sized granola bars on it. They were still steaming.

"No, but I feel no desire to do so. However, I, ah, experimented in your kitchen, coach. I hope you don't mind."

Davide shrugged, getting up. "Fine, as long as you didn't leave your mess for me."

Quincy pushed his glasses up with his free hand. "Hn, of course not. Anyway, I was hoping you would sample, my first attempt. I was trying to make up for the loss of Fract bars."

"Ah, sure, I guess so," Davide said, reaching for one of them. Val had completely hidden herself from Quincy in case he wanted *her* to be his first test subject, but abruptly jumped out.

"Wait!" she exclaimed, gaining curious looks from the others. "I mean, why not we make the losers eat them? Since they lost, they should eat them, like a penalty? Or something?" she finished, shrugging. Her teammates continued staring at her and said nothing. She tugged her hat down, and took a step back, head hung.

"Hauser is right," Cuyler said suddenly, clasping a firm hand on Val's shoulder. She almost buckled under the weight, but managed to keep her composure. "No need to waste health foods on those who have no need for them. Parrish, Roz, and all the others who lost, please take a bar."

Suddenly, Quincy came up to the couch, carrying a cookie tray, wearing a small white apron and a smirk.

"Heh, like I'm one to pass up a free meal," Percival chuckled, grabbing one. "You've done something good this time, Stylus."

Val cast a sly look at Cuyler. "Captain, you know what's in those bars, don't you?"

He turned away, bringing his cup to his lips again. "I have no idea what you are talking about, Hauser."

Val's smile was interrupted by loud footsteps and stampede of boys struggling to squeeze through the suddenly extremely crowded hallway. Unsettling gurgling noises were heard from each one of them.

"I can't die, I'm a REGULAR!"

"Water, water, water!"

"MOTHER!!!"

~~~

"Well that was *odd*," Val muttered under her breath, staring up at the evening sky as she exited the building. It was a beautiful mix of purple, pink, and gray, which would soon turn to dark blue.

Val smirked, recalling how, after ten minutes of gulping down excessive amounts of water, the handful of losers who fell prey to the self-called "Quincy Bars" were sprawled about the floor. Several, like Percival, groaned unintelligible words. Some of the unharmed players, like Hamilton, took pictures with their camera phones, and others, like the twins, prodded the fallen with half-eaten pretzel sticks. Davide was too relieved *he* was not the one on the ground to care much about his team's well-being, but he did pull out the emergency contact list and spent the next ten minutes repeating, "Hello madam, your son will be a little late coming home today…"

Quincy had taken out a HoloStick and took notes on the outcome, muttering something about "new formulas," regarding the entire ordeal as if it was nothing more than an experiment gone wrong. Cuyler, on the other hand, simply leaned against the wall, sipping at his cup of water.

Val shook her head, letting her lips curl into a small smile, as several cars passed by. She looked back to the amaranthine horizon, and began walking across the street.

"It's too bad I have a history test tomorrow," she muttered, taking off her cap, and freeing her hair from their confines. She began running her fingers through it, undoing the knots. "I was actually having a lot of f – "

"Val?" an uncertain voice asked from behind her. She immediately whipped around, panicked.

Davide, please *let it be Davide!* she prayed, squeezing her eyes shut. But when she opened her eyes again, it was not her tennis coach, but Quincy. His eyes were wide with shock, and his jaw was slack, as if trying to say something, but at a loss for the correct words to voice his bewildered thoughts. Val stared back at him, hands still curled within her hair, unable to say anything either. Her head was spinning, but she managed to ask herself what would happen to her, to her coach, and to the team?

Suddenly, a cargo truck came up from Val's right, blowing its horn. Val's eyes flickered to it briefly, and her brain registered it was her only chance to run. She turned her back to Quincy and raced across the street. He was about to chase after her, but the truck cut him off, almost slamming into his outstretched arm. The sophomore pulled it back to cover his face from flying debris. When the truck had passed, Val was just a figure, steadily becoming smaller as she ran faster than she ever had before, away from the apartment building, away from her teammate. Quincy continued staring after her, helpless, legs reduced to jelly and incapable of functioning properly.

"Val," Quincy whispered, still watching her receding outline. His forehead creased and his arm dropped to his side. "There's no way…it's just *impossible…*"

"Hey, Harris, you all right?" a voice asked, calling him from his reverie. He turned his neck slowly to face Jefferson, who wore his usual look of confusion. Quincy frowned, turning back just in time to see Val turn a corner and dash out of sight. With a sigh, he shook his head.

"No. No, I'm not."

Emile Ercole of the Yole High Podcast Presents Talk Time with the Nova Tennis Regulars! Today I'm interviewing our very own Percival Parrish! Y'all will listen well, right?

Age: 16 (sophomore)
Birthday: July 15th
Playing Style: Right handed aggressive baseliner
Racquet: Heel Firebrand
Signature Moves: Overhead Smash, Explosion
Favorite Professional Nova Tennis Player: Rurik Ivanov of Russia (Rank: 3); his power is unbelievable!
Hobbies (not including nova tennis): video games, comic books, eating, basketball
Interesting Tidbit: He used to be on the basketball team in middle school.

E: When did you get into nova tennis?
P: I was practicing basketball with some friends at the rec center when some guys came and started playing nova tennis against the wall nearby. I wasn't very interested at first, to be honest. But then this one guy showed off his special ability, and the entire auditorium shook! For real! It was totally über positive! If basketball had special abilities, I might have stayed on the team. *laughs* Ever since then, I wanted to have the same incredible amount of power, so I started playing nova tennis.

E: Why do you concentrate on power?
P: Like I said, the guy was so awesome, hitting so hard. His friends were saying there was no way any of them could return such a shot. I don't think power is the best or anything, but it sure beats accuracy. *snorts* Putting your heart and soul into a stroke that carries every ounce of energy you have, now *that's* something.

E: What sets you apart from the other regulars?
P: My power? *laughs* Other than that, I'm the only aggressive baseliner of the team. Oh, wait, that's still power. Never mind.

E: Now, the question everyone's waiting for: what's your favorite type of girl?

P: I – what? R-really? That's what everyone's waiting for? Uh, a girl who likes sports, I guess. *grins* A girl who can play nova tennis better than you, Emile! *laughs* OW!

E: Just for that, you get a Heavy Hitting question! Why are you so annoyed when people call you Porcupine or Hedgehog?
P: Oh, come on! Really? *groans* I'd really rather not answer this question!
E: B-but it's a Heavy Hitter!
(Camerawoman: E-Emile, don't make him…)
E: *signs* Fine, Lia, fine…then you get a multi-part question instead. What are your thoughts on:
Christian Cuyler?
P: The captain? He's *über* positive. The way he makes even the hardest game seem like a walk in the park is incredible, I mean, in his match against Beckham, he wasn't even sweating! And his hair never gets messed up either. Weird. I wonder if Stylus grew his hair out that long just because of the captain. Tch, suck up. But anyway, if I was to play against the captain, I wouldn't last ten minutes. No…five.
The Twins?
P: Don and Ron are EPIC. We play SO many pranks on Stylus, it's great! He's such an idiot too. 'Course, he's so weird, he hates badmouthing upperclassmen, so he takes all his anger out on me. He needs to loosen up. Oh, wait, this is about the twins, right? Well, they're great at doubles. *laughs* Val and me would get crushed to a pulp, but I'd totally own either of them at singles. Don't tell them I said that, though, or they'll just put my transcript up on LiveSpace. Again.
Quincy Harris?
P: Okay, let me get one thing straight. I do *not* hate him. He just gets on my nerves. He's so stuffy and negative and thinks he's better than everyone else. Well he's not. I'm just as good as him, and he doesn't have to go bashing on my power all the time. *smirks* And even the captain knows it now. Captain Parrish's first order of business, probably make Quincy run ten times as many sky laps as everyone else. HA!
Valen Hauser?
P: Val is frickin' sweet! Seriously, who would've thought such a skinny guy could win *anything*? I mean, I'm a little ticked his strategy's like Stylus', but hey, can't judge a book by its cover. He *did*

snap me out of my funk in that match against Poole Private, so I owe him big. Doubles really isn't my thing, but with him, it's fun. My big bro?

P: I couldn't ask for a better coach. He pushes us to do our best, and he seems to have a lot of experience and strategies. He doesn't seem to play seriously during practice, though, I wanna see him go all out! I bet he's an aggressive baseliner too!

And here are the other Regular's thoughts on Mr. Parrish!

Christian Cuyler: Parrish is a very passionate player. He will be a formidable opponent for those we face in the future.

Donald Dwyryd: Oh, but he's a good *singles* player, definitely. Totally sucks at doubles, though. After their sad performance against Poole, I can't be friends with him or Valen anymore. *grins*

Ronald Dwyryd: Porcupine's pretty awesome when it comes to pranking Stylus, but he doesn't really like messing with anyone else. It's a shame, he might see himself caught in our traps later. *smirks*

Quincy Harris: *glares* What would I have to say about *him*? That idiot needs to learn there are more things to nova tennis than power! I shall prove it to him by keeping a flawless victory record in singles! ...Besides, someone who believes *Ultimate Utopia VII* is the best has clearly never played the uncut version of *VIII*.

Valen Hauser: Perce is an amazing player. His match against Li was completely awesome. I guess we won't be playing doubles together for a while, though. Good thing, I guess, my forehead still hurts. *laughs* Which reminds me, I haven't been able to play singles officially yet. I hope your brother puts me in the lineup for singles next time. *smiles*

Davide Ercole: Perce is a tough one, that's for sure. Other teams should be wary of us. At the same time, he lets his feelings get the better of him, and his competitive spirit can make him seem cocky and overconfident. Of course, there's nothing wrong with that, as long as he wins. *laughs*

And there you have it! The personal profile of Percival Parrish! Thanks for tuning into Talk Time! Come back next week when we interview the baseball team's manager! Bye now~~~♫

Ending Theme: True to My Heart, performed by Liana Cuyler

Alan Trenton's Beginner's Guide to Nova Tennis

(So I can be as awesome as Val!)

Parts of the court

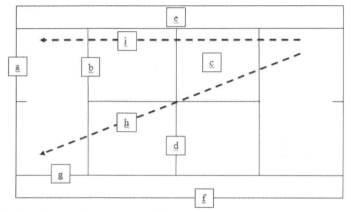

(Definitely not drawn to scale)
   a.   Baseline – where serves and most groundstrokes are hit
   b.   Service line
   c.   Service box – serve must land in here
   d.   Net
   e.   Alley – still inside in doubles
   f.   Doubles sidelines – anything past this is out in doubles
   g.   Singles sidelines – anything past this is out in singles
   h.   Crosscourt – a shot that goes from the left (or right) side of one court to the left (or right) side of the other court
           Note: Serves must go crosscourt.
   i.   Down-the-line – a shot that goes from the left (or right) side of one court to the right (or left) side of the other court

Types of shots

Groundstroke – a full stroke consisting of bringing the racquet back, hitting the ball, and following through over the shoulder
-Note: Val says that you shouldn't look at the ball until you follow through…but I want to know where it goes!
Forehand – a groundstroke made with the dominant hand on the dominant side

-Note: The Captain is left-handed, so his forehands are on the left side!

Backhand – a groundstroke made on the non-dominant side, with either both hands or only the dominant hand

Volley – a shot at the net before the ball bounces, usually hit by just bringing the racquet up to meet it

-Note: The racquet can't touch the net, though, or else you lose the point!

Serve – the shot that starts the point, done by throwing the ball into the air and bringing your racquet up to meet it

Drop shot – a short shot that brings a player from the baseline towards the net

Winner – a shot that the receiver could not even touch

Ace – a winning serve that the receiver could not even touch

Unforced error – a shot that lands out or in the net

Types of players

Counter-puncher – a player that specializes in keeping the ball in play, to tire out the opponent and/or set up a winning shot

-Note: Val says he's this type, but I think he's an all-rounder! (Look below)

Aggressive baseliner – a player that specializes in hitting really powerful groundstrokes to catch the opponent off guard

-Note: Percival and Heath are this type…and I can see why!

Serve-and-volleyer – a player that specializes in poaching (running up to) the net after the serve to catch the opponent off guard

-Note: The twins are like this, and so was that Beckham person from Outterridge, according to Val

All-rounder – a player that specializes in everything (jack-of-all-trades)

-Note: The Captain is this kind. Val says most professionals are all-rounders too, so I bet both Captain Cuyler and Val could be professional one day!

Basic Rules of Nova Tennis
1. Scoring goes 0 (Love) → 15 → 30 → 40 → Game, so each game consists of 4 points. You win a point by hitting the ball back and forth until your opponent cannot return a shot (winner), hits it out (unforced error), or the ball bounces twice (double bounce).

2. You need to win 6 games to win the set, but you need to win by 2.

>   Note: So if you're tied 5-5, you need to win the next two.

3. If a set is tied 6-6, a tiebreaker is played, in which the first player to reach 7 (winning by 2) wins the set.

4. Matches are either one set or best of three sets. Only the District tournament is best of one set. (From now on, the Regulars will have to play more!)

>   Note: In "grand slam" tournaments, men have to play best of 5 sets. I'd probably collapse before then, though…

5. Matches must be played with 3 new regulation tennis balls. Usually it's 3 balls to a can, and most manufacturers mark them with a number (like Bilson 3 or Pemm 1).

>   Note: Balls are fuzzy for some reason that Heath knows, but won't tell me. I should ask Val, but his speeches are always long-winded…

6. Players toss the tennis ball to decide who serves first by calling the color (red or blue). They alternate serving after every game.

>   Note: In doubles, if Team A's Partner 1 serves first, then Team B's Partner 1 serves next, then A's Partner 2 and B's Partner 2 before continuing with A's Partner 1.

>   Another note: Servers get two chances to get the ball in. If they miss both times, then it's a "double fault" and they lose the point.

>   A third note: If a serve hits the net, but still goes over and lands in, it's a "let" and the server takes another turn.

7. Players switch sides of the court after every odd game. They can take up to 90-second breaks during this time, and 2 minutes between sets, but only 20 seconds between points. If players go over this time, they are given a penalty which varies from a warning (high school) to losing the point (professional).

8. Sportsmanship is valued above all, so players must be honest with their shots and shake hands after a match.

>   Note: If an umpire is calling shots, then his or her say is final.

There's still so much I don't know…but I'll keep learning so that I can be a really good player one day!

Made in the USA
Charleston, SC
27 February 2013